Mari Jungstedt is one of the most successful crime fiction authors in Sweden, and has sold over 3 million copies of her books worldwide. Barry Forshaw writes that her Inspector Knutas novels are 'among the most rarefied and satisfying pleasures afforded by the field'. This is her ninth novel set on the island of Gotland and featuring Knutas.

Mari lives in Stockholm with her husband and two children.

For more information on Mari and her books, see her websites at www.jungstedtgotland.se and www.marijungstedt.se

Praise for Mari Jungstedt

'Jungstedt is the real deal . . . The plot is clever, the characters believable and the solution shocking. Jungstedt gets better and better'
The Times

'There is an icy dispassionate grip to Jungstedt's writing that recalls Henning Mankell'
Metro

'Creates the special atmosphere of Nordic crime – that land of snow and ice that fires our imagination'
Independent

'The prose has a stripped-down, utterly functional quality that is perfectly at the service of the carefully orchestrated plot. Writers such as Henning Mankell may outsell Jungstedt in the UK, but – if there is any justice – she will not remain caviar to the general'
Barry Forshaw

THE FOURTH VICTIM

MARI JUNGSTEDT

Translated from the Swedish by Tiina Nunnally

CORGI BOOKS

TRANSWORLD PUBLISHERS
61–63 Uxbridge Road, London W5 5SA
www.penguin.co.uk

Transworld is part of the Penguin Random House group of companies
whose addresses can be found at global.penguinrandomhouse.com

First published as *Det fjärde offret* in Sweden in 2011 by
Albert Bonniers Förlag
First published in Great Britain in 2016 by Doubleday
an imprint of Transworld Publishers
Corgi edition published 2017

A CIP catalogue record for this book
is available from the British Library.

ISBN
9780552168779

Typeset in 11/14pt Giovanni Book by Thomson Digital Pvt Ltd, Noida, Delhi.
Printed and bound by Clays Ltd, Bungay, Suffolk

Penguin Random House is committed to a sustainable future
for our business, our readers and our planet. This book is
made from Forest Stewardship Council® certified paper.

1 3 5 7 9 10 8 6 4 2

For Sebbe, with love

At first glance nothing seemed to be out of the ordinary. The solitary house stood on the hill inside the stone wall. The car was parked as usual on the gravel-covered space down by the rubbish bins. Scattered across the rocky ground were lingonberry shrubs and moss. The crowns of several crooked pine trees swayed restlessly in the wind. And facing the sea was the terrace, which looked cold under the overcast sky since all the patio furniture and the barbecue had been cleared away. The shutters on the ground-floor windows were closed, making it impossible to see inside. Obviously the family had arrived home late the previous night and had gone straight to bed without unpacking.

As soon as his father parked the car, the boy jumped out and raced for the front door, leaning into the gusty wind. It was the autumn half term, and they were headed for the swimming pool. He had been so happy when his best friends phoned to tell him their family would be home earlier than planned.

Yet as he got closer to the house, he hesitated and slowed his step. Something wasn't right. The door was wide open, and an upstairs window was banging back and forth. Dark patches were visible on the curving stone stairs in front of the house.

'Hello?' shouted his father as he caught up with the boy. He looked worried. 'Anybody home?'

No answer. Only the rushing of the wind in the pine trees and the roar of the waves pounding the shore far below. A light was on in the kitchen.

'Shouldn't we ring the doorbell?' asked the boy.

'Wait a minute.'

The man placed his hand on his son's shoulder and looked around. Then he signalled for him to stay where he was while he climbed the stairs. One glance inside the front hall was enough to tell him that something terrible had happened. There were more dark patches inside. A lamp had fallen to the floor, its coloured glass shattered, the shards glittering in the grey daylight coming in through the row of windows along one wall.

'What the hell—' He turned abruptly. 'Something must have happened here. Go and wait in the car while I check. And lock the doors from the inside.'

'But Pappa—'

'Go back to the car.'

His tone of voice made the boy obey. Anxiously, he began backing away but kept his eyes fixed on his father.

The tall man paused for a moment in the dimly lit front hall, listening for any sound, but he heard nothing. Then he moved forward until he came to the living room. That was when he saw her. First her bare feet, slightly suntanned, her toenails painted pink; then her legs covered by a thin nightgown with a lace hem. She was lying on the stone floor, at the bottom of the stairs.

Her eyes were wide open, staring up at the ceiling. Blood had run out of her mouth, and underneath the night-gown her chest was dark red. Almost black. Her blonde hair was dishevelled.

His expression darkened as he studied her face. Her complexion was nearly transparent. He took her cold hand in his, noticing that she had removed her wedding ring. No hint of a pulse. He touched her throat. Nothing.

He straightened up and looked around. Paintings were missing from the walls, and the bronze sculpture that always stood in the niche between the kitchen and hall was gone. The shelves were empty. He took note of everything in the room: a toppled chair, the pool of blood on the floor, the glass doors of the china cabinet standing wide open. On the stairs to the first floor he discovered the next body. Lifeless, a wound to the skull, congealed blood all around.

Outside the window the autumn leaves blazed with colour. The wind was whistling around the corners of the house. He saw his son's face inside the car. The boys, he thought. The boys. Moving higher up the stairs, he came to an abrupt halt. An arm, a bloodied pair of pyjamas. A smooth cheek, so young, so unspoiled.

Moving like a sleepwalker, he continued upstairs. His mind empty and blank, not a thought in his head.

He would never be the same.

The air was stifling, and the temperature was close to twenty-five degrees Celsius, even though it was only a little past nine in the morning. All of August had been unusually hot, nearing thirty degrees in the daytime and twenty at night. People were calling the nights tropical, even though Sweden was located almost as far away from the tropics as you could get.

Klintehamn was considered one of Gotland's most densely populated areas, with approximately 1,500 inhabitants. An idyllic, nicely maintained town on the sea along the island's west coast with an important harbour, from which woodchips, lumber and sugar beets were shipped to the mainland. And in the summertime it was from here that boats left for the island of Stora Karlsö, with its famed bird sanctuary.

The population was large enough to warrant a library, a secondary school, a social-services centre, a sports pitch and an old folks' home. But there were not enough people to justify an off-licence or a swimming pool. At the centre of town were a number of shops, and from there the municipality spread out in straight, narrow streets lined by attractive houses set amid gardens bright with flowers. On this late summer morning a quiet and sleepy atmosphere had settled over the houses. The only sounds that disturbed the cheeping of the birds in the bushes and trees were the faint clinks of coffee cups as they were set down on an outdoor table, the clattering of a lawnmower and tunes playing softly on a radio. The sounds penetrated the dense foliage of the neatly trimmed hedges.

The tourist season was almost over. The long queues at the Konsum supermarket had thinned, and the mobile fish stall in the centre of town had closed up and moved elsewhere. Only a few summertime Gotlanders remained – those who had longer holidays, or who had started them later – along with a number of seasonal workers whose contracts lasted to the end of August.

Klintehamn's modest business district on Donnersgatan was practically deserted. The ICA supermarket had just opened its doors, and a slight rattling noise could be heard as a young assistant set out the advertising signs offering newly discounted grocery prices. Through the window of the Handels Bank a couple of bank clerks were visible, preparing for the day's work. Maud's Beauty Salon was closed while the owner was on holiday, and the only restaurant on the street wouldn't open for a couple of hours. Sitting at a table outside the pastry shop was a solitary man with a cup of coffee in front of him. He seemed deeply absorbed in the local morning paper he was reading.

An elderly woman wearing a white sun hat strolled along the pavement with a poodle on a lead. A father wearing a mobile-phone earpiece pushed a pram as he strode briskly down the street. Wobbling along on a bicycle beside him was a little girl who looked to be about six years old. She was trying in vain to catch her father's attention. There was no one else in sight.

A security van came around the corner. With a slight squeal of tyres, it stopped in front of the Savings Bank next to the ICA. A uniformed guard climbed out of the back while his colleague stayed where he was, in the driver's seat. The guard, who had a crew-cut, was probably no more than thirty. He paused to scan the area before proceeding towards the bank entrance, carrying a rectangular-shaped bag holding banknotes that would fill the ATMs and the clerks' drawers, since it would soon be pay day.

At that moment the back doors flew open on a silver Ford sedan parked outside the beauty salon across the street. Two men wearing dark clothing and armed with automatic weapons rushed towards the guard.

He was just about to ring the bell, since the bank was not yet open for business, but instead he turned around. He found himself looking at a person wearing a ski mask. The bank robber signalled for the guard to drop the bag. The man seated outside the pastry shop a short distance away looked up from his newspaper. He sat there, gaping, holding a copy of the *Gotlands Allehanda* in his hands. One of the robbers had gone over to force the guard's colleague out of the vehicle. The woman walking her dog had abruptly stopped on the opposite pavement. Looking bewildered, she watched the drama unfold. Her first thought was that she must be witnessing the filming of a movie. But there were no cameras in sight. The community's two banks were located right across the street from each other – Handels Bank on one side, and the Savings Bank on the other. The staff were all at their posts and had just noticed what was happening outside the window. Someone had pushed the emergency button to summon the police. The bank clerks followed protocol and made no attempt to intervene.

The masked men pointed their guns at the guards, paying no heed to the elderly woman. The supermarket assistant had gone back inside the ICA, and the man with the pram had disappeared from view.

Without saying a word, the bank robbers signalled for both guards to unlock the back doors of their van, and there was nothing they could do but obey. The robbers instantly seized three bags of banknotes from inside. Then one of the robbers ran across the street, and another person got out of the Ford to help load the loot into the boot. When they had finished, the robbers, still without uttering a single word, forced both guards to lie face down on the ground. Holding their guns in front of them like shields, they jumped back in their car and took off. The whole thing was over in a matter of minutes.

Two seconds after the Ford disappeared around the corner and headed along Norra Kustvägen, there was a screech of brakes, followed by a shout and a thud. By the time the two guards were back on their feet and looking around to see what had happened, the robbers' car was gone. On the ground outside the Donner Library lay a motionless little girl. Her body was twisted at an odd angle. Close by was a badly mangled bicycle, and a pram with a crying baby inside had been abandoned at the kerb. Next to the little girl knelt a man whose shoulders were shaking.

Black skid marks on the asphalt were the only traces left of the robbers.

Detective Superintendent Knutas sank on to his old desk chair for the first time that morning and noticed the way his stomach bulged out over the waistband of his trousers. He'd put on weight over the summer, at least five or six pounds. That was obvious. All those barbecues with good wine had taken their toll. They'd had guests every single evening at their summer house in Lickershamn and, when he weighed himself, the scales mercilessly displayed the result. His Danish-born wife, Lina, was an unusually sociable person, and she loved having company, but Knutas had wondered why she was eager to invite so many people to share their dinner table. Almost as if she wanted to avoid being alone with him. But so far he hadn't wanted to broach the subject. He couldn't stand the thought of an argument. Of course, the children had also brought along their friends for the few days they'd spent at the summer house. But they were almost grown-up now and had other things they wanted to do during the summer holidays. Maybe Lina was finding it boring now that it was often just the two of them together in the evening. She had begun talking a lot about Denmark and how homesick she felt. She'd even started introducing some Danish traditions. All of a sudden they had to eat open sandwiches at the Midsummer celebration and sing a few Danish ballads along with the Swedish drinking songs. She had also suggested that they might go to Denmark for Christmas, even though they'd always celebrated the holidays at his parents' farm in Kappelshamn. He couldn't understand what had come over her.

He sighed heavily and pushed these thoughts aside. Then he began going through the papers stacked up on his cluttered desk. All these documents – transcripts of interviews, statements from witnesses, reports on one thing after another. He had no idea how many times he'd already taken out all the files to review the case, even though deep in his heart he knew it wouldn't lead them any further. The investigation had stalled and nothing new had come to light in more than a year.

Vera Petrov, a forty-five-year-old Russian-German woman, had settled on Gotland and had long ago become a Swedish citizen. She was married to the sea captain Stefan Norrström from the little town of Kyllaj. She was wanted for two murders committed on the island four years ago. Her husband was suspected of being an accessory to the crimes. The police had been hot on their trail, but at the last moment the couple had managed to escape on the Gotland ferry and then flee abroad. On the boat and in the midst of an intensive police hunt, Vera had given birth. The police had received several tip-offs that the couple were in the Dominican Republic, but every time they'd got close, the two had vanished again. The investigation was the biggest failure of Knutas's career.

He heard a knock on the door, and then Karin Jacobsson's slender figure appeared in the doorway. She was his closest colleague and a morning person, just as

15

he was. All the sunny days of summer had given her an attractive tan, and she was looking unusually alert for such an early hour. It wasn't even seven o'clock. She was holding two cups of steaming coffee, with a flat little package balanced on top of one of them.

'Mind if I interrupt?'

'Come on in. Have a seat over there. I'd welcome a break from all this drudgery.'

He cleared a space on his desk and took his pipe out of the top drawer. Jacobsson set down the coffee cups and placed the package in front of Knutas. She gave him a smile, revealing the gap between her front teeth.

'Congratulations!' she said.

Knutas stared at his colleague in bewilderment. She wore jeans and a hoodie with the picture of an electric guitar on the front, making her look ten years younger than her actual age of forty-six. He noticed that she'd changed her hairstyle. Lately, she'd been wearing her hair long, well past her shoulders, and he'd thought it created a softer frame for her face. Now she'd cut it short again.

'Nice haircut,' he said politely.

'Thanks.' She raised her thin hand to her forehead and tugged at a few strands of hair. 'I decided to try a fringe. I'm not used to it yet.'

'What's the occasion?' asked Knutas, picking up the package.

'It was Janne's idea. He kept telling me that I'd look good with a fringe.'

'Oh,' said Knutas. 'But I wasn't referring to your hairstyle.'

He didn't have the slightest interest in what Karin's boyfriend thought about her appearance. He held up the package and shook it a bit.

'Careful,' she warned him. 'It might be fragile. Don't you remember that today is your name day?'

'What? Not that again,' he said with a laugh.

His family didn't celebrate name days the way many people in Sweden did. And the fact that Knutas's parents, for some inexplicable reason, had chosen Bartolomeus as his middle name was something he preferred to forget. It was so typical of Karin to remember his name day. Every single year.

'But you really shouldn't have,' he said coyly as he eagerly tore off the wrapping paper.

Inside he found a black-and-yellow ribbon tied in a bow around two tickets.

'What's this?'

'Tickets to the AIK–Djurgården match at Råsunda in three weeks' time,' she told him. 'Tickets for two. And you're required to take me along.'

'But how are we going to manage that? The match is in Stockholm.'

'Have you forgotten about the weekend course we've signed up for? At the police academy? September 11 and 12. We'll go to the match on Sunday evening instead of coming back home. So we'll just have to stay an extra night.'

She gave him a mischievous look and grinned.

Jacobsson was a devoted football fan. She'd played the game her whole life, and for several years she'd been coaching the women of the Visby P18 team. It was well known that Knutas was a big AIK fan.

'What a gift! Thank you. It's really too much.'

Knutas's voice was gruff with emotion. He got up to give Karin a hug. It had been a long time since anyone had shown him such thoughtfulness.

'Hey, it's no big deal,' she admonished him. 'It was pure selfishness, believe me.'

Her eyes fell on the piles of documents on his desk.

'What are you working on?'

'The Petrov case. Trying to find a new lead.'

'Huh.'

The Petrov case was not something that Jacobsson wanted to think about. During the manhunt, she had found the couple in the ship's cabin where they were hiding. But she had let them go after first helping Vera to give birth. The explanation she'd offered to Knutas when he later discovered her secret was that she'd felt a certain sympathy for Petrov, since the woman had acted out of revenge. The two men she'd killed had raped and murdered her sister. The birth had also affected Jacobsson on a deeper level. At the age of fifteen she had become pregnant as the result of a rape, and she had been forced to give up the child for adoption immediately after birth. This was something she had regretted all her life.

Knutas, who was still the only one who knew about Jacobsson's secret, had agonized over the situation for a long time, going back and forth over how to handle the dilemma in which he found himself. Finally, he had decided not to report his colleague's actions. Of course, that had only added to his dismay over the fact that the case remained unsolved. As long as Vera Petrov was a free woman, he was forced to carry the burden of guilt on his shoulders.

Jacobsson finished her coffee and stood up.

'OK. Let me know if you need any help.'

She left the room, closing the door behind her.

Her perfume lingered in the air.

The morning light seeped in through the thin cotton curtains. The blue striped pattern was intended to give the room a nautical atmosphere. Yet they lived quite a distance from the sea, at least by Gotland standards. Emma had a childlike love of New England interior design, which brought to mind big houses along the seashore of the American East Coast. She had spent several weeks on the island of Martha's Vineyard with her parents one summer when she was a teenager, and the visit had made a strong impression on her. It had been such a fun summer holiday. So maybe that was the reason for her taste in decor.

She looked around the quiet room. White-painted pine floorboards. In the corner a brown leather armchair that was comfortably worn. A floor lamp with a wooden base, brass details and frosted-glass shade. Pillows and blankets in grey, red and blue with stars, inspired by the American flag. Not that she was especially pro-USA. She just happened to like the style. She and Johan had made their choices carefully. All the old furnishings had been replaced in order to erase any trace of her ex-husband's presence in the house. Mostly for Johan's sake, so he would feel that this was now their home. In her heart, Emma wondered if they'd succeeded. Her gaze fell on the curtains again. The fabric made her think of her parents' house on Fårö. Sometimes she had such a longing to be there.

The only sound was Johan's steady breathing. He was tangled up in the duvet, lying next to her in bed.

She got up, drew the curtains and opened the balcony doors on to the garden. Sunlight flooded the room. Johan reacted with a grunt and then pulled the covers higher. She cast a glance at the clock on the nightstand. It was only six o'clock. She often woke early, before the alarm went off. It had become a habit during all the years she'd spent teaching. She crawled back into bed, turned on to her side and looked at her husband. Only his dark, curly hair and a little of his forehead were visible. He was well and truly burrowed under the covers, as usual.

She reached out her hand and carefully crept under the duvet to nestle against his bare shoulder, gently running her fingertips along his skin and down his back. Tickling him, which she knew he liked. No reaction. She pulled her hand back and let it rest on the sheet. Then tried again. She stroked his arm, continued down over his hip and the outside of his thigh. She heard a sigh, a very obvious sigh.

'Are you awake?' she whispered.

No answer.

'Johan?'

Silence.

She lost courage and took her hand away.

It just wasn't the right time.

The winding road allowed for only one vehicle at a time, but he wasn't concerned. The risk of meeting an oncoming car in this remote spot was almost zero. Hardly anyone ever came here. The house stood all alone among the fields and meadows. As he got closer, he decreased his speed. From what he understood, the ramshackle house had been unoccupied for years. That was not uncommon on Gotland. Dwellings were left to fall into disrepair because the owners, who lived elsewhere, clung to the illusion that their children might one day want to live there. Or wanted to keep the property in the family just in case someone might be interested in taking on a renovation project in the distant future. These abandoned and tumbledown houses almost always lacked sewer lines and running water.

He drove past and then parked in a wooded area a short distance away. The spot had been carefully chosen; he had been here before to scout out the area. The car could not be seen from the road. The heat was oppressive, but for safety's sake he didn't take off the bright yellow jacket with the words 'Gotland Municipality' across the back. Just in case he should unexpectedly run into someone out here in the sticks. Wearing official attire and with the visor of his baseball cap pulled down over his forehead, he might easily be mistaken for a labourer working on the road a few kilometres away. A straight gravel path led up to the abandoned farmyard. Huge oak trees shielded the area from view. For decades, thick shrubbery had been allowed to grow wild among the tall, dense grasses. He knew he'd be able to walk the path without being seen from the house. The façade had originally been white, but the plaster was now worn off in many places. The handle of the simple wooden door was nearly rusted solid, making it difficult to use. Anyone who wanted to go inside would have to lift up the door and then give the handle a quick yank.

The house was falling apart. The chimney had crumbled, and most of the windowpanes were missing. An old toilet and a refrigerator stood in the yard. On one side of the property was a rotting grey barn with a caved-in roof. The structure was tilting so badly it looked as if it might collapse at any moment. An outdoor privy stood at the very back of the property. Still visible was a heart, now peeling, that someone had once painted on the door.

It was easy to believe that no one had set foot on the site for years. Yet three shiny motorcycles were parked out back. A light shone in the kitchen window, and the faint hum of agitated voices could be heard inside.

He paused for a moment, standing next to the wall of the house. It made him giddy to be so close. He had a good idea what they were talking about.

Quickly, he strode over to the old barn. He could hide out there.

He needed to bide his time.

Johan Berg noticed an oppressive feeling in the air when he got out of his vehicle in the car park next to the TV and radio building in Visby. He glanced up at the darkening sky. The air felt damp and muggy. He stifled a yawn as he stepped through the glass doors. He was feeling worn out, and his head ached. Elin had a bad cough that had woken him up several times during the night, while Anton was suffering from bad dreams. No wonder Johan was always tired. He couldn't remember the last time he'd slept through the night. This morning it turned out that Elin had a fever, and at first he'd considered staying at home to care for the children, but then Emma spoke to her parents, who had offered to take both children over to their home on Fårö until Elin recovered. What a relief that was. They knew how hard it was for Emma to be away from her students at the start of the school term, and he was the only reporter on the island. Of course, his colleague, the camerawoman Pia Lilja, was fully capable of conducting interviews on her own, but having to film, edit and do all the reporting work might be too much even for her.

When he entered their cramped editorial office, he found Pia talking on the phone with her long legs propped up on the desk. Her hair stuck out even more wildly than usual. The turquoise gemstone in her nose was as bright as her neon-coloured nail polish. Johan took off his jacket and slung it over the back of a chair before heading for the coffee machine to make his first espresso of the day. Pia motioned to him that she'd like one too as she continued talking loudly on the phone. It sounded like she might be speaking to a police officer.

Johan sank down on the chair across from Pia as she ended her conversation. She took a quick sip of her coffee and then explained what was going on.

'Armed robbery of a security van outside the Savings Bank in Klintehamn this morning. And right now a car is on fire in the woods in Sanda. We've got to go.'

As they approached Klintehamn, they could see big black clouds of smoke in the sky. It was clear that this was no small fire.

'The smoke seems to be coming from Hejdehållet,' said Pia. 'The question is, what would be the best route. I think we should drive past Klinte and head towards Stenkumla. There are small roads through the woods from there.'

When they reached the scene of the fire, they were stopped by the police. The area had been cordoned off, and fire engines and police vehicles were lined up along the bigger paved road that passed through the forest. They got out of the car, and Pia grabbed her camera, swiftly raising it to her shoulder. Johan managed to catch the attention of one of the policemen guarding the scene.

'Johan Berg, Regional News. What's going on here?'

'As you can see, it's a fire, and it's spreading quickly.'

'How did it start?'

'A car caught fire.'

'How'd that happen?'

'We don't know yet.'

'Do you think there's any connection with the robbery in Klinte?'

'I wouldn't care to speculate about that.'

'When did the fire start?'

'The call came in around nine thirty.'

'And the security van was robbed just after nine o'clock?'

'That's right.'

'So it seems possible that the robbers may have set their getaway vehicle on fire?'

'Again, I don't want to speculate.'

'Did the robbers leave any other clues?'

'Clues?' The policeman gestured towards the scene behind him. 'Take a look for yourself.'

Only a short distance away, the fire was raging. It had spread swiftly through the dry grass, bushes and undergrowth, igniting trees and sending flames several metres into the air. Pia caught it all on film, and they were able to get a short interview with the head of the fire crew before driving back towards Klintehamn.

On the main street it was immediately apparent that something terrible had happened. People were huddled together, talking, and police tape had been put up outside the Savings Bank building. No officer was willing to divulge any information so, for lack of anything better, Johan did his piece to camera on the street in front of the library where the robbers had run down the little girl. She was in a critical condition. When Pia changed her position as she filmed, she noticed an elderly woman sitting on a park bench nearby, holding a poodle on her lap. The woman was openly sobbing. It looked like she wanted nothing more than for someone to pay attention to her plight. Johan had also noticed her.

'I'll go over and talk to her,' said Pia. 'Wait here.'

With a certain scepticism Johan watched his colleague cross the street and head straight for the woman. Why was she bothering? They had a lot to do and, as usual, time was short. He'd just received a text message saying that the editor in charge of the noon news was hoping for a short report, or at least some photos.

Pia sat down on the bench, petted the delighted poodle and then handed the woman a little packet of tissues. Before long the old woman was leaning her head on Pia's shoulder. They made an odd couple. The camerawoman, with her wild black hair, tight jeans, heavy black eyeliner and pierced nose, was the polar opposite of the plump elderly woman in a floral-patterned dress and sun hat. Johan chose to stay where he was and let Pia handle the situation.

After a few minutes she got up and came back over to him.

'Hey, that woman was here when it happened. She's an eyewitness.'

'Really? But is she in any shape to be interviewed?'

'She's OK. And she has a lot to say. The police haven't interviewed her yet. Somehow they overlooked her, even though she was standing only a few metres from the robbers.'

'How can that be? Didn't she say anything to the police?'

'No. Apparently, she went home because her dog needed to be fed. She was in shock. I said that we could put her in touch with the police. After she talks to us, of course.'

A smile flitted across her face. There was something mocking about the look in her eyes. Pia loved this sort of thing. An exclusive story that was all their own.

'But should we really—'

'Relax,' said Pia impatiently as she put together her camera equipment. 'If the woman wants to talk, we should let her talk. She saw the whole bloody thing, for god's sake.'

Johan and Pia often had differing opinions when it came to who they should interview. She was young and hungry and wanted above all to deliver reports that were as exciting as possible to their boss back in Stockholm. Johan, on the other hand, thought more about the stressful situation in which the victim, family members and witnesses found themselves.

Even though these individuals were willing to be interviewed, they didn't always have a clear view of what the consequences might be. Especially if they were suffering from shock, which was frequently the case.

Johan followed Pia over to the old woman, who now seemed to have calmed down. He introduced himself and squatted down in front of her.

'Would you like to tell us what you saw?'

'Yes, I would. It was just about nine o'clock when I took Romeo for a walk over there on Donnersgatan.' She turned around and pointed towards the main street. 'We were on our way to the Pressbyrå news-stand because I had a craving for an ice-cream cone. I know that may sound strange, since it was so early in the day, but at my age it's all right to give in to little indulgences. And they have the world's best ice cream over there.'

She raised her head and stared into space as she went on.

'But suddenly I noticed two men standing in the middle of the street holding some sort of gun. They had on black clothing and those ski masks that robbers wear, so I couldn't see their faces at all. My first thought was that they must be making a film. But I couldn't see any cameras, and then I realized that it was real. A robbery, I mean. Right outside the bank. But it wasn't a bank robbery. They were robbing those boys who deliver money to the bank. From the security van. I think that's what it's called.'

'What did the robbers do?'

'They waved their guns about and forced the guards to open the back of the van and take out several bags. Then a third masked robber got out of the car and helped them stow the bags inside. And . . . there was something different about the third robber.'

'What do you mean?'

She looked at Johan.

'It had to be a woman.'

Johan gave a start. This was something new. On the radio and in the TV news reports, the account was consistently the same: a security van had been robbed in Klintehamn by three masked men.

'Why do you think so?'

'The way she moved. But that wasn't the only thing. She opened the boot of the car, and then the other

28

robbers brought over the bags of money. When she leaned forward to put the bags inside, I caught a glimpse of her underwear. Women's underwear. I'm quite sure about that. Pulled up high to her waist, which is the fashion these days. And they were red.'

'Are you sure it wasn't men's underwear?'

'No, no, goodness gracious. It was just a thin strip of fabric. I don't know why anyone would want to wear that kind of underwear. It must be terribly uncomfortable. Now what is it called? *Thong.* Is that the word? Yes, a thong. That's not something a man would wear. Am I right?'

The rain was pounding on the tin roof. It was Gotland's first downpour in weeks. Every now and then flashes of white light crisscrossed the roiling dark grey of the sky. Terese Larsson lit another cigarette and blew the smoke at the bare bulb hanging above the table. She tilted her chair, leaned her head back and closed her eyes. Relief spread through her body. The news reader on the local radio station had just reported that the little girl was now in a stable condition and her life was no longer in danger. What bloody good luck.

The robbery had gone off smoothly, with only one complication. As they were driving away from the bank, that child had appeared out of nowhere. She had no chance of getting out of their way. Terese recalled with horror those few seconds before the car hit her. The look of surprise on the girl's face, her eyes open wide, the cap that flew off her head, her thin arms flailing about and the thud as she collided with the car's bumper. The sound had made Terese shudder. Out of the corner of her eye she saw the father let go of the pram and come rushing over to his child. She automatically stomped on the accelerator and drove away, following their carefully devised plan. She entered the main highway to Visby but drove only a few hundred metres before exiting and heading for Sanda. It made no difference if people in the houses along the way noticed them because they were quickly going to get rid of the car, which Jocke had stolen a few days before. The last side road gradually turned into a bumpy tractor path with woods on one side and fields on the other. The branches of tall shrubs struck the windscreen as she drove too fast along the uneven ground.

They parked in a glade where the forest had been cleared to make way for a row of electricity pylons that cut right through the dense vegetation. Quickly, they removed their jackets, trousers and masks and threw everything inside the car. Then they took out the money bags and guns. After that Degen poured petrol over the car and a long stretch of the bone-dry ground and then tossed a lit match on to it. The effect was explosive. Carrying the money and guns, they'd raced off to the motorcycles that were parked a hundred metres away, close to the main road.

Later they heard on the radio that the flames had spread rapidly, causing an extensive forest fire. Since Gotland had had so little rain all summer, the fields were as dry as tinder. All traces of them should be gone by now.

Only a minute after the fire broke out, they were on the road, and from there it wasn't far to the abandoned house. This ramshackle old dwelling was perfect for their purposes. They would lie low here for a few days until things had calmed down and then leave the island, nice and easy.

The house was in a remote location, with no close neighbours and shielded from view. A perfect hiding place. They'd come out here well before the robbery

31

to check it out and leave enough food and drink to tide them over for at least a week, if necessary. Degen had even managed to get the old refrigerator working. Strangely enough, the electricity was still connected, even though the house must have stood empty for a long time. Two of the rooms were habitable: the kitchen and the bedroom next to it, with only a curtain between them. A few old pieces of furniture remained. A rickety table, several straight-backed chairs and a narrow bed. Just right for their needs. Jocke had brought over a couple of mattresses, some sleeping bags and pillows. Since the property was in such a desolate location, no one had noticed the preparations they'd made. And now they'd stolen four money bags which were, hopefully, stuffed with cash. They'd been lucky. On the news it was reported that the getaway car had been completely torched. And the little girl would live.

Terese reached for a plastic cup and took a swig from it. The alcohol warmed her stomach. She looked at her two male colleagues, who were seated at the table. Degen met her eye and grinned.

'It's too fucking good to be true,' chuckled Jocke. He held up his own dirty plastic cup in a toast. '*Skål!*' he said.

The other two raised their cups and then downed the contents. They'd put the money bags in a root cellar away from the house in case they contained some sort of transmitter. There was no reception underground.

Actually, the mobile signal was miserable out on this remote property, so the bags probably couldn't have been tracked in any case, but they couldn't be too cautious. And trying to open the bags on their own was unthinkable. They didn't have the necessary expertise.

It was almost impossible to open a money bag from a security van without activating the dye cartridges and ruining the banknotes inside. But Degen had a contact in Stockholm who claimed to know how to do it. He owed Degen a favour and had promised to help.

They'd heard that this type of money bag could contain several hundred thousand kronor. If that turned out to be true, then their problems would be instantly solved.

All three of them were acutely in need of money. Jocke's situation was the worst, since he owed his drug dealer big-time, as usual. In spite of multiple attempts over the years, he'd never been able to kick his habit. And dealers didn't take kindly to late payments or excuses. They were not about to wait.

Terese needed money for more trivial things such as food, clothing, visits to the hair salon and furniture for her new flat. Against all odds, she'd managed to get a lease on a place in Fruängen. It was her first permanent home in years, and she had no desire to be kicked out on to the street again. She was thirty-two years old, and she'd had enough. She longed for peace and quiet. Deep down, she was hoping that this robbery signalled an end to her flighty, unsettled, criminal life. She was looking for an orderly existence. Might even find herself a job, now that she had a place to live and everything. And she had finally been assigned a social worker whom she liked and actually trusted. She was tired of the drug-infested neighbourhoods, the drunken fights, the petty thefts and the stints in jail.

She'd been through plenty. She lit another cigarette and thought about what was in the money bags. Maybe they held a new life for her.

Late on Tuesday afternoon Knutas summoned his colleagues to the conference room of the criminal division for the first meeting of the investigative team. Everyone took a seat at the long table. In the middle of the table were the usual Thermos containers of coffee and a plastic tray with oatmeal biscuits on it. Out of habit, Knutas poured himself a cup of coffee before taking his regular place at the head of the table. He resisted the temptation to help himself to a biscuit.

He cast a weary glance at the row of windows along the wall. The rain was sluicing down, making it impossible to see anything of the Forum supermarket's big car park or the street outside. All the most important team members were in attendance, except for Chief Prosecutor Birger Smittenberg, who liked to be present at the meetings but this time was busy in court.

'What a sodding mess,' sighed scene of crime officer Erik Sohlman, running his hand through his thick red hair. 'First a forest fire burns up the evidence, and then a damned monsoon washes away any small traces that might have been left. And the rain starts up only a couple of hours after the robbery, in spite of the fact that it's been weeks since we've had even a drop of rain. You'd almost think the robbers were in cahoots with the higher powers.'

'I know what you mean,' Knutas agreed. 'Speaking of the robbers, what do we know about them? Karin?'

'I've collated the statements that we've taken from all the witnesses who've come here to police headquarters during the course of the day. We have information both from people who actually saw the robbery take place and from residents who heard or saw the escape vehicle. We've also talked to the employees of the two banks. There were three staff members in Handels Bank at the time, but only one clerk had arrived at the Savings Bank. The robbery took place a few minutes past nine and, according to witnesses, we're talking about three perpetrators.'

'So neither of the banks was open for business?' asked Knutas.

'No. Handels Bank opens at nine thirty, and the Savings Bank doesn't open until eleven.'

'What sort of description do we have of the robbers?'

'They wore dark clothing and black trainers, with knitted ski masks covering their faces,' Jacobsson went on. 'They were of average height, perhaps a bit shorter, and thin. One of them was bulkier than the other two, but witnesses told us that he was muscular, not fat. He also had unusually dark, almond-shaped eyes. One person said he might be of Hispanic ancestry, maybe a Spaniard or from South America.

'The witnesses all agree on the probable age of the robbers, estimating them to be between twenty-five and thirty. They were heavily armed with some sort of automatic weapons, and they behaved in a professional and organized manner. They acted quickly, without the slightest hint of hesitation. It's also important to note that none of them said a single word during the robbery. They used hand signals to indicate what they wanted.'

'Did all three of them participate in the robbery?'

'Two of them did. The third robber waited in the car and didn't get out until they were going to load the money bags inside the vehicle. That was also the person who drove.'

'And the one who hit the little girl,' interjected Detective Inspector Thomas Wittberg, the youngest of the officers at the meeting. His blue eyes looked even brighter against his perennial suntan, which was darker than ever after the long, hot summer.

'How's she doing, by the way?' asked Knutas, turning to the police spokesman, Lars Norrby, who was keeping in contact with the hospital. His long legs were crossed under the table, and he was rhythmically tapping his pen on his notepad. His long, narrow face was expressionless.

'Apparently, she's in a stable condition. She was seriously injured, of course, and she's going to have surgery this evening, but her injuries are no longer considered life-threatening.'

Jacobsson sighed with relief.

'It would have been horrible if she hadn't made it. But getting back to my report, that's as much as we know so far. The escape vehicle was seen as it took the turn towards Sanda, and it was also spotted later, heading for Hejde. A witness reported seeing a black car driving fast in the same direction only minutes later, but we have no idea whether it has any connection to the robbery. No other details, and no conclusive evidence as yet.'

'And they got the rain free of charge,' muttered Sohlman between clenched teeth, staring listlessly at the water pouring down outside the windows facing Östercentrum shopping centre.

'Do we know how much they got away with?' asked Wittberg.

'Four money bags containing two hundred thousand kronor each,' replied Knutas. 'The problem is, there's a big risk the banknotes will be destroyed the minute anyone tries to break open the bags.'

'Could it be an inside job?'

'Everyone who works for the transport company has been interviewed today and, at the present time, there's nothing to indicate that any of them were involved,' said Knutas. 'But you never know.'

'And the perps didn't leave even a scrap of evidence at the crime scene,' Sohlman lamented. 'Anything that might have been left was swiftly washed away by the damned rain.'

Wittberg was starting to get fed up with his colleague's constant complaints about the weather.

'Where could the robbers have come from?' he asked, casting an annoyed glance at Sohlman. 'It seems unlikely they would be from Gotland.'

'Hard to say,' replied Knutas. 'Since none of them uttered a word, we don't have any dialect or accent to go on.'

'I wonder why they kept silent like that,' Wittberg went on, his expression pensive.

'Maybe they don't speak Swedish,' suggested Jacobsson.

'Yet they seem to be very familiar with the local area,' said Knutas. 'They knew exactly where to strike and which escape route would be best. The robbery must have been carefully planned.'

'The question is: where are they now? They're probably lying low somewhere,' said Wittberg, looking at his watch. He had a dinner date he didn't want to miss.

Sohlman shook his head.

'Unfortunately, we have no idea what sort of car they took after setting fire to the Ford. Any evidence disappeared in the mud.'

'And the fire diverted everyone's attention, since it got so big so fast,' added Jacobsson. 'No one has reported any sightings of the robbers after that. The trail stopped there, in the woods in Sanda.'

'We've already launched a full investigation,' said Knutas. 'We've got officers knocking on doors in the area surrounding the crime scene in Klintehamn and near the site where the car was found in Sanda. We're searching all the summer cottages and other empty buildings, but that's going to take time, of course. We're also tracking down any organized crime gangs who might have had something to do with the robbery.'

'What about surveillance at the airport and ferry terminal?' asked Norrby.

'We don't have enough resources to check every individual who leaves the island. Especially since we don't really know who we're looking for.'

Silence settled over the room. Sohlman was the one who finally spoke, after first sighing with resignation.

'Oh, great. Perfect timing.'

Everyone turned to see what he was looking at outside the window.

The rain had stopped.

1994

The metro shuddered as it raced towards the city. Terese was sitting at the very back of the carriage, leaning her face against the window. She caught a glimpse of her own reflection in the glass. Long, straight hair, almost black in colour. She'd dyed it herself in the bathroom at Jessica's place. They'd swiped the box of dye from the ICA, but it wasn't a brand they were familiar with. Some cheap shit. The colour hadn't turned out anything like she'd imagined. Her greyish-blue eyes peered out from between the thick layer of waterproof black mascara she'd applied to her lashes. Her complexion was sallow from the lack of sunlight in the winter months, but at least she didn't have the pimples and blemishes most of her classmates did. She wore only a jacket over a vest. Spring was on its way, and the day felt unusually warm. She'd put on tight jeans and trainers. Initially, she'd planned to go to school, if for no other reason than to hang out in the cafeteria for a while, but as she stood outside the building she was suddenly seized with an impulse and walked on. She rang Jessica, who agreed to go into town instead. They were best friends, and both girls would much rather spend their time at Plattan, the lower plaza section of Sergels Torg, instead of in a classroom. It had been days since either had set foot in school.

Terese knew that it wouldn't be long before somebody phoned her home. She couldn't even count how many times this had happened before. Not that her mother or father cared. If they even bothered to answer the phone. They were too busy with their own problems. Both of her parents were unemployed and spent most of each day wandering around town with their pals. For as long as Terese could remember, they had been alcoholics and drug addicts. Her mother had periods when she was sober and, in some inexplicable way, she'd managed to keep the authorities from intervening too much in the family's life. She'd made a point of driving Terese to school every day, and she was somehow able to put on a good front whenever the social workers paid a visit.

If they only knew, thought Terese as she sat in her room in the flat, pretending to do her homework while some woman from the social-services office drank coffee with her mother in the living room, which would have been hastily tidied. Her father was always sent off before any social workers came over. His addiction was too easy to spot, with his missing teeth and inability to sit still.

A steady stream of people who were supposedly her parents' friends came over, just to sit around the flat. Drugs and alcohol were really the only things that drew them together, and the crowd was constantly changing. Occasionally, somebody would come into Terese's room to say hello. Lately, several of their male buddies had tried to grope her. Fortunately, so far she'd been able to fend them off, telling them to go to hell.

Even though her home situation was far from ideal, Terese hadn't tried to get help. She was determined to manage the best she could on her own. She didn't want to report her mother and father because then the authorities would pick them up and force them into a rehab facility. And she didn't even want to think about what might happen to her under those circumstances.

In her mind she conjured up a nightmare scenario in which she was locked up in a young offenders institution, with various wardens who forced her to swallow tons of pills.

In any case, Terese lived her own life and stayed away from home as much as possible. She longed for the day when she would turn eighteen and be able to leave behind that filthy flat in the Bagarmossen district. Recently, her parents' alcoholism and drug abuse had grown even worse. But there was nothing she could do about the situation. It was simply too much for her.

The place where she felt best was at Plattan in downtown Stockholm. Once a popular hang-out for junkies, it had expanded its clientele, and nowadays lots of young people had started gathering there. Kids who had nothing to do, who were unhappy at home or in school, and those who had nowhere else to go. There was a sense of camaraderie that Terese enjoyed. She didn't have to feel like a loser. No one was better than anyone else; they were all in the same boat. Luckily, her parents never went there. They never ventured beyond Bagarmossen.

When Terese and Jessica arrived at Plattan, the place was almost deserted. It was only nine thirty, and the morning rush, with all the crowds of people emerging from the metro and commuter trains to head for work, was over. And it was too early for any shoppers, since most of the stores didn't open until ten.

They sat down on the stone stairs and gazed out across the open plaza, which was surrounded by glass and concrete. For years this spot had been considered the most dangerous place in all of Stockholm. They each lit a cigarette, and for a while they sat in silence. The April sun was warm, and Terese took off her jacket. Before long a young guy came over to ask if they wanted to buy anything. Terese straightened up and gave him a smile, grateful for the attention. Finally, something was happening. He looked to be about their age, which was unusually young for a drug dealer, but she thought he was awfully cute, with his long, curly hair. He spoke Swedish with an accent.

'Where are you from?' she asked him.

'Gotland,' he said, his face lighting up. 'Tofta. Do you know where that is? It's well known because it has the most famous beach on Gotland.'

'Haven't got a clue. I've never been to Gotland.'

'You haven't? Well, you're really missing something.'

He cast an appreciative glance at her breasts under the tight T-shirt. It was amazing how that worked every time.

'So where are you from?' he asked, his eyes fixed on her low neckline.

'Bagarmossen. Do you know where that is?' she repeated his question.

'Sure. I crash with a buddy of mine in Farsta whenever I come over to the mainland. It's not far from there.' He turned to Jessica. 'Is that where you live, too?'

'I'm from Skarpnäck,' she replied sullenly. She took a deep drag on her cigarette and made a point of looking away. That was the worst thing about Jessica. She always fell into a bad mood if she wasn't the centre of attention.

'What are you doing here in Stockholm?' asked Terese, ignoring Jessica's surly behaviour.

The boy leaned forward and lowered his voice. His eyes gleamed, and he had dimples in his cheeks. He was looking cuter by the second.

'I've run away from home. But don't tell anyone.'

Terese laughed. He was really charming. And he had such a funny way of talking. A Swedish dialect that was softer, different. His voice was so nice, but he was also really cool.

'Why, if I may ask?'

'Have you ever heard of Gutemannen?'

'Gutemannen?' she repeated, opening her eyes wide. 'Who's that?'

Now even Jessica had turned around to listen.

'It's my father. In the daytime he goes around Gotland and seems just like everybody else. He goes to work, shops at the Konsum supermarket, goes home and cooks dinner with my mother, watches TV, works on his car, goes out to have a beer with his mates once in a while. But at night, when everyone is asleep, then . . .'

The boy fell silent and gave the girls a sly look. His eyes were dancing under his fringe of curls. He seemed to be enjoying the fact that he had their undivided attention.

'Then what?' they said in unison.

'Then he puts on his rubber suit, sort of like the one Spiderman wears, and he sneaks up on people to scare them to death.'

43

'How does he do that?' asked Terese, sounding sceptical.

'He rushes at them, bellowing and waving an axe in front of their eyes. It scares the shit out of them, but that's all he ever does. He's satisfied with scaring them. There have been lots of articles in the newspapers about him.'

'So why hasn't he ever been caught?'

'The cops have no idea that it's my father. I ran away from home because I couldn't keep my mouth shut any longer.'

'Oh, sure. You've got to be kidding.'

'Of course I am,' he said with a grin. 'What did you think?'

An hour later all three found themselves in a run-down flat in Farsta. The blinds had been partially lowered and smoke was slowly spiralling towards the ceiling. They'd been smoking pot, and Terese was feeling dazed and giggly. Her mouth was very dry. The cute Gotlander was rocking out on his electric guitar as Jimi Hendrix sang from the stereo, turned up full blast. The next-door neighbour pounded on the wall, but none of them paid any attention. By this time Jessica's mood had thawed, and she'd developed a real crush on their new acquaintance. Now she started dancing right in front of him. She pulled the clip out of her long hair and tossed her head back and forth. Terese was sitting in an easy chair with her legs tucked under her. She lit another joint, inhaled deeply and held the smoke in her lungs as long as she could before finally letting it out. Her head was spinning as she leaned back. This was fucking beautiful. All her problems seemed far away. Right now her classmates were sitting in school learning maths or Swedish or some other boring subject. And here she sat instead. Life was wonderful.

The other two were making out when she heard the doorbell begin ringing insistently. She listened for a while, thinking it was probably the neighbour, come to complain about the noise. Her friends didn't notice a thing. She got up and staggered over to the stereo, fumbling until she found the volume dial. When she turned down the sound, she heard a stern voice speaking through the letterbox.

'Open up! This is the police!'

Knutas walked home from work. When he opened the door to his house on Bokströmsgatan, he breathed in the aroma of homemade meatballs. A tune by the Danish rock band Gasoline was blaring from the speakers, but through the music he could hear a clattering sound from the kitchen.

'Hello!' he called as he took off his shoes and jacket in the front hall.

No answer. He went over to the kitchen and peered inside. There he saw his wife, wearing an apron patterned with large flowers and with her red hair drawn into a long plait that hung down her back. She was cooking the meatballs, tossing them into the hot frying pan. At the same time she was singing at the top of her voice and very off key along with the song 'What Do We Do Now, My Dear?'

'Hello!' he shouted again, a little louder this time. Lina turned around. Her face was flushed from the heat of the hob, making her freckles even more pronounced. She wiped the sweat from her forehead and gave him a smile.

'Hi! Are you hungry?'

He felt his heart swell with warmth as he surveyed the kitchen. Lina always went to such extremes. All the available surfaces held platters filled with fragrant, cooked meatballs, made according to her own spicy recipe. He felt his mouth watering.

'How many have you made? Five hundred?'

'I wasn't counting.'

'Why the big production?'

'I just felt like it. I had such a lovely day at work. A woman who has been in the hospital for a month because there was a risk of her having another miscarriage gave birth to her first child today. She's been so nervous the whole time. We'd planned on a Caesarean, and everything went like clockwork. She had a beautiful little boy. It was amazing.'

Knutas was listening with only half an ear as he stuffed several meatballs into his mouth. After being married for twenty years to a midwife who was passionate about her work and loved to talk about it, he'd heard just about everything. Many times over.

He studied Lina as he ate. It was great to see her looking so cheerful. That hadn't happened in quite a while. They were seldom at home together, since they were each busy with their own work. The twins were now eighteen and in their last year of secondary school. They had their own circle of friends and their own interests. Petra took an active role in the local orienteering group, both on weeknights and weekends, and she often stayed overnight with her boyfriend, who was also a member of the club. Nils spent every spare moment on his music.

And what about the two of them? Knutas and Lina had always had irregular work hours, so that was nothing new. But in the past they had still managed to find time to be together almost every day. At the moment he could hardly remember the last time he and Lina had eaten dinner together, just the two of them, in peace and quiet, or shared a bottle of wine, or even a cup of coffee.

Knutas felt a headache coming on.

'Are the kids home?'

'No. Petra has orienteering practice, and Nils is doing his homework over at Axel's place. They have a maths exam tomorrow, so they'll be staying up late. He's going to spend the night there. And Petra let me know that she'll be staying at Gustav's flat. As usual.'

She rolled her eyes and then wiped her hands on her apron.

'Is it OK if I turn down the music?' asked Knutas.

'Sure.'

Lina turned back to the worktop to make more meatballs. There was still a huge, glistening clump of meat waiting to be cooked. It looked like she'd never be finished. Her shoulders had now slumped a bit, and she was no longer singing along with the music. Knutas realized that he'd probably put a dampener on her mood. He gave her a light pat on the arm, then opened the fridge and took out the leftover pasta from yesterday's dinner. He piled pasta on a plate and heated it up in the microwave. Then he helped himself to some of the meatballs right from the frying pan. Carrying the plate and a glass of milk, he went into the living room to see if the robbery would be reported on the TV evening news.

The intro to the Regional News segment was playing. Then pictures appeared from Klintehamn, along with images of the police cordon and the car fire. Johan Berg's familiar voice narrated. Then came the traditional piece to camera showing the reporter outside the bank on Donnersgatan. 'Initially, all the indications were that the robbery was committed by three masked men, but an eyewitness has told Regional News that one of the robbers was most likely a woman.'

The camera shifted to an elderly woman with white hair sitting on a park bench and holding a poodle on her lap as Johan interviewed her. Her name was Asta Johansson, and she explained that she thought the third robber moved like a woman, not like a man. And besides, this robber had been wearing a thong.

The old woman, whom Johan Berg had brought to the police station, turned out to be a valuable witness. But when Knutas had asked her to keep what she'd seen to herself, she had proudly told him that she'd already spoken about the matter to a TV reporter.

People are hopeless, thought Knutas with a sigh. And that includes journalists.

He'd rung Berg and asked him not to make public the information that Asta Johansson had provided. The reporter had replied that he could make no promises.

The news programme was over. He finished the food on his plate, noticing how tired he felt. He belched quietly and then leaned back against the sofa cushions. That was when he discovered Lina standing in the doorway, looking at him without saying a word. He had no idea how long she'd been there. She was still wearing her apron, and her arms hung limply at her sides.

'What is it?' he asked.

He felt a nervous tightening in his stomach. She was looking at him with a serious expression on her face, and it took a moment before she replied.

'We need to talk.'

The alcohol was beginning to have its effect on Jocke. The whisky bottle was empty, and there was no more beer. Terese and Degen had started making out, but he had no desire either to watch or to participate. They paid no attention to him as Degen proceeded to pull off her jumper. She wore no bra, and her breasts gleamed in the light from the bare bulb hanging above the table. Jocke lit a cigarette and got up. Staggering, he nearly toppled over. He was very drunk.

The cramped kitchen felt stuffy and damp. He needed to take a shit. Sticking his feet in a pair of wooden clogs, he opened the door and went outside into the cool night air. He tossed his cigarette on the grass and took several deep breaths. The rain had stopped. In his mind he pictured the bundles of banknotes in the as yet inaccessible money bags. As soon as they divided up the loot, his problems would be over. First he would pay off his debts to various drug dealers, both on the mainland and here on Gotland. Then it would be time to book himself a trip abroad. He could hardly remember the last time he'd left Sweden. And he'd buy himself that Harley he'd been dreaming of. He should be able to afford it if he could get a good price for his own bike. They just had to keep the cops off their trail.

It had been a long time since he'd had such a sense of satisfaction, and he whistled to himself as he headed for the toilet. The little outhouse was old and rotting, standing among a cluster of trees at the other end of the property. He looked up at the sky. The clouds had moved away, and the moon had appeared, breaking through the darkness to cast a glow over the grass. The lonely howling of a dog echoed far away in the night; otherwise, there wasn't a sound, and nothing moved. No lights were visible from the other farms.

Jocke wondered how long they'd have to stay here and hide out. He hoped it would be only a couple of days. They'd given false names when they came over on the boat and, since they hadn't left any evidence behind and hadn't spoken a word or revealed any distinguishing traits, he assumed the police wouldn't connect them to the robbery. The other two were from the mainland. Neither of them had set foot on Gotland in years, while he lived in a bedsit in Gråbo, just outside of Visby. But he went over to the mainland as often as he could to visit friends.

Terese and Degen were the two people to whom he felt the closest. They'd known each other since they were teenagers, drinking, fucking and committing crimes together. Nobody knew him better than they did, although they tried to keep their friendship low profile. It was no one else's business.

Jocke lifted the latch and opened the door, which creaked loudly. Several old newspapers were stacked up next to the toilet, but it would be useless to try to read anything. It was too dark. Not even the moonlight reached inside, although he'd left the door open. He sank down heavily on the seat, realizing that he was constipated. This was going to take time. Fatigue overwhelmed him as he leaned back, closed his eyes and dozed.

He had no idea how long he'd been sitting there when he heard a rustling sound in the grass outside. He opened his eyes and stared out of the door. Nothing was visible in the dark but thick shrubbery, with raindrops on the wet leaves glistening in the moonlight. His muscles tensed, and he sat up straight. Held still, waiting to hear something more. It was probably nothing. A rabbit, or a hedgehog, or some other stupid little animal. And yet he listened alertly. Needed to be on his guard. More rustling. It couldn't be the bloody cops out there, sneaking about in the bushes, could it? Jocke breathed as quietly as he could while he frantically looked about for toilet paper. The roll was on the floor a short distance away. He had no intention of being caught with his trousers down, that much was certain.

As he raised himself up to reach for it, he heard a loud scraping sound, just on the other side of the wall, only centimetres away. He flinched and fell back on to the toilet seat. It was a long-drawn-out sound, as if someone were slowly dragging an object along the wall. Maybe to tease him. Or scare him. Was it Terese or Degen, playing a practical joke on him? The cops, at any rate, wouldn't behave this way.

Jocke had a hard time believing his friends would do something like this. He'd learned over the years that once they got started making out, nothing could stop them. But who could it be? Somebody who had crept out here to their hiding place and wanted to steal the loot? That seemed the most likely scenario. Fuck. That would be so damned typical. A great sense of irritation surged inside him as he tried to make his foggy brain think clearly. He needed to stand up and overpower the intruder. His current situation was too exposed, and that was putting it mildly, sitting here on the toilet as he was, with his arse bare and his jeans down around his ankles in this cramped space. A shadow rushed past outside the little window. Someone was out there, someone who didn't want to be seen. Jocke made an attempt to get up, but it was too late.

A silhouette appeared in the doorway. A knife gleamed in the moonlight.

Suddenly, it was all too clear to Jocke Eriksson that his luck had run out.

'Has something happened?' asked Knutas.

Lina closed her eyes for a second and shook her head. She brushed back a lock of hair from her forehead.

'No, not exactly. But we need to talk. Could you turn off the TV?'

She untied her apron and took it off, draping it over a chair. Then she sat down at the other end of the sofa and turned to face her husband. She rested her freckled arm along the back of the sofa and slowly began twirling a strand of hair, which was what she always did whenever she had to discuss something important. She seemed to be mustering her courage before saying anything. Knutas had a sudden urge for a cigarette. Her eyes were bright and clear, her expression determined.

'We can't go on like this,' she said.

'What do you mean?'

She threw up her hands. She always had to be so dramatic.

'We hardly spend any time with each other any more. We never do anything fun together. I want to be able to laugh with my husband. We used to do that, but nowadays it never happens.'

'But things aren't really that bad, are they?' he ventured. 'All marriages have their ups and downs. I mean, good Lord, we've been together for twenty years, so there are bound to be some low periods once in a while.'

'"Once in a while"?' Her expression was bitter. 'Our relationship has been in the dumps for a long time. I've been trying hard by suggesting various activities we could share, and offering to do things with you at the weekends. Or suggesting that we could spend a long weekend in Barcelona, or Paris, or Venice. But you always say it would cost too much, or you don't have time because you need to mow the lawn out at the summer house, or you have to paint the fence, or you have too much work, or it's much nicer just staying at home. You're not interested in any of my suggestions, but you haven't come up with any of your own. I'm sick and tired of being the engine that keeps this relationship running. If it weren't for me, nothing would ever get done in this family.'

'I think we're doing fine. But I'll definitely give some thought to what you're saying. I promise.'

'I've heard that so many times before,' she replied, sounding resigned. 'You can't just think about these matters. You have to do something. It's actions that count. You sit in an office all day, but you can't even make yourself pick up the phone and book cinema tickets as a nice surprise for me. Apparently, you don't think I'm worth even the slightest bit of effort on your part.'

'I just never get around to anything like that. Is it really so important? I do other things for you and the children. I take care of all the practical chores here at home. I make improvements at the summer house and fix things up so it'll be better for all of us. Doesn't that show you my love and consideration?'

'But it's not just about taking care of things in the house. As a woman, I need you to acknowledge me, pay attention to me. I want to feel attractive.'

Knutas felt his throat close up. Suddenly, it became clear to him what this was about.

'Have you met someone else?'

'No, of course not,' she said firmly. 'That's so typical. Just because a woman feels unhappy and decides to say what she needs, it must mean that she's met another man. You're all alike. You think you're the only ones who exist in the world.'

Red blotches had appeared on her neck, signifying either that she was upset or she was lying. Or both.

For a moment neither of them spoke. These contentious topics had been discussed many times before, with each of them saying the same things over and over. He was intimately familiar with the issues Lina had brought up, but he'd never considered them particularly serious. No marriage was perfect, and they couldn't very well expect to behave like teenagers newly in love. Although it was true there wasn't much happening in their sex life, but for some reason she hadn't opted to mention that. He could hardly remember the last time they'd made love. It must have been sometime at the beginning of summer.

'And then there's the fact that I'm homesick,' she said quietly.

'You're homesick? But this is your home.'

'I'm talking about Denmark. I miss my language, I miss the people, the food, the culture, the way of life, my old friends, my parents and my sister. I've tried to make you understand, but you never listen. And I don't want to hear about how we could celebrate Christmas in Denmark, or at least go there more often.'

'I didn't realize it was so important to you. You've lived here in Sweden for two decades. Why are you feeling homesick now?'

'I don't know,' she said, sighing. 'Maybe it's because the kids are getting older. They're busy with their own lives. And I have more space and time to think about things. To reflect on what I really want and in what way my needs haven't been met. I've come to the realization that I have to listen to myself.'

Her words died away and they were both silent.

'OK,' he said after a pause. 'So what do you think we should do?'

She didn't look him in the eye when she answered.

'I've taken a temporary position at the University Hospital in Copenhagen. It's for six months. The hospital owns a flat that I can rent while I'm there. And I can come home almost every weekend.'

Knutas stared at her in astonishment. She had planned it all out.

She was already halfway out of the door.

1994

Terese stared at the coast of Gotland as the plane descended for landing. Far below her lay the bright shoreline facing the open sea, with a few farms scattered about and hardly any roads, just flat open land. The pot party at Jocke's place in Farsta and the fact that she'd once again been taken into police custody had proved to be the last straw. The police had gone to see her parents at their flat and found both of them dead drunk, along with several drinking companions.

Social services had decided to send her to a foster family for the time being. Terese was relieved when she heard she would be placed with a family on Gotland, and not somewhere in northern Sweden, which was her greatest fear. The initial plan was for her to stay on Gotland just for the summer but, if everything went well, she would enter secondary school in Visby in the autumn.

She felt a great sense of relief when she left home, carrying a big suitcase and accompanied by two social workers, who took her to the airport. Now that she could see the coastline, it all became very real. She was about to leave her drunken parents behind, along with all the shit and turmoil in the flat in Bagarmossen. Had it ever been a home? Had she ever felt safe and secure in that place? She thought about all the years of drunken parties and the constant torment of worrying about what might happen next. At least that was no longer her concern.

And she suddenly realized that she no longer had any feelings for her parents. She didn't care what might happen to them. Through their drinking and drug use they had long ago ruined the love she had once felt for them, when she was a child. Now there was nothing left.

That was when she made up her mind, at the very moment when that insight sank in: she was never going back.

When Terese entered the arrivals hall at Visby airport, she was met by a woman named Viveka, who seemed to be her mother's age. She was short and stocky with curly hair. She smiled and shook hands with Terese, welcoming her to Gotland and speaking with a distinctive local accent that was even stronger than Jocke's.

'The car is parked outside,' said Viveka, lifting the heavy suitcase from the baggage carousel with no effort at all.

She led the way to the exit. Outside, the sun was shining in a cloudless sky. The cowslips and blue anemones blooming along the road were clear signs that summer was on its way. Terese had left behind a grey and overcast Stockholm. Somewhere, she'd heard that the sun always shone more on Gotland.

As they drove towards the city, Viveka chatted easily.

'You're lucky you've been placed with the Stenfors family. They haven't had any experience taking in foster kids. You're the first to be placed with them, but they're good people and well known here on Gotland. They own a popular restaurant in Visby. It's called Catch 22, and it's down by the harbour. Actually, it's mostly Mr Stenfors – Palle – who runs the restaurant. Mrs Stenfors – Susanne – spends most of her time at home, taking university courses by correspondence. And they have two children, twin boys, who are twelve years old. Daniel and Kristoffer. But I suppose you already know all this.'

Viveka smiled at Terese.

'Yes,' she said, 'but I don't know what they're like. I mean, as people.'

'Oh, don't you worry about that. They're nice, easy-going folks. Very pleasant to deal with, I must say. Always cheerful and friendly, and I know that they're really looking forward to having you to stay with them. They live in a big house with a view of the sea, in one of the best neighbourhoods in Visby. Well, it's actually a bit outside town,' she corrected herself. 'The area is called Högklint, and it's quite beautiful.'

Terese gave Viveka a sceptical look.

'It sounds like a perfect family. Why would they want to bother with me? Why would they take me in at all? They don't even know me.'

Viveka didn't answer.

'Where is Tofta?' Terese asked after a pause.

'Ten kilometres outside town, to the south. Why do you ask?'

'Oh, no reason. I just heard about it. That's all.'

'There's an excellent swimming beach there,' said Viveka. 'I'm sure you'll have an opportunity to go there in the summer.'

They were now approaching Visby, passing the three black towers of the cathedral and the magnificent city walls, which Terese had previously seen only in postcards. Viveka pointed out the sights and explained what they were. Soon they had driven through the city, and Terese caught a glimpse of the sea, glittering in the distance.

'We're going to take the turn here to Kneippbyn. Have you heard of it? There's a big campsite near the shore, but Kneippbyn is best known for its amusement park; it's got all sorts of attractions for children. And right next to it is a water park with lots of fun water slides. Plus, it's the location of Pippi Longstocking's house, Villa Villekulla. The Pippi films were made here on the island. But maybe you knew that?'

Terese nodded. She felt more favourably inclined towards this woman than she usually did with anyone in a position of authority. There was something appealing about Viveka's melodic Gotland accent and her friendly manner. It reminded her of Jocke, the only other person she'd met from Gotland so far, although he no longer lived on the island. He was probably still staying with that friend of his in the flat in Farsta. But he'd mentioned that he might go home for the summer. He hadn't yet found a job, and his parents still lived in the house in Tofta. He'd boasted about owning a cool motorcycle. He'd offered to give her a ride to show her around the island.

Terese's thoughts were interrupted as Viveka once again started talking.

'We're now getting to Högklint and, as I said, there's a lovely view of Visby from up there, and I'm sure the family will show it to you. We'll be there any minute now.'

The road continued climbing the slope, and the landscape seemed to get more and more desolate. She started having misgivings. How far from the city did these people live? She'd never be able to go into town on her own. She'd be like a prisoner out here.

They turned on to an even smaller gravel road and drove along the shoreline. After a few more minutes they arrived at a white limestone house, situated all alone on a hill. It looked new. The surrounding area was mostly forest. When Terese looked up at the house, she had an odd sense of foreboding. As if it were brooding over some dark secret. She quickly shook it off.

It was probably just her imagination.

Emma was looking at Johan, who sat at the table across from her. They had just finished a nice dinner and were leaning back comfortably in their chairs, each with a glass of red wine. They'd been talking about the intense activity of the first two days of the week. She had just started a new term at school, and he was working on the story about the security-van robbery in Klintehamn. She was grateful that her parents had agreed to take care of the kids. They would be in Fårö all week.

On Sunday Emma's teenaged children, Sara and Filip, would come to stay with them. They were the offspring of her first marriage to Olle. Emma had still been married when she fell in love with Johan, and her whole life was subsequently turned upside down. After her divorce, she and her ex-husband had gone through a turbulent period, but now things had settled down. No doubt in large part because Olle had met another woman, who was from Visby. By now they'd been in a relationship for several years. Sara and Filip lived part-time with each parent, which was easy enough, since Olle still lived in Roma. Sometimes Emma worried that he'd want to move to Visby, to be with his girlfriend. But there was no use fretting about that in advance.

Right now she was most concerned about Johan. He'd been very irritable lately, and seemed totally uninterested in sex. He wasn't his usual lovable self. Maybe it was because the children demanded so much of their attention. And Sara and Filip were also staying up later in the evenings, which made it more difficult for Emma and Johan to have any time to themselves. Every other week they had all four children with them, and on Sunday they'd have a full house once again.

This is our only chance for a while, she had thought earlier as she changed the bedlinen and took a long shower to wash her hair before dinner. Then she had made herself up a little, put on some mascara and lipstick. She'd even bought some new lacy underwear, which she'd put on under a clingy dress. My little surprise for him, she had thought, feeling a tingle of anticipation in her groin. It had been too long. But now that they were for once alone at home, she had opened a bottle of wine for dinner, even though it was an ordinary Tuesday evening.

She said a few words about how good the food had been and took another sip of her wine. Johan got up to clear. Even though she'd made a special attempt to dress up, he hadn't offered a single appreciative comment or compliment. He looked at her distractedly, as if nothing about her could possibly arouse his interest.

'Do you want coffee?' he asked.

'Sure.'

She helped herself to more wine, not feeling the slightest inclination to get up, now that they could sit here as long as they liked without dealing with a bunch of demanding kids. She didn't understand why Johan seemed so restless.

'Why don't you relax? We can take care of the dishes later,' she told him.

'I'm just going to put them in the dishwasher.'

Then silence.

She watched him placing the dirty crockery in the racks, her eyes fixed on his back.

'What's the matter with you?'

He turned around.

'What do you mean? Nothing.'

'You seem so distant, so uninterested in me.'

'You're exaggerating. There's just been so much going on lately, what with the kids being sick. Plus, there are so many things that need fixing in the house, and now I've got this robbery story, which means working non-stop.'

He closed the dishwasher, pressed the buttons to start the wash cycle and then came back to sit down at the table. He raised his glass to drink a toast.

'Skål!'

'Skål!'

Neither of them spoke for a moment.

'How about watching a film?' said Johan. He got up to find the newspaper. 'There's a Swedish drama on Channel 2. It's called *Three Suns*, it's directed by Richard Hobert and stars Lena Endre and Mikael Persbrandt. That might be good. Have you seen it?'

Emma shook her head. She couldn't bring herself to say anything.

He carried on studying the paper.

'Later there's an action flick on Channel 4, an American film that gets four stars. What do you feel like?'

Emma finished her wine and abruptly set down her glass.

'What do I feel like?'

Then she stomped off to the bedroom and slammed the door.

When he came home in the early hours of the morning, he slipped inside through the cellar door. He went straight to the bathroom to take a shower, and then carefully dried himself off. He had to get rid of all traces. When he was done, he checked to make sure there were no spots of blood on his body. He put his clothes in the washing machine and turned it on, frowning when he realized how much noise it made. The sound seemed so much louder at night. He closed the door to the laundry room and silently prayed that no one would wake up.

He'd parked the car in a secure spot. It had taken quite a while to clean everything, and he'd wanted to make a thorough job of it. Even though he'd wrapped the seats in plastic beforehand, there was still a risk that some bloodstains might have been left. He'd go over the car again in daylight, just to be sure.

He went back to the bathroom and looked at himself in the mirror, wanting to see if there was any change in his appearance. A fiery sensation shot through his body as he thought about what he'd done. He laughed out loud, but then fell silent. He was almost frightened by the grinning face in the mirror. He drank some water and again looked at his reflection. He stood there for a long time, going over the whole course of events. It had been easier than he'd thought. Of course, he'd had to wait for hours, but that hadn't bothered him. He'd felt unexpectedly calm. As if what he was planning was the right thing to do. Right and justified. The moment had finally arrived. He'd brought along a backpack containing sandwiches, a Thermos of coffee and a hip flask of whisky to steady his nerves. And the knife, of course.

He'd done a few tests at home. Bought some big steaks, which he'd stabbed with the knife. Just to get a feeling for how the blade would penetrate flesh. He'd also trained himself to be precise. He had tied a string around the pieces of meat and then practised cutting along it. With a firm and strong hand and not the slightest hesitation. That was what was required. When it came to the real-life situation, there would be no room for error. Then he'd simply have to go for it. And he had. He would never forget the sight of his pitiful victim. The man had sat there with his trousers down around his ankles, looking like a stupid pig. It hadn't been the least bit difficult.

Afterwards he'd had the presence of mind to follow through with his plan and quickly retreat to the root cellar. He purposely damaged one of the money bags until it began to leak dye. Then he tossed it outside in the grass, thinking it would be a good way to throw the police off his track. Let them think that those stupid robbers had started killing each other off.

Then he'd turned his attention to getting out of there.

Only now, as he looked at himself in the mirror, did he feel a great sense of relief. The pressure in his chest had eased. He was free of pain.

At least partially.

1994

As Viveka parked outside the house, a voice could be heard calling: 'They're here!'

Four people came crowding around the car before Terese even had time to take her suitcase out of the boot. The mother of the family was the first to speak. She smiled, showing her lovely white teeth.

'Hi! I'm Susanne. Welcome.'

She was slender and fair-haired, slightly shorter than Terese. No make-up aside from some pale-pink lipstick. Her hair, which just skimmed her shoulders, had been blow-dried, giving it a wavy look. She wore black linen trousers and a white top. Sandals on her bare feet. Small hands and fingernails that were perfectly manicured, long and shiny but devoid of polish. No watch or jewellery except for her engagement ring, with its huge diamond sparkling from her finger. Her body seemed sinewy and fit. She was the type of woman who presumably always looked perfect, no matter what she wore.

Terese shook hands with the woman, giving her a suspicious look from under her fringe. A faint sense of nausea rose inside her. She couldn't think of a single thing to say.

The father of the family was tall and lanky with warm brown eyes. He had on a white T-shirt with the Manhattan skyline printed in black across the front, and khaki shorts. His feet were bare, his face suntanned, with several days of stubble on his cheeks. His hand felt dry to the touch.

'Hi. My name is Palle. Well, my real name is Per-Alvar, but you can hear how pretentious that sounds. So everyone calls me Palle.' He turned towards his twin sons, who were standing nearby. 'This is Daniel, and this is Kristoffer.'

The boys looked happy, though a bit shy, as she shook their hands. It was hard to tell them apart. They had the same dark, close-cropped hair, brown eyes, and dimples in their cheeks.

'Well, I've got to leave you now, but we'll see each other tomorrow at the social-services office,' said Viveka brightly. 'At eleven o'clock. Is that OK?'

'Of course. I'll drive you in,' Susanne said to Terese. 'Then maybe I can show you around Visby.' She gave her an encouraging look.

'I'm sure that would be nice,' Viveka hurried to say. She gave Terese a quick hug, then got in the car and drove back down the hill.

Terese turned away. She took out a cigarette and lit it, immediately noticing the look of displeasure on the faces of both Palle and Susanne. She was already sullying their clean air.

'Would you like something to drink before we show you around?' Susanne rushed to ask her. 'But, of course, you should finish your cigarette first.'

She promptly fetched an ashtray from a cubbyhole in the stone wall that encircled the property. Terese took her time. She didn't give a shit what these upper-class people thought. As she smoked, she studied her surroundings. The house stood at the far end of the flat, stone-covered grounds. Extending out from the grand-looking building was a series of terraces, and there she could see patio furniture and a barbecue.

When they went inside, she was struck by how much light there was. The floor was grey stone, but everything else was white, and all the rooms had high ceilings. Windows reached from floor to ceiling. The rooms were neat and tidy, with nothing left lying about except for a blanket spread over a sheepskin-covered armchair, a glossy interior-decorating magazine and a bowl of green apples. It was like wandering through an art gallery with a few big and brightly coloured paintings on the walls. With growing unease, Terese wondered how she was ever going to be able to relax in this house.

The kitchen was spotless, with gleaming stainless-steel appliances. On the granite worktop she saw only a platter of fresh lemons and a ceramic pot holding a single green stem.

The large living room was dominated by an enormous whitewashed fireplace. In front of the hearth stood two low, light-coloured sofas facing each other, and between them was a glass coffee table with a vase filled with summer flowers. Terese had never been in such a beautiful home, and she hardly dared move.

As if Susanne had read her thoughts, she said, 'Let me just say that everything isn't usually this neat and clean. We wanted the house to look nice for you.'

'We?' Kristoffer protested. 'It was Elena.' The boy looked up at Terese. 'That's our cleaning lady. She's really nice, but she doesn't speak very good Swedish. Do you know Spanish?'

Terese shook her head.

'Mamma can speak a little. I'm going to start learning Spanish in school. That'll be great. Then I can talk to Elena.'

Susanne's smile looked a bit strained as she took out a jug from the fridge to pour a glass of water. She handed it to Terese.

'Well, usually things are left lying around everywhere. So please make yourself at home.'

What a joke, thought Terese. This place was as far from a home as anything she'd ever imagined.

She needed to pee. She couldn't hold it any longer, so she asked if she could use the toilet.

Susanne pointed her towards the bathroom door, and then the family discreetly withdrew, pretending to carry on a conversation. Terese felt like she was on stage. Like she was playing a role. The bathroom had a dimmer switch and spotlights set into the ceiling. She was impressed by the thick bath towels that were neatly folded and stacked on the shelves. A window facing the woods was open slightly, and the room smelled faintly of some sort of fruit. The fragrance came from a scented candle in a bowl.

When she came out, they continued the house tour. The whole family trooped along. The guestroom on the ground floor was to be hers, and she was glad that it wasn't upstairs with the other bedrooms. It was big and airy. Through the window she could see the crooked pine trees, and off in the distance a narrow strip of sea was visible. The bed was both higher and wider than her bed back home, with a bright coverlet and big, fluffy pillows. She had an urge to throw herself on to it right there and then. Across from the bed was a TV hanging from the ceiling, almost like in a hotel room. On a chair was a bath towel and a smaller hand towel. A white dressing gown was draped over the back of the chair. Everything was for her.

'From out here you have at least a bit of a view of the sea,' said Susanne, opening the balcony doors.

The only sound outside was a faint rustling in the trees.

'From upstairs you can see much more of the water, but I thought you might find it more important to have some privacy. You have your own bathroom here, and it's also easier for you to get to the kitchen if you want something to eat.' Susanne turned to face Terese. 'And let me say this right away: feel free to take whatever you want from the cupboards if you get hungry. Later, you'll have to tell me what you like so I can buy the right things at the supermarket tomorrow. We all have our likes and dislikes.' She laughed. 'For example, for breakfast I always have to have oatmeal with nuts and slices of kiwi and banana. On top of that I put warm raspberries with a sprinkling of cinnamon. Do you have any favourite foods for breakfast?'

'I like Havrefras cereal,' muttered Terese.

'Me too!' cried Kristoffer eagerly. 'That's what I have every morning. So you're in luck, because we already have some.'

He looked so happy she couldn't help smiling. He had the same warm eyes as his father.

'I hope you're not afraid of the dark,' said Susanne, sounding worried. 'The house is in a rather remote location. Our closest neighbour is a kilometre away.'

'No, I'm not afraid of the dark.'

Terese was starting to think that Susanne's concern was a little oppressive. Her husband, Palle, didn't say much. He mostly murmured an occasional 'uh-huh' or 'hmm'. After he had showed her how to work the TV, he left the room.

'We're planning to have dinner at seven,' said Susanne. 'Will you be all right until then?'

'Sure.'

It was already six, and she wasn't the least bit hungry.

'Afterwards I thought we could take a walk, if you'd like. So you can have a look around.'

'OK.'

'Good.'

Susanne gave her another smile and then left, closing the door behind her.

When Terese was finally alone, she sank on to the bed. It was just as comfortable as it looked. She stuffed a pillow behind her head and looked out at the terrace and woods, which she could see through the window.

What was she doing here?

Knutas was having a restless night, slipping in and out of sleep. He woke at four in the morning and couldn't get back to sleep. He lay in bed in the dim light, staring at Lina's freckled back. He wondered who she really was. Had he ever truly known her deepest thoughts and wishes?

Had their life together been only an illusion? Last night the discussion had proceeded calmly; they'd had a sensible talk without any emotional outbursts. Lina was determined to go ahead with her plan to take the temporary position at the University Hospital in Copenhagen, and she'd already made all the arrangements. She'd be leaving in a few days. She explained that she'd kept everything secret until now because she hadn't wanted to be swayed from the decision she'd made. She claimed this had nothing to do with anyone else. It was all about her.

He was having a hard time following her reasoning. They were a family, after all, the four of them, and she was one part of the whole. In his view, it seemed completely incomprehensible for someone to isolate herself from her close family members, as Lina was doing. He didn't understand, but there was nothing he could do about it. All he could do was accept the situation. He tried to convince himself that this was a mere whim, an impulse, and she would soon come to her senses. Even though they'd lost some measure of intimacy lately, he remembered all too well how much he'd missed Lina when she had spent a month on the African islands of Cape Verde the year before. He'd been so happy to have her back home, but after that their relationship had begun to falter. And they had slipped further away from each other.

Maybe it's a good thing she's leaving for a while, he thought, trying to console himself. Maybe they both needed a little distance. Any couple that had spent twenty years together needed a break, a chance to do some soul-searching and ruminating. Maybe that's all it was.

And besides, now was a good time, since he was so preoccupied with this new case and the aftermath of the robbery, and now the little girl had died, turning the incident into a murder investigation. While he and Lina had been discussing things last night, a doctor had phoned from the hospital to tell him that the girl had died unexpectedly during surgery. The news had taken the wind out of Knutas. He had sat motionless in his easy chair, unable to say a single word. A cold shiver raced down his spine as he tried to process what the doctor had just said. Everyone on the medical team was shocked and no one could explain why the girl's condition had suddenly taken a turn for the worse. Her body would be taken to the forensics lab in Solna on the following day. They were hoping the autopsy would show what had caused the death of the six-year-old.

Putting their own problems aside, he and Lina had then gone to bed. But now thoughts were again whirling through his mind.

Knutas gave up trying to get any more rest. He quietly padded downstairs and turned on the coffee maker. The cat came into the kitchen and rubbed against his legs. He bent down to lift her up, burying his face in her soft fur. Then he sat at the table, listening to the gurgling of the coffee as it brewed. Life could be so easy or so hard, depending on the situation, he thought. Why did Lina have to make things so complicated? Why couldn't they just enjoy things now that the kids were older? Enjoy each other's company without making any major demands on each other. What was wrong with having some peace and quiet? The mere act of being alive was complicated enough without looking for any new problems.

He went out to fetch the morning paper, made himself some toast and then sat down at the table to drink his coffee with the cat curled up on his lap. He gave a start when he read the headline on the front page. A close-up of Maja Rosén covered half the page. An ordinary-looking six-year-old girl with her hair plaited and a big smile that revealed several missing teeth. KILLED BY ROBBERS, it said. Knutas felt his stomach churning.

It was terrible that she had died. He couldn't even imagine how her family must feel.

His and Lina's problems would have to wait. He needed to focus all his attention on the hunt for these robbers who had caused the little girl's death.

That was the only thing that mattered.

Terese woke when sunlight settled on her face. She closed her eyes even tighter to avoid the glare. Feeling annoyed, she pushed aside Degen's warm and hairy arm, which was resting heavily on her chest. She moved away from his body, which had been pressed close to her spine and backside. The mattress was thin and lumpy, providing little protection from the stone floor. Her back ached. Her mouth was dry from the pot they'd smoked the night before, and her tongue felt like it was sticking to her gums. She needed water. Fresh air. And she had to pee.

At first she couldn't remember where she was but, slowly, everything came back to her. The robbery, the accident, racing away in the car, the fire, the money bags. With an effort she managed to pull herself into a sitting position. She cupped one hand over her forehead and squinted as she looked around the sparsely furnished room. She saw several kitchen cupboards with peeling paint that had once been a pale yellow and a few remaining knobs. The sink was covered in rust, and there was no water in the pipes. The worktop was cluttered with dirty mugs, empty tins and bottles. The small hob with the old-fashioned burners was so filthy that it was unusable, and probably had been for years. A rickety table and a few spindle-backed chairs. Piles of old junk and mouldy newspapers scattered over the floor. A narrow bed in the corner, which was where Jocke should have been. But it was empty and didn't look as if it had been slept in at all. He was nowhere in sight. Had he passed out somewhere outside? He'd probably smoked too much. As usual. And maybe he hadn't limited himself to pot. She knew full well that he was also into heavier drugs.

The nice weather had returned. The sun shone in through the broken windows. When she stood up, she suddenly saw stars, and her headache came on full force. She almost fell backwards and had to close her eyes for a moment.

She opened the door and staggered out. She was instantly enveloped by the heat of the morning. It was much cooler inside the old stone house than outdoors. She wanted to check on the money bags they'd stolen, so she headed across the property, through the tall grass, and then stumbled down the steps to the overgrown root cellar where they'd hidden them. She wanted to make sure they were still there. They were her path to a new life.

The bags lay among piles of junk in the cramped space, clammy with damp. They were dark blue and made of a hard plastic. Impregnable. Clumsily, she lifted one of them. It felt very heavy and she ran her hand over the side. Then she noticed that one of the bags was missing. She looked around in confusion, then rummaged among the junk. Where the hell was Jocke? Had he run off and taken one of the bags with him? She searched some more but then realized it was not in the cellar.

She went back up the steps and out into the sunlight. She squatted down in the grass to pee, trying to think clearly. Maybe one of the guys had taken the bag out to check on it and then forgotten to put it back. That wouldn't be so strange. The thought was reassuring.

It had to be quite late, probably past noon. When she had finished, she stood up and looked towards the road, which was clearly visible. She listened for cars but couldn't hear any traffic at all. Everything was calm and quiet. A beautiful blue butterfly fluttered around among the sunflowers that grew wild next to the house. Bumblebees buzzed. Here and there she saw a red poppy that had survived the dry summer.

The door to the outhouse was wide open, but she didn't feel like going over there. Jocke was nowhere to be seen. Maybe he'd gone into the partially collapsed barn to sleep. She'd go looking for him in a minute, but first she needed something to drink. In the fridge she found several bottles of Coke and Ramlösa mineral water. She quickly drank a whole bottle of each and began to feel better.

She picked up Jocke's old transistor radio, sat down on the steps outside and lit a cigarette. That was when she discovered the third money bag, lying in the grass a short distance away. It was dented and stained. What the fuck? she thought. She went over to get it and saw that a greenish dye had leaked out. That meant the money was ruined. Anger surged through her.

At that moment the theme music for the news bulletin began playing on the radio. She froze, listening with her heart pounding in her chest.

> The six-year-old girl who was struck by
> the fleeing getaway car after the robbery

of a security van yesterday morning in Klintehamn on the island of Gotland has died from her injuries. In the afternoon the girl was said to be in a stable condition, but later in the evening her condition worsened, and the doctors were unable to save her life.

The police have not yet tracked down the whereabouts of the robbers, but an intense manhunt is under way.

Terese had stopped listening.

The hand holding the cigarette began to shake.

'Wake up! You have to wake up!'

Terese shook Degen hard, but he tried to fend her off by flailing his arms about.

'What's going on?'

'It's a total disaster. Jocke is gone, and the girl died. Can you believe it? The little girl we ran over is dead. She was in surgery, but she didn't make it.'

'Calm down. What are you babbling on about?'

Degen sat up and rubbed the sleep out of his eyes.

'Jocke must have taken off while we were sleeping. And somebody broke into one of the bags. The money is ruined, soaked in dye, totally worthless. I don't know what he was thinking. He must have been high or something. What a fucking idiot. And now they're saying on the radio that the girl died last night. Can you believe it? We're in deep shit.'

'What the hell?' shouted Degen when he saw the dented and green-stained bag that Terese was holding up in front of him. 'There's gotta be several hundred thousand kronor in there, and he destroyed it. Shit. Well, that's his share. That's all I can say. He's not going to get even one öre of our money. Where are the other bags?'

'They're still down in the cellar. I'm going to put this one back there, too. What if it has a tracking device inside? The police could be here any minute.'

Degen grabbed her arm.

'OK, calm down. Let's take one thing at a time. I don't think we have to worry about a tracking device. There's no mobile coverage out here, so I doubt a transmitter would work either. First we need to find Jocke. Maybe he just went out for a while.'

Terese looked at him incredulously.

'Do you really think he of all people would go for a walk? Drunk and fucked up, like he was? He takes his motorcycle even if he only has to go a few metres.'

She got up, taking the money bag with her. She tossed it down into the cellar and then closed the old sheet-metal door. Just to be on the safe side. Then she rescued her mobile from the clutter on the table but, as she suspected, there was no signal.

'So what do we do now?' she said with a sigh.

'We go looking for Jocke.'

Degen got up and went outside.

Terese lit another cigarette and once again looked over at the outhouse. She remembered Jocke leaving the table in the evening, but she had no memory of him coming back. She and Degen had been so wrapped up in each other and hadn't given their friend a thought.

She was seized with a guilty conscience. What if Jocke had overdosed on some drug and blacked out somewhere? It was already past one in the afternoon. If he'd fallen asleep on the toilet sometime during the night, it seemed unlikely that he'd still be sitting there. Thoughts tumbled through her head. She took a deep drag on her cigarette and then headed over to the outhouse.

As she got nearer, she slowed her step. There was something disturbing about the worn door standing wide open. With a hammering heart, she crept closer.

The instant she caught sight of the horrible scene, she was struck dumb. She knew she should call for Degen, but she couldn't. Jocke was sitting on the toilet seat with his head tilted back against the wall. A deep gash had split open his throat, and there was blood everywhere. His whole body was drenched in it, and black pools had formed on the floor, sending up a terrible stench.

Terese jerked back so violently she toppled over on to the grass. She got to her feet and began stumbling towards the house. Her mind was empty and not a sound crossed her lips.

The scream had frozen inside her.

When the villagers in the small community with the peculiar name of Dans, in the parish of Hejde, looked up at the sky on that sunny August afternoon, it was like a repeat of the day before. A thick column of smoke rose up, and from Klintehamn came the wail of fire engines heading out. The first vehicles to arrive on the scene immediately set about putting out the fire. An old ramshackle house was engulfed in flames, and the men initially focused on preventing the fire from spreading to the other buildings on the property. Not that there were really any worth saving, since the structures looked as if they might collapse at any moment, but they wanted at all costs to avoid another forest fire like the one of the day before. It didn't take long for the firefighters to discover the dead man inside the outhouse, and at that point the police were called in.

By the time Knutas and Jacobsson arrived, less than an hour later, the firefighters had put out the flames, but they were still dealing with the smouldering remains. Only the main house had been destroyed. The fire hadn't spread to the other buildings. The grounds had been cordoned off, but a crowd of curious spectators had gathered outside the blue-and-white police tape. Several local reporters also stood there, notebooks in hand, but Knutas brushed aside the flurry of questions and made his way past without meeting their eyes. Scene of crime officer Erik Sohlman was the first to greet them.

'The victim . . . well, he's in rather bad shape,' he said with a grim expression as he turned to Jacobsson. 'I honestly don't know whether you'll be able to handle it.'

It was well known that Jacobsson had a sensitive stomach. She always had a hard time looking at dead bodies, especially if they were in a bad state. And it hadn't got any better over the years. Jacobsson wasn't happy to be reminded of her weakness, but she didn't let that show.

'Thanks for the warning, but I'll manage.'

Sohlman led the way through the overgrown yard over to the outhouse.

'I haven't really touched anything yet. The medical examiner is on his way, so I didn't want to poke around too much.'

He opened the door.

'Have a look.'

The man who was sitting in the cramped space with his trousers down around his ankles was drenched in blood. There was a deep gash in his throat. His face was also covered in blood, but they could still see that he was a young man, maybe in his thirties, with thick, curly hair and a slight build.

Jacobsson moaned and had to look away for a moment. Knutas was surprised she didn't throw up. Even he felt close to vomiting. They stood there in silence, trying to take in the awful scene.

'Do you think he could be one of the robbers?' asked Jacobsson. 'He seems about the right age and body type.'

'Very possible,' muttered Knutas.

'I haven't had a chance to search the area yet, but someone brought a big motorcycle inside the house,' said Sohlman. 'One of the firefighters said he thought it looked like a Harley.'

'Is that right?' said Knutas, raising his eyebrows. 'If the victim is one of the robbers, it could be that the other two killed him for some reason. And maybe they exchanged the getaway car for motorcycles. If that theory holds up, then we're looking for two individuals on bikes.'

He got out his mobile and hurried away.

Jacobsson and Sohlman stayed where they were, staring at the victim, who had evidently been caught by surprise as he was relieving himself.

'What a horrible way to go,' murmured Sohlman.

Jacobsson studied the man's body, taking in the slashed throat and the arms hanging limply at his sides.

'The question is: who in the world would be capable of doing something like this? Not just anybody, that's for sure.'

'There's something else I want you to see,' said Sohlman. 'Have a look at this.'

The forensics officer leaned towards the body to lift the man's left wrist. Tattooed on the inside were three initials joined together. Jacobsson bent forward as close as she dared.

'J. T. D.,' she read. 'I wonder what that stands for?'

'No clue,' said Sohlman, shaking his head. 'But it must mean something.'

Jacobsson stared at the black letters of the tattoo. The 'T' was in the middle, forming a cross with the letter 'J' on one side and 'D' on the other.

That was all.

1994

'What a fucking palace this is! Bloody hell.'

Jocke strutted through the house, sighing with envy
at everything he saw. He took in the sophisticated coffee
maker, the mixer and the wine fridge in the kitchen. He
examined the stereo system at the far end of the living
room and the original paintings done in bold colours
that hung on the wall above the expensive leather sofas
in front of the fireplace.

He sank on to the sofa across from Terese. After three
weeks with the perfect family, she was about to suffo-
cate from all the courteous behaviour, the nice manners
and the endless consideration given to everyone's feelings. She needed to be with someone she could relax
with, or she'd go mad. She had really tried, pretending
to be friendly and attempting not to show the slightest
irritation, even though the boys, and Kristoffer in particular, were always at her heels, nagging at her to play
cards or ping-pong with them, or to go out and have a
swim. Susanne had shown her around both Visby and
the whole area where they lived. She seemed so determined that everything should go well, but Terese could
hardly breathe. Palle was significantly more casual

and had mentioned that she should come over to the restaurant one day and try her hand at helping out. Maybe she could work there during the summer. And she was hoping to do that.

'Can't we do something together?' she now asked Jocke.

'Sure. Let's go over to the club, and I'll give you a ride on my bike. Some guys from an affiliated club on the mainland have come over to say hello.'

The motorcycle club was at the very end of a desolate gravel road with woods all around. It was located in a grey cement building surrounded by a high barbed-wire fence. They were greeted by two ferociously barking guard dogs that came rushing around the corner the second they touched the latch on the iron gate. Terese shrank back.

'Don't worry,' Jocke reassured her. 'Their bark is worse than their bite. Hi, boys,' he said in a gentle voice, squatting down to look at the dogs on the other side of the fence. 'It's just me. See? And I've brought a cute chick with me. Why don't you say hello to her?'

He stood up and pushed Terese forward.

'Stick out your hand so they can smell it. They don't like to let in strangers but, if I say you're OK, then it's all right with them. They just need to get to know you a bit first.'

Terese was shaking inside, but she didn't want to seem like a scaredy-cat. She leaned down towards the dogs and stared straight into their yellow eyes. They looked mean, and slobber dripped from their open jaws.

'Hey, boys, calm down,' she admonished them, as she tried to muster her courage.

Normally, she had nothing against dogs, but these two seemed downright menacing. She held out her hand and let them have a sniff. They kept at it for a while, and she was repulsed by the feel of their saliva smeared on her skin.

But at least that seemed to calm them down. The dogs backed away and started wagging their short, stumpy tails.

'All right. The coast is clear,' said Jocke, sounding relieved. 'You're accepted.'

He opened the gate. The dogs sniffed at Terese's bare legs, then lost interest and ran off around the building. Terese sighed with relief but didn't say anything. It was important to show that she could cope under pressure. Jocke had told her that he wasn't yet a full-fledged member of the club, but he'd been a Hangaround for so long he thought he should soon qualify for the next step and become a Prospect. Then he'd at least be given a few badges to put on his waistcoat, even though he'd still have to wait to get the club emblem until he was an actual member.

A Hangaround was the lowest person in the hierarchy and usually had to do all the shit jobs. He spent almost every spare hour at the club when he was on Gotland, trying hard to show that he was worthy, that he was sufficiently loyal and cooperative to be taken into the inner circle. He hadn't mentioned his drug problem, and he made a point of being sober whenever he came to the club to work on his bike or help out with odd jobs. Drug addicts were usually thrown out head-first. They were viewed as too big a security risk. In addition to tinkering with his own motorcycle, he did whatever carpentry work needed to be done. He also cleaned, painted and got the bunks ready for any visitors who happened to turn up from the mainland. They often had visitors from the Hells Angels, the Bandidos and other one-per-cent clubs, meaning those that blatantly engaged in criminal activities. The Road Warriors didn't do that, at least not openly, even though they attracted scores of Hangarounds with petty-criminal backgrounds – people who devoted all their free time to motorcycles, although it was companionship with like-minded individuals they primarily sought through the club.

'Come on. Let's go in.'

Jocke opened the door. They stepped inside a dimly lit room and then continued upstairs, hearing voices coming from above. Two guys who were a little older than they were stood at a counter holding mugs of coffee. They wore leathers and waistcoats with a skull and cross-bones on the back and with 'Road Warriors MC Visby' inscribed around the edge of the emblem. One man was tall and thin with a shaved head and a tattoo on the back of his neck. The other was heavy, with a big beer belly that bulged out below his waistcoat. He had a goatee, and he wore his long brown hair tied back in a ponytail. Both turned around when they heard footsteps on the stairs. They said hello, casting an indifferent glance at Jocke, but their faces lit up when they caught sight of Terese.

'What the hell, Jocke? Who's the cutie you've brought with you? And what's her name?' said the heavy-set guy with an overjoyed expression as he looked her up and down.

'This is Terese,' said Jocke with a certain amount of pride. 'She's only sixteen, so watch your step. Can she ride with us?'

'How could we say no?' replied the guy with the shaved head, smiling.

The first thing she noticed was the noise. The roar of the motors of ten big Harley-Davidsons, each of which weighed close to three hundred kilos, rendered her almost deaf seconds before they took off. Terese climbed on to the back pillion, following Jocke's directions to put one shoe on the foot peg and then swing her other leg over. She felt just like Modesty Blaise. And she was in full gear: leathers, dark glasses, gloves, and a big black helmet on her head. She had plaited her hair so it wouldn't fly about. She had to laugh at herself. Finally, something was happening. She was the only girl here, with ten tough motorcycle guys, about to take a ride around Gotland. This was something to tell her best friend, Jessica, about when she got back home. She wouldn't believe this. All around her were guys wearing leathers, waistcoats with the club emblem on the back and helmets with visors that made them look even tougher, cooler and meaner.

With ear-splitting thunder, the bikers set off. Jocke had told her to relax and hug the saddle between her legs as if she were riding a horse. This was especially important whenever he had to brake, so she wouldn't jostle him too much. Otherwise, she should just hang on when they swerved to make a turn and not try to help, which was a typical beginner's mistake. She had to learn to let him steer.

They rode out on to the main road, and Terese enjoyed seeing people in cars staring at them at the intersections when the whole caravan rode through. Soon they were past the city and heading south. They increased speed, and now she understood why they were all wearing shades or a visor. Otherwise, the wind whipping past their faces would have been unbearable. She relaxed and tried to remember what Jocke had told her. 'Wrap your arms around me as tight as you want, but try not to lean in the opposite direction in the turns. Just sit close and pretend your body is a sack of potatoes.'

The bike accelerated, and they drove past one car after another. When Jocke increased speed, a thrill of joy shot through her, and she had a big smile on her face. Fields, meadows, flocks of sheep and farm buildings flew past. Flowers of every colour lined the road. She felt safe somehow, because they were out here with so many other bikers. Even though she didn't know the other guys, she felt a sense of kinship with the leather waistcoats all around.

Terese pressed herself even closer to Jocke's scrawny back. She was glad they'd become friends. She couldn't believe how lucky she was that they'd met that day at Plattan and that she'd then ended up on Gotland. The very place where he was from. And here he was now on the island, and he'd be staying all summer. The sun was shining, and it felt like she didn't have a care in the world.

The cows lifted their bulky heads from the grass to stare at them as they passed. Gotland is so beautiful, she thought. Here she sat, close to Jocke, letting the landscape fly past. As if they were the only two who existed and nothing else was of any importance. It was just her and Jocke.

The two of them against the world.

All Sweden was upset to learn that six-year-old Maja Rosén had died from the injuries she'd suffered in connection with the robbery of the security van in Klintehamn. The newspaper placards screamed the headlines from the kiosks, experts on TV talk shows discussed the distressing situation and the lead story on all the news programmes was the death of the little girl.

Gotlanders began making a pilgrimage to Klintehamn, heading for the road outside the Donner Library where Maja had been struck down by the fleeing robbers. The mountain of flowers grew by the hour. Her classmates had visited the scene of the accident, along with their teachers, to leave flowers and drawings. All Wednesday tearful reports had been broadcast on both radio and TV, once the child's death had been made known.

And to top it off, a murder had been committed at a run-down property in the middle of the Gotland countryside. The very area where the Klintehamn robbers were thought to be hiding out.

At eight in the evening the investigative team gathered for a meeting. Knutas had asked the NCP, the National Criminal Police, for assistance, and they had promised to get back to him as soon as possible to tell him when the back-up forces could be put in place.

The mood in the police conference room was tense as Knutas took his seat at the head of the table. He silenced the murmur of voices with a firm wave of his hand.

'Welcome, everyone. As you all know, we find ourselves in an extremely serious situation. Last night six-year-old Maja Rosén died in hospital while undergoing surgery. In addition, we've discovered the body of a murdered man in an outhouse that belongs to a ramshackle house near the village of Dans in the parish of Hejde. That's only a few kilometres from Klintehamn and the wooded area in Sanda where the robbers' getaway car was found yesterday.'

'Do we know who the man is?' asked Wittberg.

'Yes. He was identified earlier today. His fingerprints were on file. His name is Joakim Eriksson, nicknamed Jocke. Thirty-five years old, from Tofta. He moved in criminal circles and was picked up for a series of offences over the years, including drugs and all the subsequent related crimes, such as burglary, fraud and assault. I'm sure that some of you have had dealings with him.'

Several of his colleagues sitting at the table nodded. Knutas then turned to Sohlman, who was in charge of the photos.

'Can we see his picture?'

The former police photographer turned forensics officer showed them photos of Jocke Eriksson, in both close-up and full-length shots.

'He was a well-known troublemaker,' said Jacobsson. 'But I don't think he's ever been involved in anything this serious before, has he?'

'Not as far as I know,' said Knutas sombrely. 'The outhouse where he was found will be thoroughly examined, and a large area surrounding the property has already been cordoned off. Around two this afternoon somebody set fire to the old house, and so far that has made it impossible to do an extensive search, but we did make several important discoveries. A motorcycle was brought inside the house before it was set ablaze, and a money bag was found in a root cellar on the grounds.'

'Is it the same kind that was stolen during the robbery?' asked Wittberg.

'Yup. It was damaged when someone tried to open it, so it seems the robbers attempted unsuccessfully to get at the cash. The contents were destroyed by a dye cartridge, and presumably that's why the bag was left behind.'

Knutas paused to take a sip of water from the glass on the table in front of him.

'Is there any indication that the other robbers may have also had motorcycles?' Wittberg went on.

'Yes. Traces from several bikes were found outside the house.'

'So Jocke Eriksson was murdered by his fellow robbers. Is that the theory?' asked Lars Norrby.

'That does seem to be the most likely scenario,' replied Knutas. 'Maybe they argued about how to divide up the money, or they quarrelled because Jocke tried to open the money bag, but without success, and then the banknotes inside were destroyed. Another possible contributing factor could be the death of the little girl. But, of course, we don't know that for sure.'

'How are the parents doing?' asked Jacobsson. 'Has anyone spoken to them?'

'Not yet,' said Knutas. 'She was pronounced dead at 7.37 yesterday evening. So it's only been twenty-four hours. We thought we'd wait to interview the father until tomorrow. Naturally, he's in a terrible state of shock, but he was able to return home last night. There's no mother in the picture.'

'No mother?' queried Wittberg, raising his eyebrows in surprise. 'But isn't there a baby in the family, too?'

'That's another woman's child. The father has a new relationship. The six-year-old was his daughter by his late wife. She died several years ago.'

Knutas turned to the forensics officer.

'Could you tell us about the victim's injuries?'

'Certainly,' said Sohlman, running his hand through his red hair, as he always did before speaking. 'The ME has made his initial examination at the site, and now the body has been taken to hospital. From there it will be transported to the forensics lab tomorrow. We found Jocke Eriksson sitting on the toilet in the outhouse, and it was not a pretty sight. His throat had been cut with a large knife. The perpetrator slashed a deep wound straight across his neck. No other injuries to the body, but it caused a massive loss of blood. Here, you can see for yourselves.'

Silence settled over the room as everyone studied the macabre photos from the murder scene. Even though they were all experienced officers, they had to make a concerted effort not to look away. Then Sohlman went on.

'Apparently, the perpetrator caught the victim by surprise, took a firm grip on his hair, yanked his head back and then slashed his throat. He did it forcefully and without hesitation, and I have the feeling this wasn't the first time.'

'Could we be dealing with a pro?' suggested Norrby.

'It's possible. To commit this type of murder, you'd have to be a real tough bastard. Not just anyone would be capable of doing something like this. You'd have to be doped up, a serial killer or completely insane.'

Sohlman shook his head.

'There's another thing,' he continued. 'Jocke Eriksson has a tattoo on the inside of his left wrist. You can see it here in this close-up.' He clicked a button to put the image up on the screen. 'Three initials: "J", "T" and "D".'

Knutas glanced at his watch.

'All right. The reporters will have to wait until tomorrow. I'm thinking of calling a press conference for ten o'clock in the morning. I'll take care of it. With your help, of course, Lars. Is that OK with you?'

Norrby nodded.

Knutas looked at the members of his team.

'I hope you're all feeling alert and ready to get to work. We're going to be at it around the clock. We need to catch this killer as fast as possible.'

The street of Idrottsvägen in Klintehamn was on the outskirts of town. It was a quiet residential neighbourhood with apple trees and redcurrant bushes in the gardens. Jacobsson and Knutas had decided to drive out there together because they knew it would not be an easy task to interview the father of the deceased little girl. It was impossible to predict how a parent who had lost a child might react.

The white sand-lime brick house was the last one on the block. It had a brown garage door and a well-maintained path that led to the front entrance. In the garden they saw a trampoline, and close to the house stood a pink doll's pram. Knutas was sweating in the heat. They rang the bell, hearing the muffled sound reverberate inside the house, followed by footsteps and a rattling of the lock. A brawny man in his thirties opened the door.

Patrik Rosén was clean-shaven, his hair cropped so short it was almost a crew-cut. He wore white cotton trousers and a neatly pressed black shirt open at the neck. A heavy gold chain and cross gleamed on his chest, and Knutas noted the ugly scar that ran along one cheek. He had light-blue eyes, and his expression was impassive, revealing no emotion.

Knutas and Jacobsson introduced themselves, even though they were aware that Rosén knew who they were. In the background they could see a slender woman with an olive complexion and Latin features. She was holding a baby in her arms.

'Come in,' said Rosén. 'This is my wife, Isabel.'

He led the way through the living room to a terrace at the back of the house with an oversized parasol that provided much-needed shade. After his wife brought them coffee and water, she left to take a walk with the baby.

'So you can talk in peace,' she explained in broken Swedish.

They sat down at the table. As soon as the coffee was poured, Knutas began.

'First, let me offer you our deepest condolences.'

Patrik Rosén's eyebrows twitched but, otherwise, his expression didn't change.

'We understand that this must be terribly difficult for you, but we urgently need to find out any information that might help us to track down the robbers and catch them as fast as possible. I'd like you to tell us about the morning of the robbery. Try to remember as much as you can. Even the smallest detail could be important.'

'I've already spoken to the police.'

'We know that, but since then the situation has taken on a whole new aspect, and we are interviewing everyone again. As I said, we're trying to find out as much information as we can so we can apprehend the robbers.'

'Don't you know who the dead man is?' asked Rosén.

'Yes, we do. But at the moment we'd like to hear what you can tell us,' said Knutas gently. 'What do you recall about the morning of the robbery?'

Rosén took a pack of cigarettes out of his pocket and lit one. He took a deep drag before he spoke.

'It was a completely ordinary morning. I left the house around eight thirty, after we'd eaten breakfast. I took both of the kids with me so Isabel could have some peace and quiet. She's still feeling worn out after giving birth. Simon is only three weeks old.'

'Do you have a job?' asked Jacobsson.

'Of course. But I run my own business, so I can decide on my work schedule. I'm taking time off right now so I can be at home to help Isabel with the baby. I didn't do that with Maja, but this time I want to be a better father.'

His voice shook as he said his daughter's name. He took another drag on his cigarette.

'What sort of business do you own?' Jacobsson went on.

'It's a Mexican restaurant called La Cucaracha. Isabel is from Mexico, and the plan is for her to work in the restaurant with me when Simon gets older.'

'Please tell us more about what happened on Tuesday morning,' said Knutas.

'Well, as I was saying, I took the kids with me. Simon was in the pram, and Maja insisted on taking her bicycle, so she rode alongside. She had just learned how to ride. We were going to spend some time at the playground and afterwards do the shopping at the ICA. But Maja didn't want to stay at the park. There weren't any other children playing there, so she thought it was boring. If only I'd played with her a little longer, she wouldn't have . . . But I was talking on my mobile. It kept ringing the whole time.'

102

Tears filled his eyes. Jacobsson felt so sorry for him. She could see how guilt-ridden he was.

'What happened next?'

'We had almost reached the ICA, but Maja wanted to ride her bike some more before we went inside. I was still talking on the phone, dealing with some problems at the restaurant, so that was fine with me. We didn't see the robbery take place, because by then we'd already turned off Donnersgatan, but when we reached the library I caught sight of a silver Ford coming towards us at top speed. At the same moment, Maja had veered too far into the street, but I hadn't noticed, and that's when she was hit. The car just hit her,' he repeated, his voice faltering.

'Did you see any of the people inside the vehicle?' asked Jacobsson.

'No. It all happened so fast. I hardly knew what was going on. The car just kept going. After that, I don't really remember much except that there were lots of people around me, and someone said something about a robbery, and suddenly I was sitting inside an ambulance with Maja and Simon, on the way to hospital. At first, the doctors thought about transporting her to the mainland, but then they changed their minds and thought it best if she underwent surgery here in Visby . . .'

The words faded away. The man's face was ashen grey. Knutas gave him a searching look.

'Last night we were able to identify the man who was found dead on the property where the robbers had been hiding. His name is Joakim Eriksson, and he's from here on Gotland. He was about your age, born in 1975. Do you happen to know him?'

Patrik Rosén shook his head. He was staring straight ahead, his expression blank.

'Who is he?'

'We don't know very much yet. But he came from Tofta, which isn't that far from here. I thought you might have known him, although I'm sure you didn't move in the same circles. Joakim Eriksson had been involved in criminal activity for years, and he'd been in prison several times.'

'Was he the one driving the car?' asked Rosén, his voice almost a whisper.

'We don't know who was driving,' replied Knutas. 'There were no witnesses.'

'No witnesses,' repeated Rosén distractedly. 'No one who saw Maja get hit. I didn't either. And she should have been taken to Karolinska University Hospital, right from the start. The doctors said they should have taken her to Stockholm, to the specialists over there. But they changed their minds. If they'd taken her to the mainland, she might have survived.'

He hid his face in his hands.

After their call on Patrik Rosén, Jacobsson and Knutas decided to have lunch before returning to Visby.

'Why don't we go over to Warfsholm?' said Jacobsson. 'They have good food, and I haven't been back since Eldkvarn played there last summer.'

'Me neither. Do you remember Kihlgård?'

Jacobsson giggled at the memory. Their big colleague from the NCP in Stockholm had drunk a lot of wine and decided to let rip, dancing with such enthusiasm and energy to all the tunes that the lead singer, Plura, had finally invited him up on to the outdoor stage.

'Speaking of Kihlgård, are we going to get any help from the NCP?'

'Yes, we are. The only question is when. From what I hear, they're really swamped with work.'

'Just like always.'

'Right.'

The Warfsholm Hotel was located a kilometre outside of Klintehamn on a promontory jutting out into the sea. The main building, which had once been the residence of a wealthy merchant, dated from the early nineteenth century. The façade was painted yellow, and there was a tower in the middle. Small cottages had been built on the grounds to rent out to tourists. The old bathhouse had been turned into a youth hostel, which stood a few hundred metres away. The restaurant was a popular lunch venue, and it was crowded, but they were lucky enough to find a table next to the window. Jacobsson ordered Salisbury steak with onions and cream sauce, while Knutas settled for a shrimp salad.

'So what was your impression of Patrik Rosén?' asked Knutas, as they waited for their food.

'A hard person to read. He seemed both closed off and open, both unpleasant and likeable. I got a slightly negative vibe from him. And then there was that nasty scar on his cheek. I wonder how he got it.'

'Do you think he ever had any contact with Jocke Eriksson? I see from these documents that they're exactly the same age,' said Knutas, leafing through the file he'd brought along.

'If so, it would be an unbelievable coincidence that Eriksson ran down his daughter,' said Jacobsson. 'If he was the one behind the wheel, that is.'

'Right.'

A waitress wearing a black dress and lacy white apron brought a light beer for Jacobsson and a bottle of Ramlösa for Knutas.

Absent-mindedly, he took a sip of the mineral water.

'I'm wondering about the tattoo Eriksson had on his wrist. The initials "J. T. D". I assume the "J" stands for Jocke, but the other two letters have nothing to do with his name, since his middle name is Arne and his surname is Eriksson.'

'Maybe they're the initials of his pals,' Jacobsson suggested. 'The two other robbers.'

'Could be. At least there's no "P" for Patrik.' Knutas shook his head. 'A strange man. There's something off about him, something that doesn't fit. I have a feeling he's holding things back, that he's not being completely honest. He seems off balance.'

'Good Lord, what do you expect? His daughter just died. It'd be even stranger if he seemed perfectly normal, psychologically, in this situation. Anyone who's lost a child would be completely out of it.'

'How's Hanna, by the way? You haven't mentioned her lately.'

Jacobsson's face lit up.

'She's doing great. We're slowly getting to know each other better. Have to take it one step at a time.'

It was only two years ago that Karin Jacobsson had established contact with her grown-up daughter. Hanna had seemed to accept Karin's explanation that she'd been forced by her parents to sign the adoption papers, even though she regretted her decision the moment she held her newborn baby in her arms.

'She's going to try to come over here for another visit soon,' Jacobsson went on, sounding happy. 'You have to meet her.'

'I'd like that. We never managed to get together last summer when she was here.'

'So how are you doing?' Jacobsson asked suddenly, giving Knutas a searching look. 'You seem a bit down.'

'Is it really that obvious?' He smiled ruefully. 'There have been some problems at home, actually.'

'Really? What kind of problems? Anything you want to talk about?'

'I don't know. Lina is going back to Denmark. She's taken a six-month job in Copenhagen as a midwife. Filling in for somebody who's on leave.'

A shadow passed over Karin's face. She cleared her throat but didn't say anything as the waitress brought their food. Knutas looked on enviously as his colleague dug into her serving of potatoes and Salisbury steak dripping with cream sauce as he started in on his salad.

'I see,' she said, between bites. 'So what do you think about that?'

'I don't know,' he repeated. 'Maybe it's a good idea. We haven't been getting along lately.'

'I'm sorry to hear that. When does she leave?'

'Any day now. I guess it's urgent. They want her to come as soon as she can.'

'Can she really leave her job here in Visby just like that?'

'Apparently, her colleagues at the hospital have known about her plans for much longer than I have. I don't understand her thinking. I really don't.'

He shook his head. Karin placed her hand on top of his. She couldn't think of anything to say.

They were interrupted when Knutas's mobile rang. He took the call, listened intently and then ended the conversation, having barely said a word, merely murmuring agreement. He looked at Jacobsson.

'That was Wittberg. He says that Jocke Eriksson was a member of a motorcycle club. The Road Warriors.'

'Is that right? The Road Warriors? The name makes me think it's one of those one-per-cent clubs. Or are they a law-abiding group? As far as I can recall, we've never had any trouble with that particular club.'

'Just minor incidents. A few brawls in connection with parties they've held. Plus the fact that they were selling black-market booze to their guests.'

'Who doesn't?' said Jacobsson dryly. 'That goes on at nearly every local celebration on the island.'

'Sure. But even if they're upstanding citizens, we need to follow up on this lead. This particular murder seems to indicate a crude type of guy, and there are plenty of those in the motorcycle gangs, at least among the clubs that are openly involved in criminal activity. Even if the Road Warriors don't belong in that category, they may have contacts with the underworld.'

'We really have no clue what Eriksson might have been mixed up in. Maybe he messed up somehow in the world of bikers and his murder was a form of retaliation. The way he was killed reminds me of the worst methods used by the criminal gangs.'

'We should ask our colleagues in Stockholm to take a closer look at certain motorcycle clubs,' said Knutas. He glanced out of the window and ate some more salad before going on.

'Jocke Eriksson had a criminal history, starting when he was a teenager. He'd been arrested for selling drugs, for assault, theft and possession, and he spent several years in prison. When not doing time, he lived on welfare, and he doesn't seem to have ever held a steady job. Apparently, he spent a lot of his time in Stockholm.'

'Really?' Jacobsson looked up from her food. 'Then maybe that's where we should be looking. It's not inconceivable that the other robbers are from Stockholm. Since Eriksson is so well known to the police on Gotland, it would be risky to carry out such a major heist with any of his criminal buddies from here. As you know, people in those types of circles have a hard time keeping their mouths shut.'

'You could be right about that,' said Knutas pensively. 'Let's contact the Stockholm police and ask them to check out the motorcycle clubs over there as well as Jocke's friends. We'll be interviewing his family and circle of friends on Gotland today and tomorrow. We have to hope that we'll get some leads. So far, I've only had a chance to talk to his mother very briefly.'

'So what sort of contact did he have with his family?' asked Jacobsson. 'Do you know?'

'Very sporadic. His mother couldn't even remember the last time she'd seen him. Because of his drug problems, they haven't met up very often. And his parents had been divorced a long time.'

'What about siblings?'

'Two older brothers, but we haven't been able to get in touch with them yet. One lives in a commune on the island of Fårö, and the other lives here in Visby. Neither of them rides a motorcycle or is involved in any criminal activity. At least, as far as we know.'

The premises of the Road Warriors motorcycle club were in a blocky grey, bunker-like building made of concrete in a remote field twenty kilometres or so from Visby. Johan Berg had received an anonymous tip-off that the murdered man, Jocke Eriksson, had been a member. He hadn't been able to contact the club by email or phone, since neither was listed in any public records. The club did have a website, but it gave no contact information. In general, the site seemed somewhat enigmatic, either because the club members wanted to preserve the mythic image that had arisen regarding motorcycle clubs, or because they actually had good reason not to offer too much information. The home page almost gave off the air of a closed group. Johan had the impression that the club had its own established rules, hierarchy and agenda, which were outside the scope of the usual societal norms.

Johan and Pia decided to take a chance and go out there in person. They wanted to do a follow-up story on the murder of Jocke Eriksson, so they needed to find out more about his life and what he was like. All the various news organizations had already made public the name of the victim, along with a photograph, so it was no longer necessary to protect his identity.

As they approached the grey bunker, they saw that a tall barbed-wire fence surrounded the property. On the front of the fence big signs were posted with fiery-red type proclaiming: KEEP OUT. BEWARE OF DOGS. TRESPASS AT YOUR OWN RISK. PRIVATE PROPERTY. A locked wrought-iron gate prevented any uninvited visitors from entering.

'I can't believe this place has never even been on my radar before,' said Johan. 'It seems so weird to find something like this way out here in the sticks on Gotland.'

'It's my first time here too,' said Pia. 'I've never had any reason to come out here for work, and it's not exactly on the main road.'

They stopped outside the gate and pressed the doorbell, producing a faint buzzing sound. The next instant two frantically barking Rottweilers came rushing around the corner of the building. Johan instinctively took a few steps back.

'The club certainly seems well guarded. And that's putting it mildly,' he said, keeping his voice low. 'I wonder why. Especially if the only thing they're interested in is motorcycles.'

As they stood there waiting, the dogs gradually calmed down. Then a man came into view. His bare torso was covered with tattoos, and his nipples were pierced. He wore a ring in his nose, like a bull. He looked to be in his forties. He ran his hand over his shaven skull and glared at them suspiciously from the other side of the fence.

'What do you want?'

'We're from Regional News,' Johan began, but that was as far as he got.

'No journalists allowed. Especially not on a day like today. We're in mourning. One of our brothers has passed away.'

'That's exactly why we're here. To talk to you about Jocke,' said Johan. 'And we . . .'

The man shifted his gaze from Johan to Pia. Suddenly, his expression changed, and he stared at her in astonishment for several seconds before his face lit up and he exclaimed, 'What the hell? Is that you, Pia?'

'Yeah, it's me. But who—'

Pia looked happily surprised, even though she was clearly searching her memory and trying to put a name to the guy.

The man who only seconds before had seemed like such a brute now lit up like the sun, giving her a boyish smile bordering on the shy.

'Midsummer Eve on Sudersand. When the hell was that? Maybe six, seven years ago? You had just turned eighteen. Don't you remember me? I'm Sonny!'

'Oh my God!' Pia clapped her hands. 'You've got to be kidding me. I thought you'd gone away for good.'

He unlocked the gate, ordered the dogs to stand down and then swung the gate open. The previously hostile man now stood there with his arms wide and stepped forward to give Pia a bear-hug. He was even bigger than he seemed at first glance, and Pia, who was well above average height, almost disappeared in his embrace.

'What the fuck,' he said, sighing happily. 'I never thought I'd get to hold you again.'

He buried his nose in her hair. Then he pushed her away so he could look her up and down.

'Do you know that I couldn't stop dreaming about you for six months afterwards?'

'Oh, now you're exaggerating,' she said, giggling. And yet she seemed delighted by the man's undisguised admiration.

Then she recovered her composure.

'This is my colleague, Johan. We work for TV, the Regional News programme.'

'Don't tell me you've turned into a hack journalist,' said Sonny. He cast a quick, suspicious glance at Johan and gave him a curt nod, before turning back to Pia.

'I'm a camerawoman. Johan is a journalist.'

'Oh, right. Now I remember. You talked about that. You wanted to go out into the world and film wars and disasters.'

'So far it's been nothing but interviews with dreary local guys in Visby, stubborn farmers and tourists. But a girl's got to start somewhere.'

'That's right, sweetie. Come on in and let's have a coffee. But no cameras,' he told Johan, as if he were the camera person.

Sonny put his arm around Pia and led the way towards the bunker's entrance. Johan slunk after them, keeping an alert eye on the powerful-looking dogs which, like two bodyguards, padded along behind, one on each side of the trio.

They entered a room with a sofa, several easy chairs and a coffee table cluttered with various biker-club magazines. Along one wall was a row of metal cabinets with padlocks, like in the locker room of a gym. On the wall above was a shelf holding helmets lined up in a row. A mirror, a door leading to a toilet and a shelf of boots all bore witness to the fact that this was where the members changed into their leathers before going out on their bikes.

'It's pretty empty here right now, but at the weekend it'll be packed with people. On Saturday we're going to hold a memorial service here at the club to honour our departed brother,' said Sonny solemnly. 'There'll be a big contingent from the mainland. I could show you around if you like.'

'Definitely,' said Pia. 'That would be great.'

'But no cameras,' he said again, giving Johan a stern look. Then he turned to Pia and nuzzled the back of her neck, as if that were the most natural thing in the world.

'We've just had the place revamped, and it was a hell of a job. Everybody helped out. We painted, put in a new kitchen and built a bar upstairs. Down here we have a dormitory for people who come to visit.'

They walked through the dorm, which had small, paned slits instead of proper windows and rows of iron bedsteads, like those in a military barracks. Clothing and other personal belongings were piled on top of several of the beds.

'Where are the people who are staying here now?' Johan dared to ask, even though Sonny was ignoring him completely. Instead he directed everything he said at Pia.

'They're out riding. When they come over from the mainland, they want to take advantage of the opportunity to see Gotland. Some of our club members are showing them around. But as I said, at the weekend lots more people from our mainland chapters will be coming over to attend the memorial service.'

'Chapters?' repeated Johan, puzzled.

'Our affiliated clubs in Uppsala, Gothenburg and Malmö.'

'How many members are there?'

'Here on Gotland we have ten fully fledged members. We've deliberately kept the number low. If there are too many members, it's hard to reach agreement and make decisions on various matters. Right now we also have three Prospects, meaning those who are on their way to becoming full members. And there's a bunch of Hangarounds who mostly help out with things. There's always something that needs to be done.'

'What are the requirements for becoming a member?' asked Pia.

'You have to prove your loyalty to the club, show that you're really interested and willing to take an active role. You have to win the approval of all the members and be able to get along with everybody. Otherwise, it won't work. But even if you're a perfect candidate and a hundred per cent loyal, it still takes several years.'

'Can women be members, too?' Pia wanted to know, her eyes fixed on Sonny.

'No. No birds. That just causes problems. Girlfriends can come over to work on their bikes and go along on some of the rides, but they can't be members.'

'Why not?'

'It's nothing but trouble if birds are admitted to the inner circle. Rivalries and jealousy and a bunch of shit like that. We can't afford to risk any discord among our members because of romantic quarrels.'

Pia rolled her eyes.

They moved on to the workshop and garage, located right next to the dorm. Even in there, several beds had been set up, and the whole place reeked of oil.

'What is it about Gotland that makes it so popular for motorcycle riders?' asked Johan.

A spark of interest appeared in Sonny's eyes. He stopped and for the first time turned to face Johan as he spoke.

'There are so many fucking great roads on the island, and there's hardly any traffic. And it's flat, which means you almost always have a view. You can have long stretches of road all to yourself, and you can speed whenever you feel like it. And that gives you a huge sense of freedom. Plus it's so fucking beautiful with all the beaches, the rocky shores, the *rauks* and the cliffs. Lots of ways to take in nature, and you're constantly surprised by new houses, farms, pastures with lambs, fields of poppies, or whatever the hell else you discover along the way that you've never seen before. Gotland is perfect for motorcycle rides. You wouldn't believe how much you can experience on your bike. Everything is so close.'

'Wow. I never thought of it that way,' said Johan, a bit startled to hear such a detailed and poetic description from this man with the pierced nipples.

At the back of the garage they saw a row of big, shiny motorcycles.

'These are a few of my bikes,' said Sonny proudly.

'How many do you have?' asked Pia.

'Seven. And all the same make. Harley-Davidsons.'

Sonny enunciated each syllable, trying for an American accent as he said the brand name.

'What's so special about Harleys?' Pia asked, running her finger along the shiny handlebars of one of the bikes.

'Most of all, the sound. Harleys have a lower sound than other bikes, a more muted roar. Heavier, in a way. It's because the cylinders are specially built, not like on any other bike. They're set at an angle of exactly forty-five degrees to each other, and that's where the lower, deeper sound comes from. That also means the bike vibrates more when you ride it. Some people think it's annoying, but I like it. You not only hear that you're riding a Harley, you also feel it.'

'Do all the club members ride Harleys?' asked Johan.

'All the full members do. For us, there's really no other kind of motorcycle.'

They went upstairs. There they saw a fully equipped bar, offering all manner of alcoholic drinks at a handsome counter with black-and-white tiles, and tall bar stools with chrome legs and black leather seats. A pool table stood in a separate room, which was also furnished with a sectional sofa. On the walls hung photos of Road Warrior members. They stopped in front of one showing Jocke all alone, sitting on his bike with his helmet on his lap. Wearing his waistcoat with the club's emblem, leathers and gloves, he stared at the camera with a serious expression on his face. The tough attitude didn't exactly mesh with his curly blond hair and boyish face.

'He was such a fucking good brother,' said Sonny sadly, staring at the photo. 'He hung around the club all his life. Well, at least since he was fourteen, and he ran around doing errands for everybody. We were like a family to him. He'd come over as often as he could, and he was always willing to help out. Back then he couldn't afford a Harley, but he bought a beat-up old Suzuki. That was his first bike. At that time he wasn't more than sixteen. I remember how proud he was, that boy. He was like a little brother to me.'

'What was he like as a person?' asked Pia.

'Jocke was a happy devil. And so fucking loyal. There was nothing he wouldn't do for the club. He was only nineteen when he became a Prospect, and that doesn't happen very often. By then he'd managed to get himself his first Harley. He worked like hell to scrape the money together. I don't really know how he did it. The average age of club members is fairly high. That's because it takes a number of years before anyone can afford to buy a real Harley. They cost several hundred thousand kronor. But Jocke, he got his first Harley before he was twenty. And that's damned impressive.'

'When did he become a member?'

'On his twenty-first birthday. I'll never forget it. We decided to combine it with a birthday celebration here at the club, since his family never did anything special for him on those occasions. He didn't have an easy time of it at home. The club was where he could escape; it was that simple. Anyway, he was so thrilled he could hardly contain himself. We'd bought him a new helmet as a present, and at the same time he was admitted to the club as a full member.'

'So I've been thinking,' said Pia. 'Wouldn't it be a way of honouring Jocke if you told people what he was like, all his good qualities and how he was so devoted to the club? We could do a story about him for TV. And if you'd let us film the memorial service, that would be great. Then everybody would know what a fine person

119

he was. Don't you think Jocke would have liked that? A sort of tribute to him?'

Sonny paused to consider her suggestion. When he spoke, his voice was thick with emotion.

'Maybe. Let me talk to my brothers about it.'

Johan couldn't help casting an admiring glance at Pia. Clearly, she had Sonny exactly where she wanted him.

He sat in a window seat and studied the man who was sitting across the aisle.

From here he had a good view without getting too close. He pretended to read a copy of *Metro*, now and then glancing out of the window, watching the western suburbs pass by along the metro's green line. The man, who was only a few metres away, stared listlessly out of the window. He was shabbily dressed in a stained shirt, wrinkled linen trousers and espadrilles with holes in the toes. Next to him on the seat was what looked like a sports bag. He seemed to be lost in thought. They were on their way from Vällingby, headed towards town. A journey that took a good amount of time. The train stopped at a whole series of stations before finally arriving at the central station in Stockholm.

The man stood up abruptly and got out, crossing the platform to continue on the red line. He followed.

A few seconds later a train pulled in, bound for Ropsten. The man got on but didn't bother to sit down. He merely grabbed hold of the yellow pole in the centre of the aisle.

He took a seat close to the man and stared in the opposite direction.

At Karlaplan the man got off. They made their way through the Fältöverstens shopping centre and exited on to a side street that he wasn't able to identify. He followed the man at a safe distance, pretending to talk on his mobile so as not to arouse suspicion. He had to hurry to keep the man in sight. Luckily, the man never glanced over his shoulder. The street was narrow and deserted, so it would have been impossible to hide from view.

Further up the street was a sign that said: THAI BOXING. So that was where the man was headed. A moment later the man opened the door and disappeared inside.

He stood on the street, not knowing what to do. After pondering his options, he came to the conclusion that no one knew who he was, so there shouldn't be any risk if he went inside.

A steep stone staircase led down to a small reception area with a counter that was unattended. Piled up on a rug were shoes of various shapes and showing differing amounts of wear. He recognized the shabby espadrilles, which had been carelessly tossed in a corner. He unlaced his own shoes and took them off. The air was stuffy and smelled faintly of sweat. He could hear voices and occasional shouts coming from somewhere.

Slowly, he made his way down a corridor with changing rooms for both women and men. An Asian-looking man wearing only a pair of red shorts and with sweat covering his chest came towards him. He offered a curt nod as he passed. The corridor ended at a large practice room with mats spread on the floor and several men working out. They faced each other, kicking high and uttering sounds reminiscent of the Japanese Samurai films he'd watched with his father when he was a kid. He recognized one of the men. It was him. He was a short, muscular man with tattoos on his arms and back.

Fascinated, he stopped to watch the man and his partner, who were ducking and kicking, evading and boxing around each other. He felt someone tap him on the shoulder.

'Can I help you?'

He gave an involuntary start but quickly regained his composure.

'I'm just here to have a look around. I've been thinking of joining.'

The man's face lit up.

'Then you're talking to the right person. I own the club.' He held out his hand. 'Niko.'

He was caught off guard. He hadn't counted on being asked to introduce himself.

'Jonas,' he muttered.

'So what got you interested in Thai boxing?'

'I don't know. I think it looks cool.'

Shit. The last thing he wanted was to have to talk to anybody.

'Have you ever tried it?'

'No.'

'OK. Well, you're welcome to try a workout session, if you like. Free of charge. Then you can decide if you want to keep on.'

'OK.'

'How about next Monday? It won't be so crowded then. Can you come in the daytime?'

'Sure. No problem.'

'Shall we say one o'clock? We'll be giving an introductory session to several other beginners.'

They shook hands.

Before he left the room, he turned around and cast one last glance at the man on the mat.

1994

Terese lay on her bed, listening to her favourite Ace of Base tune, 'All That She Wants', while she leafed through the latest issue of *Frida*, the magazine for teenage girls. She actually thought it was really stupid, but it was OK for whiling away the time. She was in the middle of reading an article about how to create a dream hairstyle in five minutes flat when Susanne opened the door and stuck her head in the room.

'Dinner's ready!'

There was a certain smugness in her tone of voice. As if to say: See how clever I've been again. Such a wonderful mother.

'You could at least knock first.'

'I did. Several times. But you didn't hear me.'

The house was so well insulated that if Terese had her door closed she couldn't hear a sound from the rest of the family. Sometimes she pretended that she lived there alone, that it was her house and that all her friends from Stockholm would soon be coming over for a party. Even though Susanne and Palle were nice and didn't bug her much, she was having a hard time settling in with this family. Reluctantly, she turned off the old ghetto-blaster she'd brought from home, got off the bed and sauntered out to the kitchen. The twins had already taken their customary places. Rosy-cheeked and happy, they were chattering about how hungry they were. Sometimes she felt like giving them a good slap in the face. She sat down, and a moment later Palle came into the kitchen. He'd just arrived home from the restaurant, and he smelled of grilled steak, grease and cigarette smoke. He gave Susanne a quick kiss on the cheek, which prompted a grimace from her.

'Oh, how awful you smell. And you need a shave.'

'I know that, darling. But could I eat my dinner first? It's been crazy at work. Surrounded all day by food, but I haven't had time for even a bite to eat since breakfast.'

He shook his head and smiled at Terese. Susanne set white serving platters on the table containing baked salmon with fresh asparagus and rice. Salad with a typical Gotland mustard dressing. Water in a glass pitcher with slices of lemon and ice cubes that glittered in the evening sun that flowed in through the windows.

Terese felt uncomfortable in this big, airy room with the white-painted walls. Everything was so perfectly arranged. What a difference from her parents' cramped and messy kitchen on Bagarmossen. There were always piles of dirty dishes in the sink, and the table was littered with crumbs, though the surface was barely visible underneath all the empty pizza boxes, the overflowing ashtrays, the liquor bottles and the coffee cups.

After everyone had helped themselves to some food, Susanne turned to Terese.

'So how was your day?'

'Fine.'

'What did you do?'

'Nothing special.'

'Nothing?'

Terese thought she could hear something insistent in the woman's voice. She raised her eyes from her plate and gave Susanne a defiant look.

'I haven't done a damn thing.'

'Don't swear at the dinner table,' said Susanne sternly. 'You've been gone all day, so you must have been doing something.'

'I was just hanging out with some friends.'

The twins had stopped eating and were following the conversation, wide-eyed. Palle, on the other hand, looked embarrassed and continued shovelling food into his mouth.

'Friends who ride motorbikes, right?' Susanne fixed her eyes on Terese. 'I know someone who lives in Ljugarn, and she said she saw you with a motorcycle gang at the Bruna Dörren.'

'Yeah. I hung out with them and went for a ride. Something wrong with that?'

Susanne dropped her fork on her plate, making a loud, clanking sound.

'Motorbikes? How did that happen?'

'I have a friend who owns a bike. I went for a ride with him and the guys at his club.'

Kristoffer stared at her.

'Wow. That's so cool! Did you go fast?'

'Sure. Sometimes. Over a hundred. It was fantastic.'

Terese couldn't help smiling at the boy. But she could feel uneasiness radiating from the rest of the family.

'What club do you mean?' asked Susanne. She seemed to be making a great effort to sound casual as she poked at her salad. 'What's it called?'

'The Road Warriors.'

'I'm sure they're harmless,' Palle quickly interjected. 'They may look tough, but they're not involved in anything criminal, as far as I know. They often stop at the restaurant for food. They're decent guys.'

'So who's the friend that you mentioned?' Susanne went on.

'His name is Jocke.'

'How did you meet him?'

'Through some friends in Stockholm. What is this? An interrogation?'

Terese pushed away her plate. Ready for a fight, she stared at the woman across the table.

'No, it's not,' replied Susanne sharply. 'But clearly we want to know who you spend your time with. School will be starting soon, and you need to be thinking ahead. How old is this friend of yours? Is he in school, or does he have a job? Does he live at home with his parents?'

'What the hell do you care? You're not my fucking mother!'

She got up abruptly and ran out of the room.

A little while later, as she was lying on her bed watching *Beverly Hills 90210* on TV, someone knocked lightly on the door, and a low voice said, 'Can I come in?'

It was Palle. She told him it was OK. He came in and cautiously sat down on the edge of the bed. Terese kept her eyes fixed on the TV screen.

127

'Would you mind turning that off? It's hard to talk with the TV on.'

She sighed heavily but complied.

'Things aren't so easy for Susanne. She's trying to do the best she can.'

'How nice of her.'

'I can understand that you don't like us interfering in your life too much, but you're living here with us, so of course we want to know what you do and who you see. Susanne means well. She's afraid you might end up in bad company.'

'She can't stop me from seeing my friends, damn it.'

'Of course not. We want you to have friends. We want you to be happy. But—'

'But I have to have the right kind of friends. Is that it? Or rather, only one kind. The sort that fits into your perfect life. Neat and tidy kids who never skip a day of school and spend all their free time studying.'

Terese glared at him and then went on.

'Why am I even here? What do you want from me? I'll just make a mess of things for your family, since everything here is always so goody-goody.'

Palle paused before answering. He placed his hand on the coverlet, as if wanting to come closer, but he didn't dare. She didn't move.

'Let me explain,' he said gently. 'There's a reason, though it doesn't really have anything to do with you. We like you, and we want you to be here. The boys adore you, especially Kristoffer. And you're great with them. We really appreciate that you're willing to spend time with them, play games and do things like that. But there's a reason why we want to help out a young person like yourself, and preferably a girl. At least that was something Susanne was very insistent about.'

'OK. Why? I don't get why you'd want some strange kid in your house. Someone you don't even know.'

'Here's the thing. Six months ago Susanne's niece Angelica killed herself. She was the same age as you when she died. She'd been doing drugs for several years and tried to get treatment lots of times, but nothing helped. Her parents were at their wits' end, so Anna – Susanne's sister – asked us if Angelica could live here because she needed to get away from home and have some peace and quiet. But Susanne said no. She was afraid it wouldn't be safe for Daniel and Kristoffer. A week later Angelica took an overdose. And they couldn't save her.'

Palle paused and looked at Terese. She didn't know what to say. All she wanted was to get out of there, or at least for him to leave the room so she could be alone. Her throat felt tight, as if she couldn't possibly utter a single word.

After a moment Palle went on.

'Susanne feels terribly guilty, so she made up her mind to try to help other kids, to make up for saying no to Angelica.'

'So I'm here to ease her guilty conscience?'

'You can choose to look at it that way. Or you can think about the fact that you've been given an opportunity to turn your life around while you're staying with a family that wishes you well. Keep that in mind. We wish you well.'

He gave her a searching glance. Fixed his eyes on hers. She couldn't avoid his gaze. Finally, her resistance faded.

'OK. I'll do my best,' she said.

'That's great. I'm really happy to hear that. Everything is going to be fine. I know it is. We'll all help. We like you very much. I want you to know that.'

He patted her hand.

'So I was wondering whether you'd like to come over to the restaurant and help out,' he said, in a much brisker tone of voice. 'It's about time we gave it a try. I'm sorry it's taken me so long, but I've been busy with other things. Now the high season is about to start, and next week is Almedalen Week, and things will really get crazy. I'll pay you, of course.'

Terese's face lit up.

'Sure. I'd like that.'

'All right then. You can drive in with me tomorrow. You might as well get started. There'll be plenty to do.'

'OK.'

Palle stood up.

'So, I won't bother you any more. You can go back to your TV show. Just don't stay up too late.'

At the door he hesitated for a moment, then turned around and said gently, 'I hope you understand that we really do want the best for you. We want you to be happy.'

She felt a burning sensation inside.

'I know,' she said quietly, though she didn't look at him.

When he closed the door behind him, all she wanted to do was cry.

Late Thursday night Karin Jacobsson walked home from police headquarters, her head filled with thoughts about Jocke Eriksson and who might have had the motive, determination and means of killing him in such a violent manner.

He was an ordinary troublemaker with a history of drug problems and criminal activity. He had no job or steady income, and he had lived alone in Gråbo, on the outskirts of Visby. He didn't seem to have a girlfriend. Tonight the police forensics team were also searching his flat. In addition, they were conducting interviews with Eriksson's family members and his large, loose circle of acquaintances. Most of those people were not exactly eager to talk to the police.

The issue of drugs kept coming up in the documents pertaining to his life. He'd been into drugs ever since he was a teenager, and he'd been in and out of treatment centres. Jacobsson thought that one possibility was that the murder had something to do with a drug deal. Maybe he hadn't paid some pusher in Stockholm what he owed, someone who was high up in the hierarchy. So then a junkie was sent to kill him. To set an example and scare anyone else who had dealings with that particular drug lord.

Thinking about Stockholm made her long to see Hanna. She felt a fluttering in her stomach when she pictured her daughter. Her slender figure and posture were copies of her own. Hanna had also inherited the same eyes and the gap between her front teeth. In many ways they seemed so alike, and not just in appearance. But Hanna had had a childhood that was completely different from Karin's. She'd been adopted by a wealthy family in Djursholm, where she had lived with her mother, father and younger brother, whom she loved. Of course, Karin was happy her daughter had been given such a good life, and not just in terms of material things. But she couldn't help feeling a pang when she heard Hanna call the woman in Djursholm her mother, while she addressed Karin by her first name. She understood that it was unrealistic to expect anything else, but still. Karin was extremely grateful that they'd finally made contact with each other. All of a sudden she had a new family member. At the same time, after living her whole life alone, she'd also met a man, the photographer Janne Widén.

They'd been together for a couple of years now, and that was a record for her. Janne lived on the other side of Visby, and for a while now he'd been talking about them moving in together, preferably in the house that he owned, but she found the idea frightening. How would she handle that, after living alone for all these years? The only one she'd ever lived with was Vincent, her cockatoo, and he was an undemanding flatmate. How could she live with someone else, when it meant being willing to compromise and consider the other person's

132

needs and wants? And yet she was tempted. She wanted to share her life with someone.

Jacobsson had almost reached her flat on Mellangatan when her mobile rang. It warmed her heart to hear Hanna's voice.

'Hi, Karin. Sorry for ringing so late, but I thought you might still be up.'

'Hi. It's amazing you should call me right now because I was just thinking about you. And don't worry about the time. I'm not even home yet.'

'I know. I tried your home phone first. How are things?'

'Good. Just really busy at work. How about you?'

'Fine. Just really busy at work,' she said with a laugh. 'How's it going with that awful murder case?'

'Right now we're trying to find out as much as we can about the victim. It's complicated, and we're just getting started.'

'That's actually why I'm calling you. I thought it was important, so I didn't want to wait until tomorrow. There were some big photos of him in the newspaper today, and one of my friends told me she recognizes him. She's seen him several times.'

Jacobsson stopped in her tracks.

'Really? Where?'

'At a Thai boxing club here in the city. She works out there, and she's seen him at the club.'

'Thai boxing? That's something new. We didn't know he was involved in anything like that.'

'Apparently, he wasn't. She said that he just came and watched while a friend worked out.'

'Does she know the name of this friend?'

'No. They were never introduced. But she saw the two of them together. And the other guy had black hair. Looked Hispanic.'

Jacobsson's mouth went dry. She recalled what several witnesses had reported. Dark eyes. They guessed he might be Latino. Suddenly, a visit to Stockholm seemed like a very good idea.

When Knutas got home from work he found a couple of packed suitcases in the hallway. Lina and the children were having dinner. He took his usual place at the table and helped himself from the serving dishes.

'Are you leaving already?'

'Yes. They want me to start work at the hospital tomorrow, so I have just enough time to catch the last plane to Copenhagen tonight. I know it's a bit sudden,' she said, sounding embarrassed as she gave him a quick glance.

The children didn't say anything, focusing all their attention on the food they were eating.

'When will you be back home?'

'Not this weekend. That would be too soon, and I need to get settled in the flat. But next weekend, I think. Probably on Friday afternoon, because my shift ends early that day.'

Lina looked at Petra and Nils and smiled.

Knutas realized that the three of them had already discussed everything, and that Lina had told the children what was going on between their parents. He had wanted to wait, since he and Lina weren't yet sure how they felt themselves, and he didn't want to worry the kids unnecessarily. But his wife was always so outspoken, unable to keep anything from them. He should have known.

'So what do the two of you think about all this?' he asked. 'About your mother being away for such a long time?'

'We're not kids any more,' muttered Nils. 'I suppose it's OK. And she'll be home most weekends. And we'll go over to see her during autumn break.'

'So you've already decided that?' said Knutas. 'Without even asking me?'

'What do you mean? Don't tell me that you were planning something special for us, Pappa. Were you? Maybe a trip somewhere?' Petra teased him, even though she knew full well that he'd never do anything like that.

'No,' Knutas admitted. 'But still.'

'To answer your question, of course I think it's sad that Mamma is going to be gone for so long,' Petra told him. 'But it's not far to Copenhagen. And Nils and I can get discounted youth tickets. We'll be fine.'

'It's great that you're taking this so well,' said Knutas, his voice sounding a bit caustic. 'Maybe we could all go over there together for a visit sometime soon. Is there room for us in the flat?'

Lina squirmed a bit.

'Er, well,' she said evasively. 'It's only a one-bedroom, so there aren't enough beds for everyone.'

'You mean we'll have to stay in a hotel? While you sleep in the flat?'

Knutas could hear how hurt he sounded.

'When you come to visit I can stay in the hotel with you. That's all there is to it. Could you pass me the gravy?'

Knutas stared at his wife. The same voluptuous figure, the same red hair with the corkscrew curls, the same freckles. But a totally different person. He didn't understand any of this. Yet he had to admit that he'd been noticing a change for a long time now. Maybe even for several years. But it had happened gradually, stealthily. Step by step, Lina had been moving away from him. She'd stopped spending time with him, done things on her own, prioritized her friends over him, travelled to Stockholm and even abroad. And the fact that they were spending so much time apart hadn't seemed to bother her in the slightest. Now she was on her way to disappearing for good.

He was seized with panic. Was he going to be left on his own? Would he end up sitting in the house all alone? All at once everything seemed so meaningless. Surely this couldn't be what they had struggled for all these years, he and Lina. They had made this home for themselves, scrimping and saving, working hard and doing their best to raise their children to be good people. After all the work and struggle, was the family about to fall apart, and he'd be left on his own? The thought was so unpleasant and alarming he couldn't stay seated at the table. He felt so dizzy and nauseated he had to get up. It was as if he'd suffered a terrible blow to the head.

'What's the matter?' asked Lina. 'You look so pale.'

'I think I need to lie down,' said Knutas pitifully. 'I don't feel well.'

All three helped him to the bedroom, where he sank on to the bed. Petra fetched a glass of water, and Nils ran to get some headache tablets. Lina drew the curtains to dim the light in the room. Then the doorbell rang.

'That's my taxi. I have to go.' Lina sounded both stressed and a little annoyed. As if she thought he was faking illness just to make her feel guilty. 'I hope you feel better soon.' She gave him a quick pat on the cheek. 'I'll call you later.'

He heard her giving the kids a hug in the hall. Then the front door opened. And she was gone.

138

Friday morning was exceptionally beautiful. Bright sunshine flooded over Roma and the idyllic street where they lived. Johan drew in a deep breath as he came out of the house. The birds were chirping, the lawn was newly mown as of yesterday evening, and he felt truly rested for the first time in weeks.

He had decided to go over to the editorial office extra early, taking advantage of the fact that there were no children at home right now. Emma was leaving at the same time, and he'd offered to drop her off at work. Usually, she rode her bicycle over to the small Kyrk School, which was located a short distance outside Roma.

As he stood at the gate and watched Emma coming towards him, he was seized with a real longing to take her in his arms. He gave her a big hug before they got into the car.

'Shall I do the shopping for dinner tonight?' Johan asked as he kissed her hair. 'And a good bottle of wine? I'll hurry home.'

'Sure. That would be great,' she said, pressing closer.

'Sorry I've been so tiresome lately. I promise to be nicer,' he murmured.

'That's good to hear. I've actually been worried lately. Wondering whether you might have changed your mind about me.'

'You don't ever have to worry about that. I love you, Emma.'

Johan dropped her off at the school. She looked happy as she glanced back to wave goodbye.

He turned up the music in the car, feeling more carefree than he had in a long time. A little peace and quiet – was that all we needed? he thought. A breathing space, a break from the usual daily grind. He was grateful to Emma's parents, even though he did miss the kids. It had been several days since he'd had a cuddle with them.

When he came to the straight stretch of road near Follingbo, he discovered a small bus that had come to a halt, turned sideways and partially in the ditch. The front was smashed in, and several windows were broken. The bus driver was standing in the road, frantically punching in a phone number on his mobile. Several schoolchildren were stepping out of the bus. They were crying, and one of them was holding his head, which was covered in blood.

Johan pulled over. Several other drivers did the same. The accident must have just happened. Johan was the first to reach the bus.

'Are you OK? What happened?' he asked the driver.

The man was in his sixties, his face pale as a ghost's. His voice shook when he spoke.

'We crashed into an oncoming car. He was trying to pass another vehicle and was on the wrong side of the road. I don't know how the driver's doing. Or the kids in the bus.'

'Have you called an ambulance?' asked Johan.

The man nodded mutely.

At that moment chaos erupted around them. People came running from all directions, children were screaming and crying. There was blood and broken glass everywhere, and further away a crumpled car lay in the ditch. Johan called the emergency number, 112, and then rang Pia Lilja. An accident involving a school bus had to be documented. She promised to come at once. Then Johan ran over to the car. The windscreen was shattered, the airbag had inflated and the driver's head was covered in blood. Johan managed to pull open the car door and, when he did, he knew immediately that the driver was dead. He heard sirens blaring in the distance, and the sound of agitated voices.

When Johan leaned forward, he recognized the dead driver at once.

The man behind the wheel was Emma's ex-husband, Olle.

On Friday morning Knutas chose to walk to work. The headache and nausea from the night before were now gone. On the way he spoke to the ME who had examined Maja Rosén's body, ending the conversation only a few minutes before he entered the conference room for the meeting with the investigative team.

'We now know why Maja Rosén died, even though her condition seemed to have stabilized,' Knutas began. 'She was killed by something called a fat embolism.'

'"Fat embolism"?' repeated Jacobsson.

She'd never heard of that before.

'Maja had extensive injuries to her pelvis and legs,' Knutas went on, looking down at the notes he'd made after the phone conversation. 'A fat embolism is when bone marrow and fat leak out of injured parts of the body into the bloodstream and then lodge inside the lungs. Apparently, that was what caused her death. According to the ME, it's something that's very difficult for doctors to foresee.'

'So it wouldn't have made any difference if she'd been taken to Stockholm for the surgery?' asked Jacobsson.

'Most likely not. That may be of some comfort to her family. I don't know,' said Knutas. Then he turned to Sohlman. 'Could you give us a report on Jocke Eriksson?'

'Sure. We've received the preliminary results from the autopsy. The injury to his body consisted solely of the knife wound at his throat. All indications are that the perpetrator caught him by surprise. And, by the way, the killer happens to be left-handed. According to the ME, there's no doubt about that.'

Knutas murmured something and jotted down a few notes. Sohlman continued.

'There are no defensive wounds on his arms or anything like that so it seems the victim offered no resistance. He probably died instantly. The time of death was between midnight and five in the morning on Wednesday. The weapon used was a large knife, of indeterminate brand but a type that is commonly found in butcher shops, restaurants and supermarkets; any place where meat is cut up.'

'Restaurants?' said Wittberg. 'Doesn't Maja's father own a restaurant?'

'That's right,' said Knutas.

'But are you saying he managed to go out there and kill Jocke Eriksson? If so, why would he do that?' objected Jacobsson. 'One of the other robbers could have been driving the getaway car.'

'The time frame wouldn't have presented a problem,' Knutas said. 'Maja Rosén was pronounced dead at seven thirty in the evening, and the murder was committed after midnight. Patrik Rosén was at the hospital during the operation so, naturally, he learned very quickly that his daughter had died.'

'But how the hell would he know where to go?' said Wittberg. 'Do you think that for some reason he knew where the robbers were hiding?'

'I have no idea, but we need to consider the possibility, even though it does seem like a long shot,' Knutas admitted. 'First and foremost, we need to find out whether Rosén is left-handed. And have you found out anything else about the Rosén family?'

'I was just waiting for you to ask,' said Wittberg eagerly, brushing a lock of his thick curly hair out of his eyes. 'I talked to Maja's maternal grandparents. They told me that Maja's mother – their daughter – died in mysterious circumstances when she was travelling abroad with her husband. She drowned.'

'What happened?' asked Jacobsson.

'They went swimming at night, and she disappeared. Patrik Rosén notified the police but, even though divers searched for her body, it was never found. And the woman's parents both suspect that Patrik was somehow responsible for her death. They broke off all contact with him and have never spoken to him since.'

For a moment everyone seemed too surprised to say anything. But then a buzz of voices filled the room. Knutas raised his hand to ask for silence.

'We need to investigate this matter further. But for now, let's go on. Sohlman, do you have anything to add in terms of what the forensics team found?'

'Yes. Left behind in the ramshackle old house in Dans were cups, glasses, a Thermos, beer cans, and the remains of mattresses, pillows and blankets. Everything suffered extensive fire damage. But it seems crystal clear that the robbers had been using the house as a hideout, at least for a few days. We also found a piece of a charred pizza box from the Kust Grill in Klintehamn. We went out there. It's a family-owned place. When I showed the daughter a picture of Jocke Eriksson, she confirmed that he'd been there to buy pizzas.'

'Interesting,' said Knutas. 'So it looks like they were in Klintehamn several days before the robbery. Maybe they even went into town to get groceries. We need to ask around at all the places of business in Klinte.'

'One more thing,' said Sohlman. 'We found footprints from four different shoes. Three are large sizes, between 9.5 and 10.5. But one is a size 5, which confirms our theory that one of the robbers is probably a woman.'

'I have something else to report,' Jacobsson then said.

She told her colleagues about her phone conversation with Hanna, whose friend had seen Jocke together with a dark-haired man who was working out in a Thai boxing club in Stockholm.

'When did she see him there?' asked Wittberg.

'A couple of times in the spring, and most recently in early August.'

Knutas jotted down more notes. Then he looked up at the others.

'Good job, everyone. Now we're starting to tighten the net around the individuals we're looking for.'

1994

Terese was filled with anticipation when she got into the car and sat between Daniel and Kristoffer on the way to the restaurant named Catch 22. The boys always wanted her to sit with them, even though the front passenger seat was empty.

Susanne was going to drop Terese off in the city and then go shopping with her sons. Everyone was in unusually high spirits. The radio was playing music by Magnus Uggla, who had just come out with a greatest-hits album, and Susanne was a big fan. When she recognized the intro to 'Varning på stan', she cheered and turned up the volume. Then they all sang along. The boys knew the words by heart because their mother played his records so often. Susanne really let rip, rolling down the windows in the car and whipping her head back and forth as she drove.

'Do you know that he's going to give a concert at Kneippbyn this summer?' Kristoffer had to shout to be heard over the music. 'Can we go? Please, oh, please?'

Terese nodded and laughed. She was singing at the top of her lungs and swaying in time to the music along with the boys. A feeling of warmth spread through her body. For the first time she felt genuinely happy and relaxed with the family. They were actually all very nice and sweet, even Susanne. She had to admit that. Susanne couldn't help it if she and Terese didn't exactly see eye to eye.

But more than anything, Terese couldn't help being affected by Kristoffer's undisguised adoration. He always looked at her with admiration, and he'd even given her a nickname that only he used. He called her Tessan.

When she was about to get out of the car, he insisted on going with her.

'I'm going with Tessan. She might not be able to find the restaurant from here. I'll catch up with you later.'

'OK. Meet us at Österport. Let's say in an hour, because I need to stop by the bath shop first. So two thirty at Österport. OK?'

'Sure, Mummy. I'll be there.'

He looked up at Terese, gave her a mischievous smile and stuck his hands in his pockets. She knew that he didn't usually call Susanne 'Mummy', and his mother probably didn't like it either. He was just trying to impress Terese. But Susanne didn't protest, just said, 'See you later,' and drove off.

They walked towards the harbour. Kristoffer talked and pointed, wanting to tell her about everything they passed.

The restaurant was close to the shore, just beyond Almedalen park. Kristoffer ran out on to the wharf and sat down. He took off his sandals and dipped his feet in the water.

'Come on, Tessan. It's super-nice out here!'

She went over to him and sat down, gazing out across the glittering expanse of blue water.

'Do you want an ice cream?' asked Kristoffer. 'It's my treat,' he hurried to add.

'I don't want to be late getting to the restaurant,' she told him. 'I'm supposed to be there after the lunch hour, and it's already one thirty.'

'Don't you know how late everyone eats lunch in the summer when they're on holiday? Right now it'll be packed with people, and Pappa won't have time to talk to you. You can't go over there before two. They have lots of customers at lunchtime.'

Since Palle hadn't actually given her a specific time to arrive, and Kristoffer was so convincing, she agreed.

'OK, then. I'll have an ice-cream sandwich.'

'Great.'

He jumped to his feet and ran down the wharf.

She laughed at his enthusiasm and lit a cigarette. She was really starting to like Gotland. She'd never been in a more beautiful place. She turned around to look at Almedalen, which was crowded with people sitting on blankets, eating a picnic lunch or simply sunbathing. Others strolled about or fed the ducks in the pond. Rising up beyond the park were the rugged old city walls. Kids were running around and playing on the grass. Cyclists rode past on the path behind her, and on the shore several guys were throwing a Frisbee back and forth. Cute guys, she thought, as she took another drag on her cigarette. Out of the corner of her eye she saw Kristoffer come hurrying towards her, carrying the ice cream.

'Here. Take it before it melts,' he said.

'Thanks.' She tossed away her cigarette butt and tore off the paper. 'How sweet of you to buy me an ice cream.'

'That's OK. It's only because I think you're so nice.'

'You do?' she said, surprised by the compliment. 'Well, thanks.'

'And you're cute, too,' he added, giving her a sidelong glance. 'You're the cutest girl I've ever seen.'

'Wow. Thanks.'

Terese could feel herself blushing. She hadn't expected to hear anything like that.

'Do you have a boyfriend?'

'No.'

'You should. Somebody like you, who's so cute and cool. But you'll probably meet someone here. I mean, after you get to know people a little and stuff.'

'Hmm. Maybe.'

'Do you miss your friends in Stockholm?'

'Sometimes.'

'And your mother and father?'

'Not really.'

'I bet you'll make a lot of friends here,' said Kristoffer, trying to console her as he licked his ice-cream cone.

'That may take a while.'

'Well, I'm really glad that you've come to live with us.'

Kristoffer looked at her with his warm brown eyes and smiled shyly.

Terese was so touched that tears filled her eyes.

'I'm glad to be here,' she said. 'And I like you, too.'

She put her arm around Kristoffer and gave him a hug.

Then they just sat there in silence, staring out at the sea.

Johan was sitting in his car outside the Kyrk School, trying to collect himself before he went in to tell Emma what had happened. Roma was such a small town that news and gossip spread swiftly.

After the police and medics had taken over at the scene of the accident, he had driven back to Roma. The children in the school bus seemed to have come through with only minor injuries. No one had been seriously hurt.

He still couldn't make himself get out of the car. His heart was pounding, and he shuddered as he once again pictured Olle, bleeding and leaning forward in the crumpled car. He had died in his prime. He was only a couple of years older than Johan. It could just as well have happened to him. Life was so fragile. Then he thought about Sara and Filip. They loved their father. They went to the Roma school in town, and he and Emma needed to go over there as soon as possible to pick them up. But first Emma.

He'd already smoked two cigarettes and was about to light a third, but he stopped himself. He got out of the car and crossed the schoolyard, feeling his legs trembling. He opened the front door and went to the staff room. The familiar smell of coffee wafted towards him. The school caretaker was the only person there. He wore a grey shirt and blue trousers, and he was leafing through the morning paper. According to the clock on the wall, it was eight thirty, so the first lesson of the morning was well underway.

'Hi,' said Johan. 'I need to find my wife. Emma Winarve. It's an emergency.'

'Oh?' The caretaker raised his eyebrows and looked concerned. 'I'll go and get her.'

'And Emma won't be going back to class,' Johan told the man. 'She has to go straight home, so you'll need to find someone else to take over for her.'

'All right. We'll find someone.'

The caretaker got up and hurried out of the room.

Johan sank down on one of the hard sofas and stared vacantly into space. He didn't know how he was going to tell her. He felt sick when he thought about Olle, covered in blood behind the wheel of his car.

Then he heard quick footsteps approaching.

'What is it?' cried Emma even before she came inside the staff room. 'What's happened, Johan?'

Her face was white with fear.

He stood up and held out his hand.

'Come here and sit down,' he said gently. 'Sit down next to me.'

'Has something happened to the children?' she wailed, tears welling up in her eyes. 'Not the children, Johan,' she pleaded. Her face contorted and she began to sob. 'Please, not the children.'

'No,' said Johan. 'It's nothing to do with the children. They're all fine. It's not them. It's Olle. He's been in a car accident. A really bad accident, Emma.'

Johan took a deep breath before he could get himself to tell her the rest.

'Olle is dead.'

151

The restaurant called La Cucaracha was on Lummelundsväg, a short distance beyond the city walls to the north, on the road leading to the airport. The location was a bit remote, and from the outside it didn't look very promising. A grey building with a flat roof and a small car park at the front, situated on a road that always had fairly heavy traffic. It was easy to see that it was a Mexican restaurant because of the green cactuses painted on the façade and a big sombrero hanging outside the entrance.

Jacobsson, Sohlman and Wittberg had driven to the restaurant as soon as the meeting of the investigative team was over. It was still more than an hour until their usual lunchtime but, when they stepped inside, the aroma of spicy chilli peppers prickled their nostrils and made their mouths water. Traditional mariachi music filled the empty restaurant, and a long-legged waitress with her hair pinned up in a topknot was setting a table. Jacobsson checked her watch. Only ten thirty. No wonder there weren't any customers.

When the waitress noticed their arrival, she stopped what she was doing and came over to welcome them.

They introduced themselves and asked to see Patrik Rosén.

'Sure. He's here,' said the waitress, speaking with an accent Jacobsson couldn't identify. 'He's in the kitchen. I'll go and fetch him. Please have a seat while you're waiting. Would you like coffee or something else to drink?'

'No, thanks,' they all said.

The waitress's nametag read 'Daniella'. She had a pale complexion and almond-shaped eyes. Oversized earrings dangled from her ears, and Jacobsson thought her blouse was a little too low-cut to be appropriate for the job.

They sat down at a table next to the window. The place was comfortably furnished with rustic tables made of dark wood, sun-yellow tablecloths, and chairs painted all different colours. Brightly coloured ceramic pots stood on shelves and decorating the walls were black-and-white tiles with Mexican motifs: little scantily clad children playing in the street; an elderly woman baking tortillas; a man wearing a sombrero with a donkey out in a field; three laughing men playing guitars. Jacobsson also recognized a print of a self-portrait of Frida Kahlo, the famous Mexican artist.

A few minutes later Patrik Rosén, wearing an apron, entered the room through the swinging doors next to the small bar. He looked pale and haggard, and he glanced at them uneasily as he sat down at the table.

'Has something happened?' he asked after they'd said hello.

'Yes,' said Jacobsson. 'We've discovered some new information. I'm sorry that we have to bother you again, but there's something we need to talk to you about.'

'What is it?'

'While we talk, my colleague here, Erik, would like to take a look around the restaurant and the kitchen. Is that OK?'

Rosén threw up his hands.

'Sure. Go ahead,' he said, nodding to Sohlman, who was already getting to his feet. 'I have nothing to hide.'

'First of all, I'd like you to sign your name on this piece of paper,' said Jacobsson.

'Why?'

'We just need to see your signature,' she explained, handing him a notepad and pen.

Rosén shook his head and muttered something, as if he thought the police were out of their minds.

Both Jacobsson and Wittberg saw that he took the pen in his left hand to sign his name. Jacobsson thanked him and reclaimed the notepad.

'Could you tell us about your first wife, Ulrika? Maja's mother?'

Rosén was so startled by the question he simply stared at Jacobsson without saying a word. He was silent for a whole minute. Neither of the police officers broke the silence. They waited him out, keeping their eyes fixed on his face.

Finally, he recovered his composure and said in a low voice, 'Why the hell are you asking me questions about my first wife? What does she have to do with any of this?'

'That's for us to decide,' replied Jacobsson calmly. 'How did the two of you meet?'

'Is this some sort of sick joke?'

Rosén turned to Wittberg, as if to seek his support, but the officer didn't respond.

'Answer the question,' said Jacobsson sternly.

The man across the table continued to give her a perplexed look, but then he seemed to realize she was serious. He leaned back slightly.

'What do you want to know about Ulrika?'

'Above all, we want to know how she died,' Jacobsson said bluntly.

'She drowned while we were on holiday in Greece. We were celebrating our tenth wedding anniversary. That was three years ago. The seventh of August, to be precise.'

'What happened?'

'We'd had dinner at a fancy restaurant in Naxos. We were renting a house on the beach ten kilometres or so outside of town, so we took a cab home. We opened a bottle of champagne out on the terrace, and later Ulrika wanted to go for a swim. It was almost three in the morning, so I was reluctant, but I went along because she loved to swim at night. It was what she loved best . . .'

Rosén's voice faded and he seemed to be staring at something far away. As if he'd forgotten all about his indignant reaction only a few minutes earlier. His tone of voice had changed.

'Please go on.'

'We grabbed some towels and walked down to the water. We were staying on a remote stretch of beach. There were only a few other houses and a little taverna several hundred metres away. Then we started swimming. The wind had picked up, and I thought the waves were getting too big, so I wanted to swim back to shore. But Ulrika insisted on staying in the water for a while longer, and she was a strong swimmer. I wasn't really worried. I sat down on the sand and waited for her. The air felt nice and warm. I couldn't see her because it was dark, but I could hear her. We shouted back and forth to each other, but after a while she stopped answering. I called to her several times.'

'Then what did you do?'

'I went down to the shoreline and shouted louder, but she still didn't answer. I went into the water and starting swimming, but I soon realized it was hopeless. I couldn't see anything in the dark all around me, and I had no idea where she was.'

'Then what?'

'By then I was scared, so I ran into the house and phoned the police. They searched for days, with boats, divers and helicopters, but she was never found. Ulrika disappeared out there in the waves. We'd had ten years together.'

'What about Maja?'

'She was three years old. Ulrika's parents were taking care of her while we were away. It was so hard for me to tell her that her mother was gone and was never coming back. If only I'd stood my ground and said no to going out for a swim . . .'

Rosén's previous anger had vanished. He spoke with emotion, and his anguish seemed completely genuine. Jacobsson didn't think there was any reason to pursue the subject any longer. They would have to wait until they found out more about the incident.

At that moment Erik Sohlman came out of the restaurant's kitchen. He was carrying several knives.

'I'm going to have to borrow these. I hope that's OK with you.'

'Take whatever you like,' said Rosén distractedly.

He seemed to have sunk into an entirely different mood. As if he no longer cared about anything.

156

Jacobsson leaned forward and gave him a searching look.

'How did you get that scar on your face?'

Rosén gave a start. His hand flew up automatically to touch his cheek.

'This?' he murmured. 'I've had it since I was a teenager. I was robbed when I was in Stockholm. Late one night I got shitfaced, and I got lost, wandering around the city. I was mugged in a car park. Some junkies robbed me and then stabbed me with a knife.'

'And you reported this to the police, right?'

Rosén looked at Jacobsson and shrugged.

'Actually, no. I was so damned ashamed about what happened I didn't want to go to the police.'

The street outside the restaurant was deserted. What a difference from only a few weeks ago, thought Patrik Rosén when he finally had time to step outside for a smoke. It was the same feeling every year. A void that arose after the tourists left, and the same sense of surprise that things could change so quickly. From all that hustle and bustle to emptiness and darkness. Just like in real life.

He really shouldn't be here at all. His daughter had died a mere two days ago, and the only place he should be right now was at home with Isabel and their new-born son. But he couldn't handle that at the moment. He needed to get out of the house, to keep himself busy and stick to his daily routine. Besides, he was needed more than ever at the restaurant. His best waitress had called in sick, and another was on leave because she was due to give birth at any moment.

And working seemed to help. It grounded him. He felt better stirring the pots, chopping vegetables, warming tortillas, cooking beans, cutting meat. And setting the tables, serving the food, clearing away the dishes. Moving back and forth between the kitchen and the dining room.

As the owner of the small restaurant, he did everything, helping out wherever he was needed. The Mexican cook was hard-working and made fabulous food, but he needed assistance.

La Cucaracha was a popular place, known for its atmosphere and good food. Even though it was in an out-of-the-way location, customers always found their way to the restaurant. This Friday evening it had been packed almost the whole time, and he had barely had even a minute for a break. But that was precisely what he'd needed. Working kept him from thinking about Maja and offered him some much-needed respite.

Now it was pitch dark outside, and the pavement was deserted. He glanced at his watch. Five past eleven. Almost another hour until they closed, at midnight. He'd just sent the waitress home, and the chef was also about to leave. The kitchen closed at ten, and he had almost finished clearing up. Still sitting at one of the tables was a group of friends who'd been carrying on a lively conversation all evening. And at a table in the corner were a couple who were obviously in love. They'd been sipping their wine and staring deep into each other's eyes ever since they'd finished eating.

The group of friends had now paid their bill, and Rosén was hoping that the couple would also pay and leave soon, so he could close a little early. He was dead tired, and his feet ached. All he wanted was to go home and sleep.

He ground out his cigarette under the sole of his shoe and cast a glance through the restaurant window. The group got up and headed for the door, but the couple still sat in the light of the candle, dreamily staring at each other. They made no move to leave, and he couldn't very well turn them out before closing time.

He got out another cigarette and had just lit up when he heard the sound of an engine in the distance. It was a muffled rumble far away but approaching rapidly. An unmistakable sound. Several motorcycles appeared on the road. Four leather-clad men slowed down and then parked nearby.

Rosén froze but didn't move from his position, leaning against the wall. The group of friends came out of the restaurant and thanked him as they left. They strolled off towards town, enjoying the warmth of the late-summer evening. Don't go, he thought. He took a nervous drag on his cigarette. What the hell did these damned hooligans want? Were they just here for some food? Or did they have something else in mind? He'd never had any trouble with any of the motorcycle clubs on the island, but these guys didn't seem like locals.

Shit. First, the police stomping around earlier in the day, and now this. He stayed where he was and continued to smoke, pretending to be unperturbed, although he was watching the bikers out of the corner of his eye as they took off their helmets. He'd never seen them before. Four rough-looking guys came striding towards him. Fear surged through Rosén, and his mouth went dry. He could see that their eyes were ice cold.

He tossed his cigarette away and turned to open the front door of the restaurant.

A heavy hand grabbed him by the shoulder.

1994

After saying goodbye to Kristoffer, Terese stepped inside the Catch 22 restaurant and was instantly impressed by its unpretentious style. The place was still packed, and a pleasant buzz of voices filled her ears as soon as she opened the door. To her right she saw a bar that ran the length of the restaurant. Music posters hung on the walls, and the rustic furniture was made of dark-stained wood. There was very little space between the tables, which had no tablecloths. Only salt and pepper shakers, along with bottles of ketchup and steak sauce. The waitresses were rushing around with trays loaded down with plates of food. An aroma of grilled meat filled the noisy place, and Terese liked the music that was blaring from the loudspeakers, although she didn't recognize any of the tunes.

She looked around uncertainly, and her bewilderment must have been clear to see because the guy behind the bar called out to her.

'Hi, sweetheart. Can I help you?'

'I'm supposed to meet Palle.'

'He's probably in the kitchen. Have a seat and I'll go and tell him you're here. I'm not sure he'll be able to get away at the moment, because we're pretty busy right now. What's your name?'

'Terese.'

The bartender gave her a smile, and she noticed to her embarrassment that she was blushing. He was tall and had a special way of looking at her that made her stomach flutter. It might actually be fun to work here, she thought. He finished filling the beer glasses in front of him and set them on a tray before disappearing through a swinging door. A few seconds later he was back.

'Palle says he'll be with you as soon as he can, but to have something to drink while you're waiting. What would you like?'

'A Diet Coke,' she said, sinking down on to a vacant bar stool.

'I'm Dennis.'

The guy behind the bar held out his hand.

'Dennis,' she repeated, and laughed. She'd never met anybody with that name before.

'My mother loved the comic-book character Dennis the Menace when she was a kid. But it's probably not a comic you'd know.'

'No, I don't,' she admitted.

She shook his hand, which felt slightly sweaty. Then Dennis went back to work. He was swamped, moving fast as he got out bottles and filled glasses with draught beer. The waitresses kept coming to the bar in a steady stream to call out their orders. Terese was amazed the bartender could keep track of them all.

As she sipped her Coke, which seemed extra festive because it was served with ice cubes and a slice of lemon, she tried to guess how old Dennis was. No more than thirty-five, she thought. But at least twenty-two or twenty-three.

She looked around the restaurant and discovered a door leading out to a terrace, where customers were also seated. The waitresses scurried back and forth, going in and out and making their way between the tables, carrying their trays of food and drinks. She noticed two younger guys whose job it was to clear away the dirty dishes and wipe the tables. That was probably what Palle had in mind for her. She'd never be able to handle a waitressing job in such a busy place.

Then Palle came through the swinging doors, wiping sweat from his forehead. He gave her a smile.

'Sorry for making you wait. I hadn't counted on so many customers this late in the day. The lunch rush is usually over by two.'

'That's OK.'

She smiled to show that she meant it.

'I see that Dennis has been looking after you. Are you hungry?'

'I can wait a while.'

'How about if I show you around, and then we can sit down and have a bite to eat. I'm starving, and it's a good idea for you to try out our menu, since you're going to be working here.'

She nodded.

Things were starting to calm down. The customers at one table after another got up and left. Everyone seemed pleased and took the time to say goodbye to Dennis before going out of the door. Palle asked for a bottle of Ramlösa, which he poured into a glass. He took a menu from a rack at the bar and opened it to show Terese.

'We've got an American-style menu here, as I'm sure you've already noticed. We serve mostly hamburgers. That's what we're famous for,' he added with pride. 'You won't find a better burger in all of Sweden. We have two American cooks, who really know how to make them right. Our appetizers are also popular, especially the buffalo wings, mozzarella sticks and potato skins. And in the evening we serve hot dishes cooked on the coal-fired grill outside. I'll show it to you later. We've got various chicken and beef dishes on the menu, as well as lamb and salmon.'

Terese studied the menu, anxious to seem interested. Hardly any of the available selections were familiar to her, but her mouth watered as she listened to Palle describe the food.

When most of the customers had left, he showed her around. The outdoor terrace was much bigger than she'd thought. It wrapped around almost the entire building. And the view of the water was fantastic. A stage occupied one end.

'In the summertime we have live music every night except Sunday,' Palle explained. 'Mostly, a great American band of old guys who play soul music.'

'Cool,' she said, even though she thought it sounded boring.

A little while later they were seated at a table outside. In front of each of them was a basket holding a juicy burger and the biggest portion of French fries she'd ever seen.

'So what do you think about working here?' asked Palle, between bites. 'You can start by clearing tables. Is that OK?'

'When can I start?'

'Tomorrow, if you like. It's probably better if you work the lunch shift, because it's even busier in the evening.'

She couldn't see how that could be possible. Every table had been taken when she came in.

'Great. I'd like that.'

She looked over at the bar and met Dennis's eye.

'You open?'

The man who asked the question wore a leather waistcoat with an emblem from a motorcycle club that Patrik Rosén didn't recognize. The biker had a huge belly and a black beard gathered in a long, skinny plait that hung from his chin.

'Yes, but the kitchen is closed,' replied Rosén, embarrassed to hear that his voice quavered.

'We're not interested in eating, are we, boys?'

The big man turned to his fellow bikers.

'Don't say that,' said one of them, laughing. His head was shaved, and a tattoo covered half his face. 'It depends what they're serving.'

They brusquely hustled Rosén inside the restaurant but backed off when they saw the couple sitting at the table in the corner.

'I guess we'll settle for something to drink for the time being,' said the man with the plaited beard, casting an annoyed glance at the amorous lovers. 'Four strong beers. Pints.'

Rosén swallowed hard and hurried behind the bar. His pulse was racing. What the hell should he do? He could hardly ring the police just because four guys wearing leathers wanted beer. But there was something menacing

166

about them, and the couple had apparently noticed it too. The young man motioned to Rosén for the bill after he served the pints. Reluctantly, he accepted the money, and then the couple quickly left the restaurant.

The four bikers drank their beer in silence. The man with the facial tattoo stared at Rosén, who was clearing away the last dirty dishes. His heart was hammering in his chest. He went into the small kitchen, put the plates in the dishwasher and turned it on. The familiar rumbling sound as it started up calmed him down a bit. What if the bikers really just wanted a beer? What if they just got a kick out of scaring people? They probably had no idea who he was, or what he and Jocke had been up to. How could these guys possibly know anything about it?

The two of them had been so careful to keep it secret. Neither of them wanted anyone to know. According to their agreement, Jocke had sworn never to say a word about their dealings to anybody, especially not any members of the motorcycle club. If he did, the whole arrangement would come to an abrupt end. Rosén had been very clear about that. And things had been fine for years. Why would they suddenly seek him out? Especially now that Jocke was dead.

An ice-cold shiver raced through Rosén as he thought of something. Did they think he was the killer? He stared at the swing door that led to the restaurant. The Los Lobos CD had stopped playing, and an uneasy silence had settled over the place.

Then he heard the metallic click of the lock on the front door, and the sound of the blinds being lowered in the windows facing the street.

Frantically, he looked around for something to defend himself with. Above the range hung a long row of newly purchased knives he'd brought over today after the police confiscated the old ones. He grabbed the biggest one. At that moment the door swung open and three of the bikers stood there, blocking any exit. The man with the plaited beard glared at him hostilely.

'What do we have to do to get another beer around here?'

Silence. Patrik Rosén looked with surprise at the three brutes and realized he didn't have a chance.

'What do you want?' he managed to ask.

'What do we want? What do you say, brothers?' said the man with the paunch, who seemed to be the leader of the group. 'What do we want?' he repeated. Then he frowned. 'Hey, that knife looks dangerous. Sort of like the knife some bastard used to murder our friend Jocke. Wasn't it the same kind of knife in that picture in the newspaper?'

The other bikers nodded.

The man stepped forward.

'We know what you did, you bastard,' he snarled.

The three other men also moved forward. In a last desperate attempt to flee, Rosén threw himself at the back door.

Before he even managed to press down the handle, everything went black before his eyes.

On Saturday morning Knutas was sitting alone over breakfast, having his first cup of coffee of the day, when the phone rang. The children were still asleep, and Lina was in Copenhagen. He would just have to get used to that. He felt a warmth come over him when he heard Karin Jacobsson's voice, but he could tell at once that something had happened.

'Hi,' she said. 'You need to come in. Patrik Rosén was badly beaten up at his restaurant last night.'

'What? Any arrests made yet?'

'No. We don't know a thing at the moment. Only that someone beat him up and then trashed the restaurant.'

An hour later Knutas joined Jacobsson and Wittberg in the conference room at police headquarters. Jacobsson, who had arrived early, told them what she knew.

'Late last night or in the early hours of this morning, Patrik Rosén was assaulted at La Cucaracha. The injuries he suffered are severe but not life-threatening. He was taken to hospital and, according to the doctors, he's in no condition to be interviewed for at least a couple of days.'

'How was he assaulted?' asked Knutas.

'He seems to have been kicked and punched, but no weapon was used. He suffered bruises all over his body but no internal injuries except to his head. Apparently, there's a slight swelling in his brain, and that has to ease before we'll be able to question him.'

'Was he alone in the restaurant when this happened?' asked Wittberg.

'I spoke to his wife, Isabel, who was in a state of shock.' Jacobsson shook her head. 'That poor woman. Rosén was supposed to work all evening and close the restaurant at midnight. Both the waitress and the cook had gone home by the time the beating took place. Rosén wasn't expected home until one in the morning, so Isabel had gone to bed and hadn't realized that he hadn't come home. She was awakened by the phone call from our duty officer, who told her what happened to her husband.'

'Who phoned the police?' asked Knutas.

'The restaurant is in a rather out-of-the-way location. It's not in the middle of any residential neighbourhood, so it took a while before anyone noticed. Some teenagers happened to pass by, and they were the ones who rang the police. The restaurant is a shambles, but it's mostly a question of broken plates and glasses. The guys who did this didn't waste a lot of time on destroying the place.'

'Guys? Do we know that more than one person was involved?' said Knutas.

'That's what Sohlman thinks. He's out there right now, and I talked to him a little while ago.'

'Any witnesses?' asked Knutas.

Jacobsson shook her head.

'Not a single witness has notified the police so far. We can only hope that will change during the course of the day. We need to start knocking on the doors of the nearest houses and office buildings, and also see if we can track down any customers who were at the restaurant last night. That shouldn't be hard, since almost everybody pays by credit card these days.'

'Who else works at the restaurant?'

'We actually met both of them yesterday morning when we went out there,' replied Jacobsson, with a nod towards Wittberg. 'The Mexican cook, Rafael, and a lovely waitress named Daniella. She spoke Swedish with a strange accent. Could you tell where she was from?' she asked Wittberg.

'No. I wasn't listening to what she said. I was too busy looking at her.'

Jacobsson couldn't help smiling.

'You're hopeless.'

'OK,' said Knutas, clapping his hands. 'We need to get on this right away. It seems highly likely that the assault on Patrik Rosén has something to do with the case we're working on. The question is: what's the connection?'

Guilt gnawed at Johan on Saturday morning as he got in his car to drive over to the editorial office. He didn't like leaving Emma alone, but today was the memorial service for Jocke Eriksson, and he needed to go to work.

All yesterday had passed in a fog. After his wife had heard the terrible news, she finally calmed down sufficiently for them to be able to drive over to the Roma school to pick up Sara and Filip. Johan had phoned ahead to speak to their teachers, asking them to take the children out of class. But Emma didn't want to tell them about Olle until they got home.

The news of their father's death was a great shock, of course. Luckily, Emma's parents had come over from Fårö, bringing the younger children with them. Johan was able to leave the chaos in their hands.

When he checked his mobile, he saw a text that Pia had sent earlier in the morning, asking him to call if he had time. Taking into account the tragedy that had struck his family, she hadn't wanted to disturb him by phoning. He rang her number, and she answered at once. After they'd talked for a moment about the awful turn of events, Johan asked Pia why she'd been trying to get hold of him.

'Something happened last night,' she began. 'Patrik Rosén was assaulted at his restaurant, La Cucaracha. He was badly injured and taken to hospital.'

'You're kidding. Do they know who did it?'

'No. And the police aren't saying a word. I went over to the restaurant to get some footage, but only outside. And I talked to some people who live fairly close, but no one seems to have seen or heard anything.'

'OK. I'll see you soon.'

The sun was shining on the blocky concrete building of the motorcycle club and the leather-clad bikers when Johan and Pia arrived an hour later. On Sonny's orders a stage had been set up outside, along with a beer tent, and two women were grilling burgers non-stop. They looked nearly identical, with dyed blonde hair and black leather skirts, each with a cigarette hanging from her lips and sunglasses perched on her head.

Johan and Pia did their best not to draw attention to themselves, but they noticed suspicious glances and scowling expressions directed their way. Sonny had explained that, in these circles, there was a great deal of scepticism about journalists. Yet he'd managed to convince the club leaders that it would be advantageous to allow them to do a story on the memorial service. And, eventually, all the members had agreed. Johan was secretly wondering whether they'd be able to get any of them to be interviewed on camera. But he decided to wait until after the ceremony. Everyone seemed to be keeping a close watch on Pia and her camera, turning their backs the minute she started filming.

173

'How are we going to do this if they keep avoiding us like the plague?' she hissed in Johan's ear.

'Let's just wait for a while. Maybe they'll thaw out.'

At that moment Sonny appeared on stage. A framed photo of Jocke stood on the table next to him. The crowd of bikers drew closer until they were all standing there together, their eyes fixed on Sonny. There was no microphone, but he spoke in a loud, clear voice that could be heard by everyone listening. Johan counted thirty people. He knew that members of other motor-cycle clubs were also present.

Pia now began moving confidently among the crowd. She'd decided the best policy was to ignore their belligerent attitude. And for some inexplicable reason this strategy seemed to work. After a while no one seemed to care any more about the camera. Everyone was listening to Sonny's emotional speech and forgot all about Pia. They must have been like real brothers, thought Johan, as the man on stage spoke. The club members had always called each other brothers, but this went beyond that. Sonny spoke of Jocke as if they'd been best friends, and yet there was a strong sense of an even deeper connection that might almost be called love. Johan couldn't figure the guy out. If Sonny hadn't flirted with Pia the way he had done, Johan might have thought he was gay, in spite of his macho appearance. Outwardly, the leader of the Road Warriors looked tough, with his numerous tattoos and shaven head, his leather waistcoat, his boots with all the rivets, and his pride at owning no fewer than seven Harleys. But, inwardly, he seemed both sensitive and boyish, sniggering childishly as soon as Pia said anything funny. He had waxed lyrical when he described the experience of racing along on his motorcycle and talked about nature and wildlife and the beauty of the island.

Sonny was an authority figure and leader in the motorcycle world, and Johan realized that he was widely admired and respected. But there seemed to be a whole different side to this man. At any rate, right now he was giving a lengthy and touching eulogy for his deceased friend. When he finished, he was greeted with loud applause. Then members from various clubs climbed up on stage to add a few words of their own. When everyone had finished, Sonny again took the stage and looked out at the audience.

'All right, boys. Now we're going to do what I know Jocke would have wanted us to do.' He raised the bottle of beer he was holding. 'We're going to get fucking drunk! *Skål!*'

Pia managed to get hold of Sonny as he got down from the stage, and they did an interview with him, asking him to talk about what Jocke had meant to the club and vice versa.

'Who was his best friend here, aside from you?' asked Pia afterwards.

'Maddis,' said Sonny without hesitation.

'Maddis? That sounds like a girl's name.'

'It is.' Sonny gave Pia an embarrassed look. 'She's my woman. We've been together for several years now. You're not disappointed, are you?'

'Not at all,' said Pia with a laugh. 'I wasn't exactly planning to repeat what we did the last time we met.'

'If I was free, I wouldn't hesitate for a second,' said Sonny, grinning.

They found Maddis behind the bar in the beer tent. A woman in her forties with long dark hair, she was almost painfully thin. She wore jeans, high-heeled boots and a black top.

'Could we interview you?' asked Pia. 'Sonny told us you were good friends with Jocke.'

'That's right, I was. Sure. I don't mind talking about him,' said Maddis, smiling. 'That's why we're here, you know. Do you guys want a beer? I'm thinking of having one. If we're lucky, they're still cold.'

They each took a beer and went outside to sit down at a table.

'Is it OK if we start filming now?' asked Pia. 'You already know what we want to talk about.'

'It'll seem more spontaneous that way,' Johan explained, holding out the microphone towards Maddis.

'Sure,' she agreed. 'Where should I look?'

'Just look at me,' said Johan. 'We'll pretend the camera's not even here. It's just you and me.'

'OK.' Maddis smiled again. 'In that case, I'm going to have a smoke. Is that allowed on TV?'

'Of course.'

Johan noticed that her hands shook when she lit the cigarette.

'What was your reaction when you heard that Jocke had been murdered?'

'At first, I couldn't believe it. He was the kind of person everybody liked. Then I felt horribly sad, and horribly angry, too.'

'What kind of thoughts went through your mind?'

'Well, I wondered if the murder had something to do with the robbery. So bloody stupid. Jocke had a

176

tendency to land in a lot of trouble, but deep inside he was a good-hearted and kind person.'

'Who did he hang out with?'

'I don't really know. He didn't ever talk much about any of his friends outside the club. And he rarely brought any outsiders over here. I asked him why, and he told me that he didn't want to mix the rest of his life with his life in the club. This place was sacred to him. He didn't want to muddy it up with any other shit. He did bring a couple of friends over a few times, a guy and a girl, but that was long ago.'

She fell silent and took a deep drag on her cigarette.

'So, I think that's enough,' she said, turning to Pia. 'Can you turn off the camera now?'

Pia lifted her eyes away from the viewfinder to give Maddis a surprised look.

'Sure, if that's what you want, but—'

'Of course we'll stop if you're feeling uncomfortable,' Johan intervened. 'Shut it off,' he said to Pia, and then turned back to Maddis.

'OK. So we're not going to film this part, and I won't mention what you tell me in my report. Word of honour. But do you have any idea who the friends were that he brought here?'

'I don't even know if they live here on the island or not. I had a feeling he was still seeing them, but he never talked about them.'

Johan sensed that this could be important. Jocke was one of the robbers, and the other two were supposedly a guy and a girl. The robbers had seemed like a real team, coordinating their efforts with great efficiency.

As if they knew each other well.

On Sunday the police heard from the first witness regarding the assault on Patrik Rosén in La Cucaracha. An elderly man who happened to live in the neighbourhood, across the road, had phoned the police to say that he'd heard the roar of motorcycles late on Friday night. He had been in bed with a bad cold, and his cough had kept him awake. The witness heard the sound of the bikes twice. First around eleven thirty that night, and then an hour later. Because the man also had a high fever, he hadn't had the energy to get up to have a look out of the window.

The man contacted the police because he'd heard on the radio about what had happened and that the authorities were asking any witnesses to come forward.

At the same time, members of the Road Warriors and any current visitors to the club had been brought down to police headquarters to be interviewed over the weekend, but without any significant result. They flatly denied any involvement in the assault and provided alibis for each other. Since the perpetrators had not left behind any evidence, the police were fumbling in the dark so far. Having one witness who'd heard motorcycles that night was not sufficient to make an arrest. And the customers who had eaten at the restaurant had nothing to say. They'd enjoyed a pleasant dinner but hadn't seen any bikers or other suspicious individuals. The police hadn't yet been able to contact the last restaurant customer, who had paid his bill at 11.22 p.m.

Knutas and Jacobsson went out to have a look at the destruction at La Cucaracha, but they hadn't yet been allowed to speak to Rosén. He was still too weak to be interviewed. His wife firmly denied that Patrik had anything to do with motorcycle clubs.

As the work day drew to a close, Knutas and Jacobsson were both tired and hungry. They decided to go out and grab a bite to eat.

The warm summer evening smelled of asphalt and the sea. It was a relief to get out of police headquarters and leave all their worries behind. At least for a while.

They strolled down to the harbour and found a window table in a restaurant that faced the water. The speciality was American-type appetizers. They ordered several to share, along with a bottle of wine. The sun hung like a crimson globe above the sea.

'Autumn isn't far off,' said Knutas, 'even though that's hard to imagine.'

The waitress brought their food, and they hungrily started eating. Neither of them felt like talking about the investigation, so they ate in silence.

'So how's it going with Lina?' asked Jacobsson after a while.

'I don't really know. She's gone to Copenhagen to start that temporary job. We've hardly talked since she left.'

'How are you feeling about that?'

'Empty. Strange. It's like I've been suddenly hurled into a dark void. Nothing makes sense, nothing seems permanent. My life feels like a house of cards that could collapse at any moment.'

'Why do you think I've lived by myself for so long?' said Jacobsson, giving him a wry smile.

'Thanks. That's really comforting,' said Knutas dryly, as he gnawed on another spicy chicken wing.

'Sorry. I didn't mean it like that. I know things seem tough right now, but maybe something positive will come of it in the long run. Sometimes it's good to shake things up a bit, open new doors, let in some fresh air. Try something new and change your perspective.'

'Good Lord, you're full of advice. So how are things with you and Janne?'

'Good. He wants us to move in together.'

Knutas dropped the chicken wing on his plate and wiped his mouth with a napkin. The next second, he had a coughing fit.

He took several gulps of water, and the coughing subsided. When he was able to look at Jacobsson again, she noticed that his eyes were filled with tears, probably from all the coughing.

'Move in together?' Knutas said. 'What do you think about that?'

'It scares me, but it's also tempting, of course. Sometimes I just get so tired of being alone. I'd love to share my life with someone.'

'Does it have to be Janne?'

Jacobsson looked at Knutas. He felt himself getting lost in her big brown eyes.

'Do you have someone else in mind?' she said.

She took another sip of wine. Kept her eyes fixed on his.

Suddenly, the air was filled with tension. The conversation had taken a turn neither of them had anticipated. Knutas didn't know what to say. He drank some more wine to buy time. There had always been something special about Karin, and at the moment he felt like throwing himself at her.

Then Jacobsson's mobile rang.

'Speak of the devil,' she said, rolling her eyes. 'Hi. Yes, I'm finished with work for the day. Anders and I are sitting here at Catch 22 on the harbour having a bite to eat and talking about the case. Oh, really? You're nearby? Sure, come on over. Of course. That's great. See you.'

She ended the call and looked at Knutas.

'That was Janne. He's coming over.'

'I've got to go,' said Knutas, standing up abruptly. 'I'll pay the bill on my way out. See you tomorrow. OK?'

He left before Jacobsson could say a word.

1994

Jocke picked Terese up at four in the afternoon. She had lied to Susanne, telling her that she was going to sleep over at Linda's house. Linda was a girl who sometimes worked in the kitchen at Catch 22, and they'd met there several times. Linda had promised to cover for Terese if Susanne happened to ring. Terese had said she would take the bus to town, so she left the house on foot, headed for the main road.

Jocke picked her up at the bus stop. He was driving a beat-up old Amazon he'd borrowed from his brother. It was painted a screaming orange with a smattering of green flowers. Jocke said that one of his brothers was a hippie who lived in a commune on Fårö and spent all his time smoking grass. The other was the total opposite. He was studying economics at Stockholm University and was head of the student organization. He'd never dream of lending his car or anything else to his little brother.

They were going to drive over to Klintehamn and pick up one of Jocke's friends before they went to the Road Warriors party.

Terese had spent a large part of the afternoon getting ready. She'd washed her hair and plucked her eyebrows.

Painted her nails and shaved her legs. Stood in front of the mirror for hours, trying to decide between two different outfits.

As soon as she got in the car and they were heading south towards Klintehamn, Jocke tossed her a can of beer. The windows were open, and he turned up the stereo full blast.

'Time to party!' he shouted out of the window.

Terese was seized with an overwhelming sense of freedom. She took several big swigs of beer before lighting up a cigarette. She turned down the music, which made the speakers buzz, and then turned to face Jocke.

'Who are we picking up?'

'My buddy Degen. You'll like him. His real name is Diego. He's from Chile, but he's lived here in Sweden since he was a kid.'

'Does he live with his parents?'

'No way. He had a tough time at home, just like you and me.' Jocke gave Terese a swift smile. 'And he got into some trouble. He did a few burglaries and stole some cars and then got nailed for assaulting his father. Degen finally got fed up with his old man beating up his mother, so he let him have it. Then he got sent to one of those young offenders homes, or whatever they're called, in Klintehamn. But it's not a secure unit. He can come and go as he likes, and it actually seems OK. He lives in a house with a few other people and works in a bakery in Klinte.'

'How old is he?'

'Nineteen. Same as me. You're the baby of the group.'

'Is he from Gotland, too?'

'No, he's not. They probably sent him here to get him as far away from home as possible. He's from Stockholm. From Vällingby. Do you know where that is?'

'Sure. It's west of the city. I'm from a neighbourhood to the south.'

She tossed her cigarette butt out of the window and opened another beer. She longed to get drunk. It had been weeks since the last time. She'd been playing the good-girl role for so long she was just about to go crazy. She'd worked several days at Catch 22, and that had been fun, but it was hard work and she was exhausted by the time she got home in the evening. It turned out that the cute bartender, Dennis, only had eyes for his girlfriend, so that was a big disappointment. But she had earned several hundred kronor each day, and she received the wages in cash after every shift. Dennis simply took the money out of the till. So now Terese had money of her own, and she'd treated herself to a whole carton of cigarettes, which Jocke had got for her cheap. She'd hidden it in her wardrobe. He'd also bought some weed, which they were going to smoke later in the evening. Tomorrow was Sunday and she didn't have to go to work so she could sleep all day if she liked.

'So what kind of party is this?' she asked.

'Oh, just you wait and see. There's going to be a shitload of people. The Road Warriors' summer party is famous. Everyone in the motorcycle world who has friends in the club will be there – people from other chapters, or affiliated clubs on the mainland, plus a gang of real tough guys from the Hells Angels and the Outlaws. But lots of them are nicer than they look,' he added with a grin.

They drove past Tofta, and a view of the sea opened up along one side of the road.

'This is where I'm from,' said Jocke, a certain pride evident in his voice. 'I was baptized in the Tofta church, and we live close by. I'll show you sometime.'

Terese nodded. She would like that.

The water glittered, and off in the distance they could see both Big and Little Karlsö rising out of the sea. The air was hazy, so they could only glimpse a vague outline of the islands. But after several days of overcast skies and rain, the sun was finally peeking out from the clouds.

A short time later they reached Klintehamn and turned on to the main street through town.

'So this is downtown Klinte,' joked Jocke, as they passed the ICA on one side and a hairdresser's salon on the other. They saw several workmen having a beer, sitting at a table outside the only restaurant. They parked the car near a grand nineteenth-century house set amid a beautiful garden.

'This is where Degen lives,' said Jocke, getting out of the car. 'He's staying with the people who run the young offenders home here. They're pretty decent. Even though they've got their own kids, they let troublemakers like Degen stay with them. Not many people would do that.'

Terese felt a pang of guilt when she thought about how she'd behaved towards Susanne. She and Palle were decent people, too.

As soon as they set foot on the property, they heard a voice calling out: 'Jocke? What the hell!'

A dark-haired guy wearing tattered jeans and one earring came out of the big house, holding his arms wide open.

185

'Hi, Degen!'

They patted each other on the back a bit clumsily, the way guys usually do. Then Degen looked at Terese. He had warm, dark eyes. He wasn't very tall, but quite muscular. His biceps bulged under the short-sleeved T-shirt he had on. Jocke introduced Terese.

'I've heard a lot about you. My name's Diego, but everybody calls me Degen.'

'Shall we go?' said Jocke.

'Sure. I'm as ready as I'll ever be.'

Without hesitation Degen headed for the car and chivalrously held the door open for Terese. Then he jumped into the back seat.

186

Knutas stretched out his hand to Lina's side of the bed and gently stroked the sheet. An empty feeling came over him. At the same time, he thought about Karin. He'd never been able to sort out his feelings for her. Up until now he'd merely accepted the situation for what it was and dismissed any glimmerings of attraction or the fact that he'd started thinking of her more as a woman than a colleague.

Today the reinforcements from the NCP would arrive, so Jacobsson was going to take the opportunity to go over to Stockholm and visit the Thai boxing club where Jocke Eriksson had been seen with a friend. It was just as well she'd be away. Knutas's brain was feeling besieged enough.

He walked to police headquarters. It was still dark, with no one around, and the morning air felt refreshing after the stifling heat they'd been having lately. A solitary cat sat in the middle of the street and stared at him as he passed. The paper boy, who was riding his bike among the houses, waved his hand in greeting.

When Knutas entered the police station, he said hello to the duty officer seated in his glass booth. The man couldn't help asking him what had to be a rhetorical question.

'You're up awfully early, aren't you?'

'Yup. That I am.'

As soon as Knutas sat down at his desk, he got out his pipe from the top drawer and carefully filled it with tobacco as he looked at the piles of paper in front of him. For once he was actually going to light the pipe and have a smoke. Smoking was not allowed inside the building, except in the interrogation rooms. The staff room designated for smoking had been closed long ago, but occasionally he would stand at an open window, light his pipe, and take a few puffs. It was an absurd situation. Here he was, a high-ranking police chief in charge of the entire criminal division, yet he was forced to sneak a smoke like a teenage boy. What a country we live in, he thought.

He wondered if it was the same in Denmark. Probably not. The Danes were more broad-minded than the Swedes. Over there even the queen smoked openly, without showing the slightest embarrassment. If anyone in the Swedish royal family was ever caught with a cigarette, the picture would be on the front page of all the tabloids.

Denmark. Lina had gone back to her roots. And something told him she'd gone there for good.

He opened a window, sat down on the ledge and lit his pipe. In his mind he pictured her face. Her wise eyes, her lovely white teeth when she smiled. Which she often did – at least she used to, before this last year. Her freckles. Her red hair, which tumbled in a thick mane down her back. How he had loved her. He still did. She was the mother of his children and the woman in his life he felt closest to. She was also the person who knew him best. He thought about all the days they'd shared. All the meals they'd eaten together. Memories rushed through his mind, of summer holidays they'd enjoyed, birthdays they'd celebrated and coffee breaks they'd taken out in the country. Moments in their lives that were ingrained for ever in his memory. Her expression when she gave birth to their children. How happy they'd been when they took the babies out in the pram for the very first time. The time when they could finally afford to buy the summer cottage. Together, they had planned and refurbished it. What was to become of everything now?

Knutas realized that he had started to weep.

The bright nights of the summer were fading, and it was dark at this late hour. Several cabs drove slowly down the street and stopped outside, dropping off their customers. Some were more formally dressed, wearing suits. Others had on jeans and polo shirts. The people who slipped inside the nondescript entrance were of varying ages and no doubt had a wide range of professions and backgrounds. But there was one thing they did have in common. They were all men.

The striptease club was located in a well-to-do part of town, right across from one of the most splendid churches. It was now past midnight, and a crowd was streaming into the establishment that had made its name as one of Stockholm's most daring clubs. Sexual intercourse on stage had been outlawed long ago, but here they went as far as they could go within the limits of the law. Yet no one talked about what went on inside the private sex booths in between police raids.

He came walking from the metro station, having kept the person in front of him in his sights for the past hour. The man he was following had been joined by another man in a pub in the centre of town, and now they were heading for the discreet door with the club's name etched on it in small gold letters. From what he understood, the place also had a reputation as a hangout for criminals of the more sophisticated ilk. Yet that was probably not the main reason for the man's interest. He was not a big-time crook or someone with power, money and status. Maybe he was on his way up in the hierarchy. The man who had joined him seemed to indicate as much. He was a real gangster type, with his big nose and slicked-back hair. He wore an expensive suit and a gold watch. The two men were carrying on an intense conversation, though he couldn't hear a word they said. Judging by the way they were waving their arms about, it was a topic of great interest to both of them. Neither seemed to notice his presence.

When they went inside the club, he followed. He paid the entrance fee of three hundred kronor and then slipped inside, where the walls were covered with velvet. He was immediately approached by a bare-breasted blonde with pouting lips. She was carrying a tray of glasses filled with champagne. The bubbly was included in the fee. He took a glass from the tray and made his way further into the club. He was astonished to see how many people there were, and it took a few minutes for him to find a vacant table, which was a good distance from the stage. There he saw half-naked women wriggling around the shiny silver poles shaped like erect penises with flashing lights. How sodding symbolic, he thought. That was the focus, of course, the centre of the universe. Power plays, prostitution and warfare were all based on that tender organ. So much misery in the world was caused by the male sexual performance. God, it made him sick; it gave him a deep sense of contempt for his own gender.

He sipped his champagne and looked around for the man. The women on stage did nothing for him. If he tried to feel anything at all, it was sympathy mixed with disgust. It took a while before he sighted his target and he worried that the man might have got away again. But then the man appeared from a side room some distance away, still in the company of the man with the big nose. They went over to the bar and were instantly served drinks. They seemed to be regular customers.

He was suddenly seized with a great urge to approach the man, to look him in the eye and say something. He gulped down the last of the champagne, got up and went over to the bar. The music was getting more seductive, and on stage the last remnants of clothing disappeared as the audience whistled and applauded. But he hardly even noticed. His eyes were fixed on the man leaning against the bar, having a serious conversation with his companion.

He had an urge to stuff the glass down his throat. At that moment he happened to jostle a customer in a suit, who gave him such an apprehensive look that he came to his senses. Was his anger that apparent? He needed to calm down. He took a deep breath. He had to do something, but he avoided looking at the bastard because, if he did, he knew he wouldn't be able to hold back from launching himself at the man. Right here and now. And to hell with the consequences.

Mustering all his self-control, he walked over to the other end of the bar and ordered a large glass of beer. Then he took a swig before he headed over to those two idiots, pretending to stumble along the way so that he ended up pouring his whole beer over the man he hated. At the same time, he stomped on the man's foot as hard as he could. In the dark and crowded room, no one noticed what had happened until they heard a howl pierce the thudding of the music.

Before anyone could stop him, he raced across the club and out through the door, and walked quickly up the street. When he had rounded the corner and made sure that no one was following him, he took out a cigarette and lit it with trembling fingers. He realized he wasn't going to be able to control himself any longer. When they next met, it would be time.

The hotel stood in an out-of-the-way cobblestoned lane in Gamla Stan, the old town district in the heart of Stockholm. Jacobsson looked up at the sculptures flanking the front entrance and the anchors embedded in the façade. This was where she always stayed when she was in the city. Hanna had offered to let her use one of the guestrooms in her huge flat in Söder, but Karin preferred the hotel. She didn't want to move too fast. Her relationship with her daughter was still so fragile. She wasn't sure whether Hanna, in her heart, had forgiven her mother for giving her up for adoption at birth. Was it even possible to forgive such a betrayal? And Karin had no desire to talk about Hanna's father. He was a riding master and had raped her when she was only fifteen. He was never reported to the police, and he was able to continue living a peaceful life with his wife and children, giving riding lessons to young girls. Karin didn't know much about him, except that he was a stern man with a military bearing who kept his pupils at arm's length. A man with a formal demeanour. Except on that one occasion.

She hated it when these thoughts appeared in her mind.

Sometimes they could drag her down into the deepest abyss. Into black holes. Maybe that was why she had lived alone for most of her life. She didn't dare enter into any intimate relationships, because sooner or later she would feel vulnerable, forced to expose her true self and begin to care about the other person too much. Better to avoid such situations, she'd always thought. Not subject herself to that sort of danger. She could go on living her simple, uncomplicated life without any emotional upsets. And besides, her job presented enough challenges. She had good colleagues – especially Anders Knutas. She was very fond of him. They worked well together. He was her boss, and they each had their role, which created a sense of order that she found reassuring. She refused to allow any other feelings. And supervising the practice sessions with the women's football league kept her busy several evenings a week. Her parents still lived in Tingstäde, about thirty kilometres north, but she rarely visited them. They'd never been close, and their actions after the rape and during the subsequent course of events had not improved Karin's relationship with them. There weren't many people she socialized with, nor did she feel any need for a big circle of friends. She liked being alone.

Then she'd met Janne. It was wonderful to find someone who cared about her, who said she was important to him. Maybe this change in her attitude was a result of getting older.

She pictured Janne's face as she unpacked her suitcase in the hotel. His sensitive eyes, his warm hands, his deep voice. He'd asked her to move in with him. Good Lord. Live together? Sharing everything, having to compromise on so many things, from what to cook for dinner to what TV show to watch. How would she be able to handle that after being so used to doing everything on her own?

And then there was Anders. Lina had moved away. Their marriage seemed on the verge of collapse. Karin stopped what she was doing and sank down on to the bed, her washbag on her lap. She stared with unseeing eyes at the floral pattern on the gold wallpaper. A whole new scenario had presented itself. New rules of the game. New possibilities.

She sat there staring into space for a long time.

Knutas was feeling restless after the morning meeting ended. Everyone was busy working on different fronts. Yet he couldn't bring himself to stay at his desk, even though that was what he should have done, since his job was to act as the coordinating hub between the various entities as the work progressed.

The reinforcements from the NCP were expected to arrive later, in the afternoon. A meeting with them and the rest of the investigative team was scheduled for three o'clock. Until then, he really didn't need to sit and stew in his office.

The photograph of Lina standing on the beach in Lickershamn in the summer sun mocked him. He put it away in the desk drawer and shut it with a bang. He didn't feel like thinking about his personal problems. He got up and left headquarters, saying that he'd be gone for several hours but could be reached on his mobile.

He got into his beloved Mercedes, a vintage model from 1965 that was still running. Lina had never understood his great love for the old vehicle. She couldn't see its charm, nor did she appreciate the worn red vinyl of the seats, the ivory-coloured steering wheel, the smell of oil, or the gear shift with its dull knob made from Bakelite, now cracked with age.

He chugged out of the car park and headed south. The heat was back and, since he had no air conditioning, he rolled down the window and popped his favourite CD – Paul Simon's *Graceland* – into the player. That was the only modern convenience he had in his car.

The wind blew through his hair, and his mood began to improve. He tried to concentrate on the case. In his mind, he went over the chain of events. First the robbery, then the collision with the little girl, which had ended so tragically. The fire in the woods, the murder in the outhouse, the abandoned money bag which someone had tried to force open, the motorcycle, the footprints, and the statements from witnesses describing a woman, and a man who appeared to be Latino. And the assault on Patrik Rosén – if that had any connection with the case. Jocke Eriksson's membership of the motorcycle club; the initials tattooed on his wrist; his contacts with the criminal world, both in Visby and Stockholm. What was the significance of that? Eriksson had been confined to a young offenders institution for several spells, and he'd also done time at Svartsjö prison, outside of Stockholm. Was that where he'd met his fellow robbers? The prison also had a section for women. Maybe he ought to ask Karin to pay a visit to the place, since she was in Stockholm.

Knutas suddenly pictured his colleague's face. Her eyes, the gap between her teeth. She'd been seeing that Janne Widén for a while now. A dreary man, totally lacking in personality. Knutas had met him a few times, but only briefly, just enough to say hello and exchange a few words.

He brushed aside these thoughts, which were making him feel cross. He would phone Karin later. Right now he just wanted to be alone. He turned up the volume and let the music envelop him. He was listening to the tune 'You Can Call Me Al'. The lyrics suited his situation perfectly – this mid-life crisis of his and the feeling of disintegration that had taken over.

All he could do was sing along.

1994

Terese had never seen so many motorcycles in one place. There had to be at least fifty parked close together on the gravel lot in front of Kuben, as the club building was called. Everywhere were groups of men drinking beer, all of them wearing leather waistcoats with various club emblems on the back. Some were younger – maybe around twenty-five, she guessed – but most were older men in their forties. Jocke had told her that the waistcoat was a status symbol and an indication of membership, signalling that the man was one of the brothers. All members wore the waistcoats for official occasions. His own was still devoid of any insignia, and he dreamed of the day when he'd be granted the honour of wearing the club's emblem on his back. Then he would be a full member who had been accepted into the brotherhood for all eternity. On equal standing with the others. Then he wouldn't need anything else in the world. His life would be perfect.

There were also some girls, most of them wearing skirts and tight tops, their long hair hanging loose down their backs. Hard rock was streaming through the open windows from the bar upstairs, and Terese felt her excitement rise when she saw that the place was packed. The minute they got out of the car Jocke had taken out his hip flask. The alcohol stung her throat. She lit a cigarette and looked about with curiosity. Someone waved, and she recognized the guy with the shaven head from the motorcycle ride a few days earlier. Jocke was greeting people right and left, and he introduced her again to the guy with the shaven head. Now she learned that his name was Sonny, and she realized he was some sort of leader of the club. Everyone was in high spirits, pounding each other on the back and laughing raucously.

'Come on. We need something else to drink,' said Degen, ushering them into the bar, which was full of people. The music was deafening.

Several beers and shots of tequila later, she was feeling incredibly drunk. She was hanging on to Degen, enjoying being soused, glad to be there and to be so close to him. Suddenly, the music stopped, and Sonny climbed on to an overturned beer crate. He waved a flag with the club's emblem, urging everybody to listen.

'OK, brothers. All my brothers,' he shouted, when the crowd was sufficiently quiet. 'And sisters,' he added with a grin, pinching the arse of a girl standing nearby and prompting a loud cheer from the men. 'We'll get back to partying soon, but there are a few announcements we need to make tonight.'

Now Terese noticed that Sonny was holding something in his hand, though she couldn't tell what it was.

'First of all, congratulations are in order to Big Johnny Boy on five years of membership. Congrats! Where are you, you fat devil?'

More bellows of laughter.

A man with a huge beer belly stepped forward. He was given a little pin to fasten to his waistcoat. It read 'Five-year member'. That unleashed a standing ovation which practically raised the roof. Then it was time for another announcement. Sonny looked out at the crowd. He seemed to be enjoying all the attention.

'There's a boy here who has been working hard for the club for several years. Actually, he's been hanging out here ever since he stopped clinging to his mother's apron strings, and I'll be damned if we're ever going to get rid of him. And even though he's only a little shit, he's a fucking great little shit. Tonight he's the youngest in club history ever to be promoted from Hangaround to Prospect, and the little shit's name is Jocke.'

More applause. Terese looked for Jocke, but at first she couldn't find him among all the beards and leather waistcoats in the dimly lit bar. Then she saw him emerge, and he looked so genuinely happy she almost cried. He stepped forward to receive his pin from Sonny. Triumphantly, he held it up for all to see, pumping his fist in the air.

Sonny handed Jocke a glass and they drank a toast, downing the drink in one and then tossing the glasses over their shoulders. Loud cheering erupted, and several big guys grabbed Jocke and threw him towards the ceiling again and again.

Terese and Degen pushed their way towards him when he was finally released.

'I'm so fucking happy!' shouted Jocke. 'So fucking happy!'

But they didn't have Jocke to themselves for long, because girls were soon flocking around him. At one stroke, his status had been raised significantly. Now his path was clear to full membership. And to the birds. Degen paid for more drinks, and they drank a toast to their friend. Terese looked deep into Degen's eyes. He looked cuter with every drink she had. He lifted her chin and gave her a long kiss. She felt dizzy and shouted into his ear that she needed to sit down. She could tell she'd had way too much to drink.

People were starting to dance, and Degen steered her through the sea of swaying, sweaty bodies. They went upstairs and down a long corridor to an empty room with a sofa and TV. They started kissing, and he ran his hands over her body. Before she knew it, she was lying on the sofa and Degen was pulling off her knickers. His tongue pressed harder, and he groped under her top and then undid her bra, gasping with pleasure when he felt the fullness of her breasts. He kissed and licked them as he pulled her top over her head.

She was lying naked on the sofa with Degen's head between her legs when the door opened. Two dark figures appeared in the doorway.

'And what have we here?' said one of them. 'Looks like some action going on. The chickie has lost her knickers. But what's the little dago doing?'

Degen froze and drew back. He looked up at the two men. They were much older, and he didn't recognize either of them. They weren't wearing waistcoats, so they weren't members of any of the invited clubs.

'We're not interrupting anything, are we?' said the other man. 'You wouldn't mind some company, would you?'

Terese was still lying on the sofa, making no attempt to move and hardly daring to breathe.

'OK. Sorry, buddy,' one of the men hissed in Degen's ear. 'But we'll take over now. Two real men can do a better job with this little pussy than a puny guy like you.'

He grabbed Degen by the hair and dragged him to the door. Degen yelled and kicked wildly, but it was like trying to use a fly swatter against the muscular bruiser. The other man gathered up Degen's clothes as he leered at Terese, who was lying on the sofa, frozen in terror.

'Nice boobs. Not bad at all. This little chickie has a lot to offer.'

'Yeah, you've got that right,' said the other. 'But you, you little shit, you're out of here. And not a word to anybody or we'll kill you. Got that into that monkey brain of yours?'

He kicked Degen hard in the stomach before opening the door and tossing him out in the hall along with his clothes. Then he slammed the door and locked it on the inside.

Degen grabbed the door handle and tugged, but the door wouldn't budge. What the hell should he do now? The music was blaring and he could hear roaring from the floor below. The party was in full swing. He had to find Jocke. Quickly, he put on his clothes and then raced downstairs. He found his friend and a girl wrapped in a tight embrace on the dance floor. He had to tear Jocke out of her arms.

'Two bastards are raping Terese upstairs!' he shouted into Jocke's ear. 'They've locked themselves in with her.'

'What the hell are you saying? Who are they?'

'No idea. I don't think they're from here.'

It took them only minutes to run around to the back of the building and climb a ladder up to the room where the two strangers had Terese. Jocke struck the window with an iron bar he'd grabbed on the way. The sound of breaking glass startled both men.

'What the hell?'

Before they had time to react, Jocke was in the room, with Degen right behind. Wielding the iron bar, punching and kicking, they brought both men to their knees. Then Jocke grabbed a piece of glass and slashed one of them in the face, making blood spray in all directions. The fight was over.

Degen helped Terese put on her clothes, and then all three climbed back down the ladder and ran for their car.

Jocke drove as fast as he dared through the dark. He was still drunk, but he was also in shock because of what had just happened. He could feel himself shaking all over. Degen sat in the back seat with his arms around Terese.

'We'll go to my house,' Jocke decided. 'My parents are away.'

Half an hour later he parked the car in front of the house in Tofta. It was in a remote location out in the country with no near neighbours.

'You need to give me something,' Terese pleaded. 'Something to calm me down.'

'Don't worry,' said Degen gently as he helped her out of the car. 'We've got pills and grass.'

'Give me all of it.'

'Sure, sweetheart. Anything you want.'

'But first I need to take a shower.'

'All right.'

When Terese came out of the bathroom with a towel wrapped around her body, Degen took her hand and led her to the sofa in the living room.

'OK if we smoke some stuff in here?' he asked Jocke.

'Sure. They've gone to the Canary Islands for a week. Plenty of time to air the place.'

After a couple of joints and several glasses of wine, they had all begun to relax.

'Who were those bastards?' asked Degen.

'No clue. They must be from the mainland.'

'Let's hope they're not from the Hells Angels or anything,' said Degen. 'If they are, you're in real trouble, Jocke. It's not a pretty sight, what you did to that bastard's face.'

'They're not. I'm sure of it,' said Jocke. 'I remember seeing them strutting about in the bar earlier. Shouting and showing off. They weren't wearing waistcoats, and I didn't recognize them, so they could be brand-new Hangarounds from some club here on Gotland, because only club members came over from the mainland, aside from the chicks. Or else they came with someone they knew. I'm not really sure. I've never seen them before. Those fucking bastards.'

Jocke rolled another joint. Terese lay on the sofa with her eyes half closed. It felt good to be high. She was in a fog, happy to be lying here, leaning against Degen's shoulder. He stroked her cheek.

'How are you doing, girl?'

'OK now. Fine,' she told him, slurring her words.

'Those arseholes. Did they hurt you?'

'They didn't have time to do anything. You're my heroes,' she murmured. 'We'll stick together for ever, the three of us. Promise?'

'Hell, yes. We promise,' said Jocke.

'Of course. We'll always take care of you,' whispered Degen.

'Always,' said Terese, before closing her eyes and falling asleep.

As Knutas drove his car along the main street in Klintehamn, the dramatic events that had occurred in the town a week earlier seemed totally unreal. How could something like that have happened in this peaceful setting? Slowly, he drove past the library, the ICA, the banks and the pastry shop. He turned at the Konsum supermarket on the other side, passed the Kustgrill and the Pressbyrå news-stand.

He didn't bother to get out of the car to talk to anyone. He didn't have the energy for that right now. And besides, other police officers had been assigned to interview the townspeople. He continued driving back to Visby and then took the on-ramp towards Sanda. Just as the robbers had done. At the exit to Hejde, a witness had seen a black car driving at high speed after the getaway car. The question was whether that was mere coincidence. Was the car actually following the robbers? And was the driver yet another accessory to the crime? In spite of repeated appeals from the police for information regarding the black car, no other witness had turned up, nor had the driver come forward.

Knutas reached the glade in the woods where the robbers' car had been set ablaze. He turned off the engine and got out. The ground was scorched from the fire, and all the encroaching vegetation had been burned. The trunks of the nearby trees were blackened, their branches charred. The police tape was still there, drooping disconsolately between several bent poles. Not a sound from anywhere.

He walked around with his eyes on the ground, searching in vain for even the smallest trace the forensics team might have missed. He headed along the tractor path, which led into the woods, and continued up to the main road. Somewhere along here three motorcycles had been parked. He didn't know exactly where, so he searched the area at random. Three motorcycles. One had been found inside the abandoned house; the other two had vanished, as if swallowed up by the earth.

So far the police had turned up nothing in their investigation of the motorcycle clubs in Stockholm. Jocke Eriksson didn't seem to have had much to do with the clubs on the mainland, even though he did know some of the members, especially among the Road Warriors' affiliated clubs. And the members of his own club seemed to know very little about his personal life. In fact, they knew almost nothing except that Jocke had had a difficult childhood and was rarely in contact with his parents. They did suspect that he'd occasionally taken drugs. But as long as his drug use didn't affect them, they hadn't paid it much attention. It could be that the club members took a more lenient attitude towards Jocke because he'd hung out at the club since he was a kid and they all knew how much the place meant to him.

Knutas wiped the sweat from his forehead and sat down on a tree stump in the shade. He took his pipe out of his jacket pocket and lit it. With a sigh of pleasure, he took a long puff and let the smoke fill his lungs. The surrounding trees stood there as silent witnesses.

Suddenly, he heard a twig snap behind him. A teenage boy appeared, using a sturdy branch as a walking stick. His face was covered in freckles, and he wore big glasses with heavy black frames. His red hair stuck straight up, and he had on a bright yellow T-shirt and mint-green shorts, and plasters on both knees. He stopped and stared at Knutas suspiciously.

'Hi,' said the detective superintendent.

'Hi. Who are you?'

'I'm a police officer. My name is Anders Knutas.'

'What are you doing out here in the woods?'

'Just checking on things. What are you doing here?'

'Hiking. That's what I do every day.'

The boy scratched a mosquito bite on his arm.

'Don't you go to school?'

'I have a tutor who comes to my house.'

'Oh.'

Knutas didn't want to ask any more questions about that. There was something odd about this slight boy standing in front of him.

'Did you see the fire there was here recently?' he asked.

'Sure, I did. Both here and over in Dans. I usually hike for several hours a day.'

'Do you think maybe you saw something that might help the police?'

'I once saw three motorcycles near that house in Dans that later burned down.'

Knutas gave a start.

'Did you see who was riding them?'

'No. They wore leathers and helmets, so I couldn't see their faces.'

'Could you show me where?'

'It's too far to walk. For you, anyway.'

'We can take my car.'

Knutas nodded towards his Mercedes.

'I'm not allowed to ride in cars with strangers.'

Knutas smiled.

'I can understand that. Here's my police ID. We can also ring your parents to ask them permission. What's your name?'

'Svante.'

The boy turned the ID card this way and that.

'You're a detective superintendent? How cool. I like Inspector Beck. From the books by Sjöwall and Wahlöö, you know. Are you hunting for a murderer?'

'That's my job. That's why I'm here in the woods right now. Looking for leads.'

'I've seen a bad guy, too.'

'Where was that?'

'Near the house in Dans. A different time I was there. At first, I thought he was a city workman because he was wearing one of those vests that roadworkers wear. One of those bright yellow vests. But he didn't seem to be doing any work. He just kept walking around the house. I followed him and watched him peering in the windows and trying to open the door. That time there weren't any motorcycles around.'

Knutas listened with growing interest to what this peculiar boy was saying.

'When was this? Do you remember what day you saw him?'

'It was last Sunday, because I was out all day. When I have free time I can stay outdoors for hours. I bring a packed lunch with me.'

Knutas took out his mobile.

'I think we'd better not waste any more time. Let's ring your parents.'

Johan was slumped in front of his computer in the editorial office, searching the news wires and daily papers for anything new about the hunt for the robbers and Jocke Eriksson's killer. He was having a hard time concentrating. The weekend had been a nightmare. Emma was devastated, the kids couldn't stop crying, his parents-in-law were shocked and grief-stricken. And there he was in the middle of it all, having to take control of things, make sure the children were fed, and see to the younger kids, who had no idea what was going on.

Last night after Emma had fallen asleep he had lain in bed and stared into the darkness, unable to sleep. He couldn't believe how much he missed Stockholm, especially now that everything was in such turmoil here on Gotland. Of course, he felt terribly sorry for Emma, and it was awful that Olle had died, but sometimes he couldn't help feeling that too much of their life together revolved around Emma and her former marriage to Olle.

Pia came stomping into the office, rousing him from his daydream.

'Hey, I just talked to Sonny at the Road Warriors. He says he doesn't know a thing about the assault on Patrik Rosén. The motorcycles that people heard could have come from anywhere. There are lots of folks who ride bikes here on the island.'

'I suppose he's right,' said Johan distractedly. 'On the other hand, I don't think he'd tell us if he was involved in any way. Does anyone know whether Rosén had anything to do with the motorcycle clubs? Or with Jocke Eriksson, for that matter?'

'No, but there's no getting around the fact that they were born in the same year and come from neighbouring towns,' said Pia. 'It's only about ten kilometres between Tofta and Klintehamn. Maybe they went to the same primary school. Or secondary.'

'That should be easy to check.'

'By the way, Sonny is on his way over here,' said Pia, looking pleased. 'He said there's something he wants to tell us.'

Johan looked up from his computer with interest.

'Sonny? Really?'

'I've been pestering him about those two other friends of Jocke's. Maybe all my nagging paid off.'

'Good job, at any rate,' said Johan appreciatively. He couldn't help being impressed by his colleague's powers of persuasion.

An hour later Sonny Jonsson was sitting at their conference table with a cup of coffee in front of him. With his leather outfit, and multiple tattoos and piercings, he definitely looked out of place in the office setting. He sighed heavily and then began.

'I've talked to Maddis, and she thought this might be important. But I'm not sure. She wanted me to go to the cops, but I refused. I don't trust those bastards.'

'OK,' said Johan, giving Sonny his full attention. 'We're listening.'

'Jocke had a pal named Degen that he brought over to the club several times. And a girl, too. But I don't remember her name.'

Pia and Johan exchanged glances but didn't make a sound, not wanting to interrupt Sonny's story.

'The three of them were as thick as thieves, even though they didn't see each other regularly. And they'd been friends for a long time, ever since they were teenagers. I think they got really close after something that happened at the club.'

'What?'

'The chick came to one of our summer parties. It was a big bash and a lot of folks from the mainland came over. She got real drunk, and later that night two bastards tried to rape her in a room upstairs. Jocke and Degen managed to overpower them. Jocke sliced up the face of one of the guys with a piece of glass. I found out about all this much later. No one at the party noticed a thing.'

'Did the guy who got his face slashed report it to the police?' asked Johan with interest.

'No. Probably because then the guy might have been accused of attempted rape. But those yobbos came poking around the club several more times, trying to get hold of Jocke. As luck would have it, they always turned up whenever he wasn't around. And neither Degen nor that girl ever came back to the club.'

'How did you find out about this?' asked Pia.

'One evening we were sitting around drinking and Jocke told me what happened. The guy he cut was permanently disfigured. And I can't help wondering whether what happened back then has something to do with Jocke's murder.'

'You mean that guy whose face was cut wanted revenge, and so he killed Jocke?' said Johan, sounding dubious. 'And now the others are next in line?'

Sonny shrugged.

'Something like that.'

'When exactly did this happen?'

'A hell of a long time ago. Before Jocke became a full member, and that was when he turned twenty-one. So sometime before that. Maybe one or two years earlier, I guess.'

'So about fifteen years ago,' said Johan, doing a quick calculation in his head. 'Why would he strike now?'

'No idea. It does seem like a long shot,' Sonny admitted. 'But after that, Jocke changed. He got real tight with Degen and that chick, and he was sort of secretive about them. I got the feeling there was something more that he didn't want to tell me about those two, but I don't know what it was.'

Jacobsson had never been to a Thai boxing club before. She went down the steps that led to a basement entryway littered with shoes tossed in heaps. The small reception area was squeezed into a corner. A young guy wearing a knitted cap in garish colours greeted her. How can he wear that in this heat? she thought. She introduced herself and asked to see the boss. She had an appointment. Unfortunately, he wasn't there at the moment, but he was supposed to arrive soon. She could go inside and watch while she waited, although first she needed to remove her shoes. Obediently, she unlaced her trainers and took them off.

Inside the workout room a group of beginners was getting ready for a session. It was mostly guys in their twenties, but also a couple of girls who looked to be a few years older. They wore sleeveless tops and leggings, and they'd pulled their hair back into ponytails. The guys wore shorts and T-shirts. The basement room had a low ceiling and no windows. The floor was covered with hard green mats. The walls were lined with mirrors and posters showing a number of Thai boxers. Jacobsson surmised they must be stars of the sport, although she knew absolutely nothing about it. Dusty pipes were visible on the ceiling, and in several places hung various rings and sandbags that were used for training.

Hard-rock music blared from the speakers, but the twenty or so students who were warming up were completely focused on what they were doing. The instructor was a short, thin, muscular guy who wore his thick, curly hair in a topknot. He was scurrying around the room, keeping an eagle eye on everyone to make sure they were doing everything properly.

'Faster, faster!' he shouted to be heard over the music. 'Keep up the pace. This is not a playground. You can sleep at night. Move, move, move.'

Everyone was training hard, doing push-ups, sit-ups and shadow-boxing. Jacobsson sat down on a stool to watch, impressed with the level of energy in the room.

Then the actual session started, and the instructor kept up the same frenzied pace as he guided and motivated his students. He tried to get them to work even harder by making use of some rather strange metaphors, which to Jacobsson's ears sounded like a real stretch.

'Footwork, people, footwork! Babies crawl, we walk. Faster, faster! Shoulders down, turn, chin down, eyes up. Think water. Water flows.'

Sweat was pouring off everyone. Some of the participants moved mechanically, trying to imitate the instructor's movements as best they could. Others seemed naturally more aggressive and gave it their all, bloodthirsty looks in their eyes.

Jacobsson was so fascinated by it all that she almost forgot why she'd come. But then a man who appeared to be close to her own age approached, and she remembered why she was there.

'Hi. Sorry I'm late. I'm Niko,' he said, speaking loudly and leaning close to her ear so she would hear him over the music.

He motioned for her to follow him, and they went into the clubroom and sat down.

Niko wore black slacks and a wrestler's top. He had a dark complexion and bulging muscles. Jacobsson did her best not to stare.

'I'm looking for a man who works out here,' she began. 'He's in his thirties and probably Latino.'

'Lots of guys like that here. Don't you know his name?'

'No. But several times he's brought along a guy from Gotland. A guy with thick, curly blond hair.'

Jacobsson handed him a photograph of Jocke Eriksson.

Niko took a moment to study the picture but then shook his head.

'No idea. We have a lot of people coming and going here. Do you know how long he's been training? Is he a beginner or advanced?'

'I think he's been training for a while, at least, but that's just a guess on my part. I don't really know.'

'We have several groups for advanced boxers, and three different instructors, so maybe one of them would know the person you're talking about.' He glanced at his watch. 'Joa will be done with the beginners soon, so you can talk to him yourself. Amanda has the group after his, so she'll be busy for the next hour. Are you in a hurry?'

'I can wait.'

When Joa was finished with the session, the participants all seemed completely wrung out and there was a strong smell of sweat in the room. If the air smelled this bad after the first class, Jacobsson wondered what it would be like for the poor students in the last class. Clearly, there was no air-conditioning.

Joa was a young man with a serious expression. His whole appearance seemed somehow unreal, with his pale complexion, curly hair and slender and fine-limbed body under the sinewy muscles. Even though he'd just performed the role of a hard-nosed instructor, there was something delicate, almost angelic, about him. As he stood facing her, Jacobsson realized that she was experiencing something that had never happened to her before. For the first time in her life, she was meeting a man who was not taller than she was, and who probably weighed about the same – five foot two and 110 pounds. An inappropriate thought flitted through her mind. I wonder what it would be like to have sex with a man the same size as me, she thought. But the idea vanished as quickly as it had appeared.

They shook hands, and she explained what she wanted to know. Then they sat down on stools in the workout room. The next group of students was getting ready. Several people were sitting or hanging about, talking to each other and watching those who were working out. An adjoining alcove was furnished with a sofa, several chairs, a table and a vending machine.

'Do a lot of people who aren't students come here?' Jacobsson asked.

'No. Everyone is active in the club. But there's a bunch that likes to come here even when they're not training. The students get to be friends after a while.'

'How long have you worked here?'

'Since I was seventeen, and I'm twenty-three now. I was the Swedish champion in 2008, and the Nordic champion in 2009 in my weight division. Pretty soon I'll be leaving for Thailand to take part in the world championships.'

'Wow,' said Jacobsson. 'That's impressive.'

'Thanks.'

He gave her a fleeting smile. He's so cute, she thought. Like a doll. She couldn't get rid of the unreal feeling.

'I'm looking for someone who works out here and who might be Spanish or Latin American. He was seen here at the club with a friend whose name is Joakim Eriksson, nicknamed Jocke. Last week Jocke was murdered on Gotland. You may have seen photos of him in the newspapers. This is what he looks like.'

She held up the photograph of Jocke.

'Yeah. I recognize him,' said Joa quietly.

Jacobsson's heart skipped a beat.

'Are you sure?'

'He's been here several times. And I talked to him. So he's the one who was murdered? I didn't realize that. I remember him because he was the type of person who talked to everybody. And he was so obviously from Gotland. Plus, he has the same name as me. My real name is Joakim.'

Jacobsson could hardly sit still. Forcing herself to stay calm, she then asked, 'What about the guy who brought him here? The guy who works out?'

'He's called Degen. I don't know what his real name is. Wait a minute, and I'll check.'

Joa got up abruptly and headed for the reception area. Jacobsson followed. He switched on the computer.

'We keep on file the name and address and phone number of everyone who has a membership card, so it shouldn't be hard to find him.'

Suddenly, he looked up with alarm, as if a terrible thought had just occurred to him.

'Degen's not the one who did it, is he?'

'We don't have any suspects at the moment, but obviously we'd like to ask him some questions.'

Joa seemed satisfied with her explanation. Apparently, he hadn't kept up with the news stories that mentioned possible links between the murder and the robbery of the security van. Or maybe he simply hadn't thought that far.

Jacobsson was struck by an idea. The initials on Jocke's wrist were J. T. D. Could the D stand for Degen?

'Do you happen to know whether this Degen has a tattoo?' she asked as Joa was searching the computer files.

He paused.

'A tattoo? I don't really know. But if he did, what sort of tattoo would it be?'

'Not very big.' Jacobsson held up her thumb and index finger to indicate the size. 'And just three initials: "J", "T" and "D".' She stretched out her arm and pushed back the sleeve of her shirt. 'Right here. On the inside of his wrist.'

'No. I've never noticed anything like that. But we always wear gloves when we're working out, so it'd be hard to see. And I'm not his trainer. You should ask Amanda when she's finished her session. She's Degen's trainer.'

Joa returned his attention to the computer and went back to searching the files. It took a while. Then

222

he uttered an exclamation and stopped, staring at the screen in bewilderment.

'What's the problem?' asked Jacobsson.

'I can't find him. Just a minute.'

He turned around and reached for an old-fashioned ledger box containing dusty black binders and placed it on the counter with a thud.

'We keep this as a back-up,' he said with a wry expression. 'Just in case the computer gets fried.'

Jacobsson could hardly contain her impatience.

Joa slowly and meticulously went through the folders, leafing through the pages with ever-growing concern.

'I don't get it. I've looked at the names of everyone who started on the beginner course last spring, just like he did. But he's not here. This is really strange. He's gone.'

Joa turned around and shouted to the young guy with the gaudy cap. It seemed that everyone could see how annoyed Jacobsson was getting, because even Niko turned up and was apprised of the situation. After all three had spent another fifteen minutes searching the pages, Jacobsson began to lose patience.

'How can a member of your club simply disappear? How could he be erased from all the files?'

'I really can't explain what's happened. Obviously, we won't be able to clear up this mystery right now,' said Niko apologetically. 'But give us time to work it out. I'll talk to the other employees who have access to the files, and then I'll phone you as soon as we find this Degen. Or anyone who knows more about him. Amanda Sierra is the instructor for his group, but she's just gone home sick.'

Jacobsson stared at the man standing in front of her. She was practically bursting with impatience. To be so close, and yet.

'See that you do find him. And if he happens to turn up here, ring the police at once.'

She handed him her card and then quickly climbed the stairs. If she stayed even a second longer, she would explode.

Svante Hedström looked about with curiosity as he entered one of the interview rooms. He was accompanied by his mother. She had been at home when Knutas phoned, and she had agreed to come with her son to police headquarters. She had explained that Svante suffered from a mild form of Asperger's syndrome and, for the time being, he was being taught at home. He'd had a difficult time fitting in with his classmates at school.

Knutas did his best to create a nice, relaxed mood in the cramped room. He chatted a bit and offered coffee for Mrs Hedström and a soda for Svante. It was always important to make a witness feel comfortable, because otherwise it could be difficult for the person to remember details. But in this case that didn't seem to be a problem. Svante appeared to be elated about his role as witness and completely unaffected by the sterile and inhospitable setting. He kept clasping and unclasping his hands as he gazed about, wide-eyed. Thomas Wittberg sat in as an observer, even though this wasn't an official interview but more of a conversation in an effort to glean more information about the suspicious man Svante had seen outside the ramshackle house. A police sketch artist was also present to try to make a drawing of the man from the details the boy provided.

Knutas switched on the tape recorder, made the usual introductory remarks and then leaned back in his chair.

'So you saw a man near the house in Hejde on Sunday, 22 August. What time was that?'

'It was in the afternoon, maybe around three or four.'

'What was he doing?'

'He walked around, looking at the house, and then he tried the door several times. He peered in through the broken windows, but they're too small to climb through, or he probably would have tried that. It looked like he wanted to, but he would never have fitted. He was too big and heavy.'

'What did he look like?'

'He was pretty tall. Taller than Pappa, I think. And he's six feet, isn't he?' He looked at his mother, and she nodded. 'And he was bigger than Pappa, too. Heavier. Not fat, just big.'

'How old do you think he was, if you compare him to your father?'

'Pappa is forty-three, but I think this man was younger.'

'What colour hair did he have?'

'I didn't see it, because he was wearing a baseball cap, so his hair was hidden underneath.'

'What was he wearing?'

'Jeans, of course. And a vest.' Again the boy turned to look at his mother. 'You know, the kind of vest that city workmen wear? Greenish yellow, really bright.' Then he looked at Knutas. 'It said "Gotland Municipality" on the back.'

'Did you notice anything else about him? Did you get a look at his face?'

226

'It was hard because of the baseball cap. I could only see the lower part. But I know he didn't have a beard.'

Knutas took out of his jacket pocket a photograph of Patrik Rosén and placed it on the table in front of the boy.

'Is this the man you saw at the house?'

The boy studied the picture for several minutes.

'I don't really know. It could be him, but I'm not sure.'

'How long did he stay on the property?'

'I don't know. Maybe fifteen minutes.'

'Then what did he do?'

'He went back out to the main road and walked along it for a bit. Then he turned on to another smaller gravel road heading into the woods. He went over to a car that was parked in a clearing. Then he got in and drove off.'

'And you followed him all that way? That was brave of you.'

'I guess. Maybe.' Svante smiled shyly.

'Did you see what colour the car was, or even what kind it might have been?'

'It was a yellow Toyota Corolla. The licence number was OLW437.'

'Are you sure?' exclaimed Knutas, surprised.

'Yes. I remember "OLW" because it's just like the brand of cheese snacks we usually buy. And Pappa is forty-three, and we live at Ängsvägen 7.'

Knutas took a deep breath.

1994

'Where have you been? Answer me!'

Susanne's eyes were blazing with anger as she confronted Terese. It was three in the morning, and Terese was very drunk. All she wanted was to fall into bed, but the bitch was blocking her way.

Palle was at work, and the kids were asleep.

A month had passed since the attempted rape at the motorcycle club, and Terese had been trying ever since to shake off the memory of what happened. She'd been out partying a lot. She was still only sixteen years old, but did they really think she was going to stay at home and sit in front of the TV with them every single night?

'Leave me alone,' said Terese, slurring her words. 'None of your damn business.'

She tried to slip past, but Susanne refused to budge.

'This has got to stop. Do you hear me? I can't do this any more. You don't pay any attention to what I say, you drink and smoke, and it wouldn't surprise me if you've been taking drugs, too.'

'Leave me alone,' Terese repeated. 'I want to go to bed. I'm so fucking tired. I need to get some sleep.'

'Me, me, me,' said Susanne. 'All you think about is yourself. You don't care about anyone else. I've done everything in my power to make sure you're happy here, but what do I get in return? Nothing. You never help out here at home with any of the cleaning or cooking. You don't even bother to make your own bed. You never offer to babysit, even though you know full well that Palle and I would love to get out of the house once in a while. But we're always so careful not to ask for your help. God forbid that you should feel as if you owed us anything, or that you felt any sort of pressure. That would be too much for you, since you're such a delicate little creature. But going out and partying all night? Oh, sure, that's just fine. You've got plenty of energy for that!'

Susanne's face was white with anger. Terese had never seen her so furious. She looked sort of funny the way she was standing there, that perfect woman, with her hair sticking out all over and wearing that ridiculous nightgown with the angel pattern. Terese couldn't help laughing.

'How dare you laugh at me when I'm wide awake in the middle of the night, worried out of my mind! You have no feelings at all. I don't think you could even spell the word "empathy". And you're such a liar. Like when you said you were going to spend the night at Linda's and instead you went to a party at the motorcycle club. With all those gangsters! And you're a thief, too. I haven't wanted to say anything, because God knows we're supposed to be so bloody considerate of your feelings. But Palle and I both know that you've been stealing money from us. Don't you think I notice when hundred-kronor bills disappear from my wallet, or that you've been taking money out of the tin in the kitchen? Or that Palle's jar of coins suddenly contains only one-krona and fifty-öra coins? You swiped all the five- and ten-kronor pieces. I can't believe you had the nerve to do something like that. Especially after we've been so generous. We give you a much bigger allowance than social services said we should. But are you grateful? No, not at all. You just keep taking more and more.'

Crestfallen, Terese stood in the living room and stared at Susanne without saying a word. So now it was finally coming out. Susanne was saying what she really felt. As if Terese hadn't known all along. They didn't want her here. And now it was out in the open.

Rage surged inside her, blinding her. The bitch wouldn't stop talking. She would never stop. Terese had to make her shut up. She raised her hand and punched Susanne right in the mouth. She must have used more force than she intended, because the woman toppled backwards on to the floor.

'What the hell do you think you're doing? Are you out of your mind? Get out! Get out of my house!'

She got up and launched herself at Terese, pounding the girl with her fists. Terese tore herself away and ran to her room, locking the door behind her. With shaking fingers, she got out her mobile and tapped in Jocke's number.

'The bitch has gone crazy. Can you come and get me?'

'Sure. I'll be right there.'

Then she fled the house, slamming the door so hard that all the windows rattled.

On Monday afternoon reinforcements finally arrived from the NCP. Martin Kihlgård made his usual boisterous entrance at the criminal division, with two other colleagues in tow. By this time the big, good-natured detective was a familiar figure at police headquarters in Visby. Over the past few years his cheerful and jovial demeanour had made him popular with everyone to whom he'd offered assistance on various homicide cases on Gotland. The fact that he was also a skilled detective merely added to his appeal.

Knutas had made sure fresh cinnamon rolls were served with the coffee, even though he would personally abstain. But he knew it wouldn't have taken more than fifteen minutes before Kihlgård started to grumble if there were no pastries on the table.

The investigative team greeted the new arrivals, and then the meeting began. A good deal of information had been collected, and they needed to pick up several loose threads.

Knutas started by reporting on what Svante Hedström had told him during the interview. The car was now their hottest lead.

'It turns out the car was rented from Avis at the airport on the twentieth of August, which means five days

231

before Jocke Eriksson was murdered. At nine thirty in the morning, under the name of Alvar Björkman. But that name doesn't appear on any airline passenger list, and there's only one Alvar Björkman living on Gotland. A ninety-five-year-old man who lives on Fårö. Of course, we plan to check him out, along with the three other Alvar Björkmans who live elsewhere in Sweden, but it seems most likely that the car was rented under a false name.'

'Has anyone talked to the employee who dealt with this Björkman?' asked Kihlgård as he reached for a cinnamon roll.

Knutas's stomach growled. They smelled so good, like they'd come right out of the oven.

'No. The car-rental agency is looking into the matter, and they'll contact me as soon as they get hold of the person in question.'

'Is there any CCTV from when he rented the car?' asked Prosecutor Smittenberg.

'There are cameras set up in various places in the airport, but not at that specific location. So I'm afraid there's no hope of that.'

'What about the car?' asked Wittberg. 'Where is it now?'

'It's been impounded and will be transported here this afternoon so that forensics can go over it.'

'When was it returned?'

'On Thursday morning the agency employees found the car keys in the box at the airport. The keys weren't there on Wednesday when they emptied the box at around 6 p.m., so he must have turned in the car sometime between six on Wednesday evening and eight o'clock on Thursday morning.'

'In that case, there might be witnesses who saw him out at the airport, right?' said Wittberg.

'It's possible. That's one of the things we need to check. Could you do that?'

'Of course. Might give me a chance to talk to a few cute check-in girls at the same time,' he said with a grin.

Everyone chose to ignore his comment. Ever since Wittberg's latest summer romance had ended, he'd been behaving even worse than usual. His colleagues all wondered when the youngest member of their team would finally settle down. Wittberg was now thirty-five, but when it came to women his development seemed to have stalled somewhere around the age of twenty.

'Was the car rented to anyone else after this Alvar Björkman returned it?' asked Kihlgård as he ate another cinnamon roll. Crumbs had spilled on to his shirt.

'No. It was at the airport all weekend, and they hadn't even got around to cleaning it. So we're in luck. In the best-case scenario, we'll find some traces that were left behind,' said Knutas.

'Speaking of cleaning, has anyone checked with any of the car-wash places in town?' asked Sohlman.

'Do you think the perp could have been that daring?' Wittberg wondered out loud. 'Do you think he actually went to a petrol station to have the vehicle cleaned?'

'I don't know, but maybe there wasn't much to see on the outside of the car. Maybe he didn't think it was such a risky thing to do.'

Sohlman threw up his hands. He seemed to be in a bad mood. Possibly because none of the crime scenes had produced anything of interest in terms of evidence.

'When will Karin be back from Stockholm?' asked Kihlgård.

'That depends on what happens. She might be back as early as tomorrow,' said Knutas.

'For our part, we've investigated any connections that Jocke Eriksson might have had in Stockholm,' Kihlgård went on. 'He was the flatmate of a known drug dealer in Farsta. Only a small-time crook, but very active. At least, he used to be. His name is Milovan Djokovic. He's been in trouble with the law for years, and he's spent a large part of his life in prison.'

'Djokovic?' said Wittberg. 'Like the tennis player?'

'What?' Kihlgård gave him a puzzled look.

'Forget it,' said Wittberg. 'Go on.'

'OK, well . . .' Kihlgård cleared his throat. He seemed to have momentarily lost his train of thought. 'Of course, we've talked to this Djokovic, and he claims not to know anything about Jocke's private life, except that he was a junkie and had been mixed up in some minor crimes and drug deals. Djokovic maintains that he personally got out of that racket a long time ago. We haven't discovered any solid leads, but we're still working on it. What does Eriksson's family have to say?'

'We need to talk to his parents again,' Knutas admitted. 'We've only spoken to them once, and they were both rather vague. Couldn't really tell us anything about their son's life other than things we already knew. For example, they said he didn't have a girlfriend, or at least not as far as they knew, and he spent most of his time in Stockholm. His last relationship ended six months ago, and we haven't yet been able to contact the girl.'

'What's her name?' asked Kihlgård.

'Kitty Adamsson.'

'We'll find her,' said Kihlgård, with his mouth full. He nodded to his two colleagues from Stockholm, who sat quietly, letting their boss do the talking, since he had been here before.

'Finally, we have the assault on Patrik Rosén,' said Knutas. 'We were able to interview him today, but he claims not to remember anything about the attack, except that four men came in and ordered beer. After that, he recalls only being hit over the head.'

'Was he able to describe the men?' asked Kihlgård.

'Not really. All he could tell us was that they were middle-aged and wearing dark clothing. But we did get hold of the last customer to pay his bill at the restaurant on Friday night. A young man who ate at the restaurant with his girlfriend. He said that four tough-looking bikers came in late that night. They sat down and ordered beers. He and his girlfriend felt so threatened by them that they paid their bill and left.'

'That's interesting,' said Kihlgård, wiping his mouth with a paper napkin. 'What does Rosén say about that?'

Knutas gave Kihlgård an annoyed look. Didn't the man ever stop eating?

'He claims not to remember any of that. It looks like we're not going to get much further with that particular case right now. But we've got plenty of other things to keep us busy at the moment.'

'Then we'd better get started,' said Kihlgård, getting up. He swiped one more cinnamon roll before leaving the room.

By Knutas's calculation, it was his fourth.

Karin and Hanna had agreed to meet outside Ramblas, a Spanish tapas restaurant near Hornstull in the Södermalm district of Stockholm. Karin was favourably impressed the minute she stepped inside. The place had a casual and cosy atmosphere. Dark wooden panelling on the walls, simple rustic tables with plain tableware. Yellow and red napkins sticking out of the glasses. The decor included fishing nets, guitars, wine racks and red lanterns, as well as candles in all the windows. Spanish music streamed from the speakers at a volume that allowed for conversation. The place was crowded, even though it was an ordinary Monday evening.

That was one thing about Stockholm that Karin sometimes missed. There were always people everywhere, lots of new people. The city was always jumping, at any hour of the day or night and all year long, not like Visby, which seemed half asleep most of the time, at least when it came to nightlife. After the shops closed at 6 p.m. the streets were practically deserted during the ten months outside the tourist season.

Hanna had made a reservation, and they were shown to a table next to the window facing the street. The waitress wore black, and her hair was pinned up, revealing a tattoo on the back of her neck. They ordered Spanish wine and water. Karin studied her daughter as Hanna leafed through the menu. She looked so sweet, with her classical features. She was twenty-nine but looked ten years younger. Her slender figure added to the impression. The same was true of Karin. They were amazingly alike, and not just in appearance. Both wore jeans, sleeveless T-shirts and trainers.

'What are you going to have?' asked Hanna. 'They have lots of good tapas here. We could order several different kinds. And there are plenty of things I can eat, too.'

Hanna didn't eat meat, fish, shellfish or eggs.

They agreed on a number of dishes, and Hanna ordered in Spanish, which she spoke fluently.

Karin listened appreciatively. There were some clear differences between them. Hanna was so educated. She spoke several languages, read voraciously and had gone to university, both in Stockholm and in Luleå, where she'd earned a degree in structural engineering. She had also travelled all over the world with her family. Karin would never have been able to offer her daughter such experiences.

'Here's to seeing each other again,' she said now, raising her glass. Sometimes she felt inferior to Hanna. They came from such different worlds.

'*Skål*. How'd it go at the Thai boxing club?'

'Good. It was very productive. Thanks for your help. It was an excellent tip-off.'

'So tell me about it,' Hanna went on. 'Did you find the guy?'

'All I can say is that things are moving along, but not as fast as I'd like,' replied Karin evasively. 'But I probably need to stay in Stockholm for another day. And keep looking for those robbers. They're probably just small fry. Maybe they robbed the security van to increase their status and climb up the ladder. That happens.'

'What do you mean? People commit robberies just to show they're capable of something like that?'

'Exactly. And never mind any collateral damage along the way.'

'That's disgusting,' said Hanna. 'Just think about that little girl who died.'

'Yes. That was really terrible. We're doing everything we can to catch them.'

The food arrived, and Hanna explained what was on each plate. Oven-roasted and salted potatoes with a spicy red sauce; marinated artichokes; potato omelette; chickpea-and-olive-oil spread; prawns in garlic sauce. Karin felt her mouth water at the sight of such delicacies. It was past eight in the evening, and she hadn't eaten anything since lunch.

'So tell me how you've been,' she asked.

'Not much going on right now. I've just been working. We're in the middle of a big project: blocks of flats in Värtahamnen. As you probably know, there's going to be a lot of construction in that area over the next few years. And Kim and I are thinking of moving in together. She's wanted to do that for a long time, but I've been wavering. Partly because she's so much younger than me – only twenty-one – but also because everything would be on my terms if she moves into my flat. And I'm afraid that would upset the balance in our relationship and make things even more unequal than they are already because of the age difference. But she keeps talking about it. The sweet girl still lives at home with her parents.'

'It's strange to hear that you and I are in the same situation, except in reverse,' said Karin. 'Janne wants me to move in with him.'

'And give up that lovely flat of yours?' exclaimed Hanna in dismay. She had fallen in love with Karin's simple but charming attic flat with its view of the sea and the rooftops of Visby. She and Kim had visited Karin earlier in the summer.

'No, I'd never do that. I would rent it out. Besides, it's a housing association flat.'

'But do you want to do that? Move in with him, I mean?'

'I don't know. I'm very fond of him, of course, and sometimes I get so tired of being alone. But I'm scared of having to make compromises and take someone else into consideration. I'm not sure I can handle that. I've lived alone all my life.'

Hanna took a sip of wine and gave Karin a searching look.

'But why? Why haven't you ever had any long-term relationships?'

Karin hesitated before answering.

'I have a hard time with intimacy. I was never very close to my parents, and then, after what happened . . . Well . . . I guess I ended up scared of men.'

'There's an alternative, you know.'

'Yes, but I've never been sexually attracted to women. That's just how it is – although plenty of people have assumed that I'm a lesbian. I'm a police officer, I live alone, I'm a coach for a women's football team and I don't wear particularly feminine clothes. I guess I fit all the old stereotypes.'

Karin fixed her gaze on a gigantic painting that dominated the opposite wall. It showed a restaurant scene in which a flamenco dancer in a red dress was proudly raising her arms above her head.

Hanna laughed.

'Looks like you passed that inclination on to me instead.'

'Have you ever been interested in guys?'

'I dated a few when I was a teenager. More or less to try it out, even though I didn't find them especially interesting. I've always thought women were much cuter and more attractive. Then I was at a party and a girl kissed me, and that was it. I haven't had a boyfriend since. Not as a love interest, I mean.'

'How old were you when that happened?'

'Seventeen.'

'How did your parents react?'

'They're OK with it. A little shocked at first, and in their hearts I think they're sad they won't have any grandchildren by me. At least not in the usual way. But they've never said anything like that. And they're very fond of Kim.'

'That's good.'

Karin looked at her daughter across the table. They'd never talked about such personal matters before. By now they'd finished eating, and the wine bottle was empty. Hanna ordered each of them a cognac to have with their coffee. She looked at Karin warmly as she raised her glass.

'Skål, Mamma.'

A fiery jolt shot through Karin. Hanna had never called her Mamma before. Tears started streaming down her face, and there was nothing she could do to stop them.

'Mamma, what is it?' said Hanna, leaning forward to stroke Karin's cheek. 'I love you, and I like the fact that you're tough. I admire you. I'm so glad that you decided to find me. I'm sorry I was so unfriendly at first. I didn't know how to handle things. So many different emotions came up. Of course, I've always wondered who you were, and I wanted to make contact, but I was so afraid of what I might find out. Maybe you wouldn't have wanted anything to do with me. And that would have been unbearable.'

Now Karin was crying uncontrollably. She couldn't restrain herself. Everything she'd kept bottled up inside all these years spilled out, everything she'd tried to keep under control. She just sat there, sobbing into the napkin. Then she felt Hanna's arms around her.

'Can you ever forgive me for giving you away?' Karin asked, her face pressed against her daughter's throat.

'I forgave you a long time ago.'

For the first time since that brief moment in the maternity ward when Hanna was a newborn baby, Karin now held her child in her arms.

It had taken nearly thirty years.

The Solberg pool was empty except for a young girl who was practising her butterfly stroke in the lane reserved for fast swimmers. Knutas was swimming one length after another at a steady pace and in his usual section of the pool. Outside the big glass windows facing the street the sun had taken on a more autumnal shimmer. Almost two weeks had passed since the security van had been robbed and Jocke Eriksson murdered. In spite of receiving assistance from the NCP, the investigative team had not made any significant progress. Jacobsson had reached a dead end in Stockholm. She had not been able to track down the man known as Degen who worked out at the Thai boxing club. But the fact that his name was Degen was definitely of interest, since the letter 'D' was one of the initials tattooed on Eriksson's wrist. Knutas pictured the tattoo: 'J' stood for Jocke; 'D' most likely for Degen. So only the 'T' remained. If the third robber was a woman, then the 'T' had to be the initial of her first name.

What sort of relationship did those three individuals have? They seemed to have been so secretive and he couldn't work out why. Many of Jocke's motley group of acquaintances had mentioned that he had a couple of friends in Stockholm, a guy and a girl. But the only lead the police had managed to ferret out so far was the club where Degen trained. Yet there the search had stopped.

The interview with his trainer, Amanda, had yielded nothing. She claimed to have instructed Degen without ever having any personal conversations with him. She admitted that she might have forgotten to register him in the club files.

At any rate, Karin had now returned from Stockholm. Knutas was happy to have her back, even though lately he was finding it hard to behave normally in her presence. He was overly conscious of everything he said, how he moved and how he looked. Since Lina had left, he'd started working out several times a week. In the evening when he got home, he would lie on a mat on the living-room floor and watch the news on TV as he did sit-ups and arm exercises. The kids couldn't resist teasing him. To them he undoubtedly looked like a pathetically dumpy middle-aged man who was making desperate attempts to improve his appearance.

He began swimming faster without even thinking about it. In the water he was weightless and free and he could think more clearly.

In his mind he went over the investigative work of the past week. The car that had been rented under the name of Alvar Björkman still had traces of blood on the seats and the floor. Analysis showed that the blood belonged to Jocke Eriksson. The SCL, the Swedish Crime Laboratory in Linköping, had outdone itself and produced the report unbelievably fast. So there was no longer any doubt that the killer had rented that Toyota.

The police had contacted all the car-wash places, but without any results. None of the employees could remember seeing anyone bring in a Toyota Corolla to be washed during the relevant time period, and no one had noticed anything unusual. The young boy named Svante who had seen the perpetrator was unable to provide enough details to allow the police sketch artist to create a viable drawing.

As for Patrik Rosén, the father of the little girl who had been killed, he continued to maintain that he remembered nothing about the men who had assaulted him except that they'd worn leathers. He had no idea why they had attacked him. And the police had made no progress in the investigation of the incident.

Right now Knutas was feeling generally worn out. To top it all, his colleague Kurt Fogestam in Stockholm had phoned this week and reminded him of a case that was still weighing on his conscience: the Petrov investigation. According to a witness, Vera Petrov and her husband had now been sighted in Las Palmas on Gran Canaria. The information might prove to be accurate; at any rate, the local police would check it out. For now, they would just have to wait and see, said Fogestam. That was exactly what Knutas had been doing for four years. Waiting. And it was taking a toll on his nerves.

Having finished his thousand metres, he climbed out of the pool. In the locker room he went over and stood naked in front of the mirror. He twisted and turned, noting with disappointment that there was hardly any difference in his stomach even though, lately, he'd been so careful about what he ate. He leaned forward to study his face and hair. He was still nicely tanned from the summer sun. Of course, there were lines around his eyes, especially when he smiled or laughed, but they didn't really bother him. Worse were the grey streaks in his hair, even though they were still hardly visible. He tugged at a few strands. The skin under his chin had begun to sag a bit more, but what could he do about that? He just had to accept it. The last thing he needed was to get so desperate that he decided to have plastic surgery. Did men even do that sort of thing? He'd never thought about it before, although he did know that some men had Botox treatments. He'd seen it on TV.

Suddenly, it occurred to him that he was beginning to worry about looking older. He never had before. Karin's face appeared in his mind. Was this because of his growing interest in his colleague, who was twelve years younger than he was? Good Lord, he really needed to pull himself together. All of this, just because Lina was going to be gone for six months.

He was starting to get used to the fact that she wasn't at home. Petra and Nils were being unusually helpful. They had offered to cook, do the shopping and clean up more than they normally did. Maybe they felt sorry for him and wanted to make things easier. So one unexpected benefit of the situation was that it had brought him closer to his children. They had started having coffee together in the evening and talked in a whole different way than when Lina was home.

Karin. Several times lately he'd been surprised by how strongly he was attracted to her, especially when they were alone.

He had caught himself fantasizing about having sex with her. He didn't know what had come over him. He never used to think about other women that way. For so many years, Lina had been the only one for him. But there had always been something special about Karin.

And I'm not going to feel guilty, he thought defiantly. Lina had no one but herself to blame.

1994

When Terese awoke, she at first couldn't work out where she was. She looked up at the ceiling, peering bleary-eyed at a beetle. Slowly, it crawled across the ceiling and down the opposite wall. She was hot and kicked off the covers, then turned on to her side and found herself looking at Degen's handsome face. His features were relaxed as he slept, his eyebrows thick and dark, his lips soft, with a clearly defined Cupid's bow. His nose was straight and lovely. He lay on his side in a foetal position, his arms hugging his chest. He looked so fragile, and she was overwhelmed with a deep sense of tenderness.

He had been so kind to her ever since the attempted rape, looking out for her comfort and well-being, making sure that she was OK. He had even asked if she wanted to report the incident to the police.

Not on her life. She would never subject herself to that sort of thing. Or Degen either. He was the one, after all, who had taken her upstairs to that room and undressed her. The police might blame him for what had happened. And if she filed a report, then Jocke would be arrested for slashing the guy's face with a piece of glass.

247

She, Jocke and Degen had grown so close over the past few weeks. It felt as if they'd known each other all their lives; the two young men were now her best friends. They had become the family she'd never had. And they had all had their first initials tattooed on to their wrists as proof that they would always stick together. As soon as she and Degen got out of their respective foster homes, they were planning to move to Stockholm to live with Jocke. And then all the grown-ups could go to hell.

She sighed and again glanced at the beetle. It had reached the window and was now moving around the frame, on its way back up to the ceiling.

She wondered if she was going to continue living with the Stenfors family. Susanne refused to speak to her. She was also furious about the tattoo, which Terese had got without asking permission. Tomorrow she and Susanne and Palle were all supposed to turn up for an emergency meeting at the social-services office.

Her stomach churned when she thought about how that might go. Maybe she would be moved to another family. That wasn't really what she wanted. She had Jocke and Degen here, she liked the twins, and she had no complaints about Palle. Susanne was the only real problem. What did she expect? That Terese would be transformed into an angel just because she was allowed to stay with her amazing family?

But the bitch also happened to be right. She had in fact stolen money and alcohol, even though Susanne and Palle had been more than generous. She needed to clean up her act. She felt guilty when she thought about Kristoffer's look of disappointment when she once again told him that she didn't want to play any computer games, ping-pong or Parcheesi. She needed to try a little harder. If they let her, she wanted to stay here on Gotland until she turned eighteen, and then she would move in with Jocke and Degen.

Terese was convinced that everything would be fine after they'd been to the social-services office the next day, but it didn't work out as she'd expected. Palle and Susanne had already made up their minds. It didn't matter what she said.

'Well, it looks like we're not going to get any further,' Viveka finally concluded, casting a worried glance at Terese, who sat across the table from her. 'If this is how Palle and Susanne feel, there's not much I can do.'

Humiliation burned on Terese's cheeks. She had tried to explain to them that she was sorry for her outburst and for her behaviour in general, that she intended to do better. She promised not to steal from them again. But nothing she said had helped. They were intractable. Susanne looked at her entreatingly as she tried to explain her viewpoint.

'Terese, I'm very fond of you, I really am, but this isn't going to work any more. I've been tiptoeing about for months now, doing my best to make sure you feel comfortable and welcome in our home. But when I see how you've started taking over the family more and more, and how everyone is always trying to please you, I just don't want to continue like this any longer. I also have a responsibility as a parent; I need to think of my own children and their well-being. You are not a good influence on them. You swear and smoke and slam doors and get angry about the smallest things, and I can see how the boys are retreating. They disappear into their rooms as soon as dinner is over. There's no family time together any more. I've noticed how seldom I hear them laugh, and it's clear they're having a hard time relaxing. They need to feel safe and secure in their own home. I also have a strong suspicion that you've been taking drugs. Palle thinks so, too, by the way.'

Terese stared blankly at the ugly green curtains hanging at the window, tears welling up in her eyes.

'It's really a shame, but there's nothing to be done about it,' Palle added. 'I'm sure you understand that you're largely responsible for the way things have turned out. You also stole money from the restaurant.'

'That's a fucking lie!' shouted Terese, and now she couldn't hold back any longer. Tears poured down her face. 'You can both go to hell! I hate you!'

She leapt to her feet, tore open the door and fled from the building. Outside on the street the sun was shining mercilessly in a clear blue sky. She fumbled to get out a cigarette as she ran as far away from the social-services office as she could go. They would never catch her. From now on, she would take care of herself.

Johan and Pia were in the car, on their way to Tofta church and Jocke Eriksson's funeral. In spite of all the digging they'd done over the past week, they hadn't managed to find out anything more about who the friends of the murdered man might be. So far, all they knew was what Sonny had told them.

Johan had asked the Stockholm editorial team for help in checking into the criminal elements in the city, as well as the motorcycle clubs, but that hadn't produced anything useful. Maybe their search hadn't been thorough enough, thought Johan, since he was very familiar with the limited resources available to the local-news division at television headquarters. Time was never wasted on something that wouldn't produce guaranteed results, meaning information that could contribute to the day's broadcast. There was simply no time for anything else.

The research they'd done on Gotland had also proved fruitless. They'd looked into the circles Jocke had moved in, but not a single person seemed to know either Degen or the girl. Jocke must have kept his friendships with them secret. The question was: why?

But now they were on the way to his funeral. Pia was singing along with the pop tunes playing on the Mix Megapol radio programme. At regular intervals the smarmy voice of the DJ would announce that the station was mixing current hits with golden oldies. Pia stopped singing when Tofta church came into view. It was situated in the middle of a field in which purplish-red poppies bloomed.

'Wow, that's beautiful,' she said.

The church was built in the typical Gotland style, with a whitewashed façade and a dark tower. It was visible from the coast road that ran south from Visby and was surrounded by meadows filled with flocks of grazing black sheep.

About forty people had gathered for the funeral. All the members of the Road Warriors were present, wearing their leather waistcoats, which would have pleased Jocke. Others who were frequent visitors to the club had also come to pay their respects to their deceased friend. Several individuals from affiliated chapters on the mainland had arrived via Nynäshamn. Like the Road Warriors, they wore leathers and sported long hair, tattoos and multiple piercings.

After Pia and Johan had parked their car, they were greeted by Sonny and his girlfriend, Maddis, who were having a smoke with a bunch of other motorcycle-club members. Johan asked if he could interview them afterwards, and they agreed. But he decided to wait to approach Jocke's family, wanting to see how they might be feeling after the service.

When Pia got out her camera, several people turned their backs to her. She pretended not to notice and continued to set up the tripod, then proceeded to film. Johan walked among the people gathered outside the church, though he was mostly observing. He didn't want to bother anyone before the service started.

When the bells in the church tower began to toll, he headed for the entrance.

'I'll stay out here,' Pia told him. 'I hate funerals. And we can't film inside the church anyway. You go ahead.'

She sat down on top of the stone wall that enclosed the gravel space in front of the church.

'OK,' said Johan. 'See you afterwards.'

'Sure.'

Johan was the last person to enter the church. He took a seat in one of the pews at the back. Since he was there in the capacity of a journalist, he wanted to keep a low profile. Sometimes his job made him feel a bit sleazy. As if he were there to take advantage of other people's grief. Trying to be discreet, he studied the mourners.

He couldn't help thinking of Olle. Soon it would be time for his funeral, too. Poor kids. Poor Emma. Olle's life had ended when he was in his prime. Johan recalled how they had talked only a few days before the accident about how Olle was looking forward to a trip to New York in the autumn. He was going to take Sara and Filip there during their school holiday.

Johan thought about how quickly life could change. The victim of that accident could just as easily have been him. The thought was disturbing and incomprehensible. What did it mean to cease to exist? Never to have a chance to see his children grow up, never share any more joys or sorrows with Emma – never experience anything else at all. Death was a strange phenomenon. How was it possible to live and work, to bring children into the world, to be part of a community with friends and family, to mean something to others and then merely die? Disappear for good. And yet the days continued onward, weeks turned into months and years. But for the one who had died, there was only darkness. He simply didn't exist. Life proceeded more or less normally for everyone else, while the dead person was a skeleton in the grave or ashes in an urn.

He was pulled from his reverie when a woman cautiously took a seat next to him, perching on the very edge of the pew. Half her face was hidden behind big sunglasses, which she made no move to take off. She sat motionless, her head held high. She wore a hat, and her hair was pinned up underneath, so he couldn't see what colour it was. She seemed to be about his age, maybe a little younger. He looked down at the dark trousers covering her slender legs. Oddly enough, she was wearing black trainers. As she wrung her hands, Johan noticed a tattoo on one wrist.

After a while he heard her sobbing, and he couldn't help turning his head to take a surreptitious look at her. Tears were running down the woman's face.

On impulse he reached out to pat her hand.

There they both sat, each without a clue who the other was.

Knutas and Jacobsson had set up their folding chairs in the loft next to the organ pipes inside Tofta church, not wanting to be seen by the mourners. They wanted to take their time to observe everyone present. They had both brought binoculars in order to zoom in on the faces of those who had come to Jocke Eriksson's funeral. Jacobsson also had a camera, and she was taking photos of everyone. There was a possibility that Jocke's two friends might be bold enough to risk turning up for the service. For that reason, both officers were armed and wearing bullet-proof vests.

Nothing more had been broadcast on the news about who the police might be looking for, and there had been very little mention of the case at all during the past week. When there were no new developments in an investigation, reporters quickly lost interest. But the silence in the press might mean that the two friends would feel safer.

In the front pew sat Jocke's immediate family. His parents looked rather shabby. Their clothes were wrinkled, their shoes scuffed with wear. The mother seemed nervous and kept shifting her gaze, while the father was pale and balding, displaying clear signs of alcoholism in the fine network of blood vessels on his face. Their two other sons sat beside them. The older one, whose name was Göran, was a real hippie type with long, blond dreadlocks and a black batik shirt with a peace sign on the chest. He lived in a commune on Fårö and made his living selling handmade jewellery on the beaches in the summertime. He spent the winters in Jamaica, where he had a wife and child.

The middle brother, Jörgen, was the best dressed member of the family. He lived an entirely different sort of life and, as far as Knutas knew, he'd never been involved in any illegal activities. When interviewed, he had stated that he reviled anything to do with drugs, criminals and the motorcycle world. He was married, had two children and lived in a house on Endreväg, just outside the Visby city walls. He was an economist for a large corporation. He and his wife were seated between his parents. He wore a black suit, a nicely pressed white shirt with starched collar and a white tie. He was tall and solidly built; his dark hair was combed back, and he bore no resemblance to Jocke whatsoever. He was clean-shaven and presented a dignified appearance. It was hard to imagine that he was the brother of the other two.

Knutas moved his gaze to the others gathered in the church. It was a motley crowd, to put it mildly: tough-looking bikers; spruced-up relatives; hippie types; neatly dressed former classmates; as well as a bunch of known criminals and junkies who were obviously doing their best to look respectable, as much as that was possible. They wore clothing that had mostly come from rubbish bins and Red Cross collection drives.

The service began, accompanied by occasional sobs from individuals seated in the pews. As organ music played, the mourners fumbled their way through the words of the hymns, revealing either a limited education or a certain shyness.

Through their binoculars, Knutas and Jacobsson studied every single person, without really knowing what they were looking for. Suddenly, Jacobsson drew her colleague's attention by giving him a slight poke in the ribs.

'Look at the next-to-last row of pews on the left,' she hissed. 'The woman who seems to be alone, over on the side. That spot was empty before, so she must have come in after everyone else. And look who's sitting next to her.'

Knutas aimed his binoculars at the place Jacobsson had pointed out.

There he saw a young woman wearing a hat and big sunglasses. She was discreetly dressed in a dark jacket and trousers. What made her stand out was the fact that she occasionally raised one hand to use a handkerchief to wipe away the tears streaming down her face. Otherwise, she sat motionless, her hands in her lap.

'Could we really be that lucky?' whispered Knutas. 'Do you think the third robber would actually dare to come to the funeral?'

He shifted his gaze to the left. Seated in the pew right next to her was none other than Johan Berg.

'Look at the last row,' Jacobsson went on. 'The guy sitting right behind her, wearing a hat. He wasn't there before either.'

Knutas eagerly directed his attention to the last row. There he saw a man in his thirties who was also wearing sunglasses, which he'd not taken off once inside the church. His shoulder-length hair was black, his complexion a golden brown. He looked like he could be Latino. He leaned forward to pass a tissue to the woman sitting in front of him. Knutas squinted as he peered intently through the binoculars. When the man handed over the tissue, the sleeve of his jacket rode up and revealed a tattoo on his wrist.

'Bloody hell! He has the same tattoo as Jocke Eriksson. That's got to be Degen,' said Knutas. He and Jacobsson instantly jumped to their feet.

In his rush to get up, Knutas knocked over his chair. The loud bang made people turn their heads to look up at the organ loft, since the music had stopped and, at the same moment, the pastor had paused in his speech. Both police officers stood there, clearly visible.

The reaction from the man and woman at the back of the church was instantaneous. They leapt up and ran for the entrance. Everyone turned around to stare in surprise at the two people as they dashed towards the closed door, pushed it open and then disappeared. Even the pastor was caught off guard and stared in bewilderment at what was going on. A moment later the two plain-clothes officers came storming down from the organ loft and gave chase.

The church door slammed shut behind them, and then they were gone.

He could feel the sweat running down his spine, making his shirt stick to his back under his jacket. He discreetly wiped away some drops of sweat from his forehead and upper lip. He had to make it through this. Maintain control. This was an important moment, an emotional puzzle piece in the whole process. That much he understood.

While everyone had gathered outside the church, he had kept his eyes open for the man he was looking for, but he hadn't seen him. Maybe Diego González had sensed something was wrong. He hadn't turned up at the strip club again, and he'd kept away from the Thai boxing club. Nor had González set foot in his flat for several days.

He'd started feeling desperate and hadn't managed to find out where Degen could be hiding.

Then it was time for the funeral, and he'd set his hopes on seeing González at the church. He'd almost given up when the service was interrupted by two people rushing out – first a woman wearing a hat, and then a man. Before the church door closed, he'd managed to catch a glimpse of the man out of the corner of his eye, and he recognized Diego González. There was no doubt about it. When two individuals who could only be police officers chased after them, he excused himself, saying that he needed to see what was going on. Then, without a glance at anyone, he hurried up the centre aisle of the church.

1994

The flat was on the ground floor of a building in the centre of Vällingby. It was a one-bedroom with a small patio facing a space shared by all the tenants. The place was a bit run-down, and the bathroom was filthy, but it was theirs. At least for the time being. Degen had sublet it from a friend, who in turn had sublet it from someone else who had moved in with a girl living somewhere in Bålsta but had still wanted to hang on to the flat.

Terese could hardly believe it was true. Everything had happened much more quickly and easily than she'd ever dared hope. Now they had their own place. For two months she'd been staying with friends and other chance acquaintances. She had stubbornly refused to move home, and her parents seemed to think it was just as well she didn't. Since she would soon turn eighteen, social services had offered no objections.

Not that she cared what anyone thought. She had both Degen and Jocke to defend her. The tattoos that all three of them bore on their wrists proved they belonged together. They had sworn their loyalty in blood and fucked many times when they were all high as kites. There was nothing she wouldn't do for Degen and Jocke.

Something had changed after the attempted rape at the motorcycle club. They had become friends for life. She hardly thought about the assault any more; it had faded in her mind like a vague memory. It no longer seemed real. She would never find out who those two men were, but she didn't really care. Best to let it go and get on with things. Life goes on, as Jocke had said. Now the three of them were finally together, and their dream had been realized sooner than any of them had expected. Degen had just been released from the young offenders home on Gotland. He had served his time.

And now all three of them were standing in the living room and looking around.

The flat was furnished, but the lumpy sofa with the brown corduroy upholstery was covered with stains. On the floor lay two mattresses made of yellowing foam rubber. The flat seemed to have been used as a refuge by junkies and the homeless. Degen's mate had warned them about this so they wouldn't be surprised if people rang the bell at all hours of the day and night, wanting to come inside. It would probably be a good idea to change the lock as soon as possible.

The bedroom, which faced the street, had a double bed that looked like it had been found on a rubbish heap and a shoddy old wardrobe that tilted ominously. It seemed ready to fall apart at any moment. The bathroom had dark-green vinyl wallpaper that was meant to look like tiles and hung in shreds. The bathtub was black with dirt, as were the sink and the toilet.

'Wonder if the TV works,' muttered Degen as he started turning the knobs. A moment later he had managed to get both sound and a picture. 'Shit, that's great!'

he exclaimed, looking so thrilled in spite of the dreary surroundings that Terese had to give him a hug. He put his arms around her and surveyed the room.

'OK, it's not exactly pretty, but we can make this place look good, you know. All it needs is some elbow grease.'

'First I need a fix,' said Jocke, sitting down cross-legged on the floor.

He got out some foil and a lighter and began preparing a needle. He'd gone over to the hard stuff, and heroin was his new love. That worried Degen and Terese. Jocke already owed huge sums of money to several drug dealers.

Now all three of them sat on the floor in a circle, and Degen rolled a joint for him and Terese to share.

'We need to get some cash so we can pay off our debts – especially yours, Jocke,' said Degen, taking a long toke. 'Otherwise you're going to be in big trouble. And we have to come up with the rent in advance. I'll be damned if I know how we're going to manage,' he said, looking at Terese.

'OK, OK,' whined Jocke as he emptied the syringe into the crook of his arm. 'That bastard Sillen threatened to kill me the last time I couldn't pay him. Fuck him. I'll work it out.'

Terese and Degen exchanged glances. He was obviously talking shit. They all knew that Sillen and his cronies were deadly dangerous. One way or another, they needed to come up with the cash, and soon. Terese puffed on the joint and held the smoke in her mouth until tears filled her eyes and she grimaced. Slowly, she exhaled, staring pensively at the others. Then she said in a low voice, 'I've got an idea.'

When Knutas and Jacobsson came running out through the church door, they saw the fleeing couple only a short distance away.

'Stop! Police!' shouted Knutas, running as fast as he could.

They were so close on the heels of the man and woman that the pair didn't have a chance to get in a car or hop on a motorcycle, even though there were plenty of them parked outside the church.

Further along, the road split into two, and the couple took off in separate directions. The police did the same. Jacobsson followed the woman, while Knutas set his sights on the man.

A barn stood on one side of the road, and the man, who it seemed was the suspect known as Degen, had disappeared behind it.

When Knutas rounded the corner, the man was gone. He saw an enormous pile of manure and then he noticed that the barn door stood open. He must have slipped inside, thought Knutas, drawing his service weapon. He took off the safety catch and crept through the door. The sharp smell of manure filled his nostrils. He was breathing hard but hoped that his gasping for air wouldn't be heard. Inside the barn he found himself in an aisle between rows of empty stalls; the livestock was still out grazing in the summertime pastures. Cautiously, he crept forward, anticipating that Degen might be hiding in one of the stalls. But after several minutes he had to conclude he was wrong.

With all his senses on alert, Knutas continued on. Further along, he came to a stable with horses in it that neighed softly when he came in, which of course gave away his presence. He realized that he needed to call for back-up, if Jacobsson hadn't already done so. His heart was pounding as he took out his mobile and tapped in the number for the desk sergeant at headquarters. Whispering, he explained the situation and gave his location. Tofta was only ten kilometres from Visby, so it shouldn't take long for help to arrive. Then Knutas slowly continued forward, peering into each stall as he passed. No Degen.

The stable was quiet, not a person in sight; only horses, their jaws moving, all of them chewing non-stop. Apparently, they had recently been given their dinner of hay or oats. They raised their heads and stared at Knutas as he passed. A black cat sat in the middle of the stable floor, licking its paws, and he gave a start when a couple of kittens came scampering towards him.

Where the hell could the man have gone? He might have doubled back, slipped out the other side and run far away while Knutas was sneaking about like James Bond among all the wheelbarrows, kittens and feed bins. Knutas was starting to feel frustrated. If only he could catch the man, the whole case might be solved at one fell swoop. It was vexing, to say the least, knowing that Degen was so close and yet Knutas couldn't find him. He paused for a second, listening intently for any sound.

The blow came from behind and was so forceful that Knutas flew forward and then slammed on to the cement floor.

The woman that Jacobsson was chasing lost her hat, and a long plait danced back and forth on her back as she ran. The boy named Svante Hedström had said that the female biker he'd seen near the run-down house had worn her dark hair in a plait. Thoughts swirled through Jacobsson's mind as she raced along. Was this woman one of the robbers who had run over little Maja Rosén, and who might also have killed Jocke Eriksson, even though she'd been crying as she sat in the church? If so, she was chasing a person who was tough as nails and very dangerous. Jacobsson sincerely hoped Knutas had called for back-up; she wasn't convinced she'd be able to handle this person on her own. But right now she was the only one running after the woman, whom they hadn't yet been able to identify. In fact, they knew absolutely nothing about her, except that her name presumably started with the letter 'T'.

Jacobsson was gaining on the woman, but she was still a good thirty metres away. Then they left the pastures, poppy fields and meadows behind and were surrounded by woods. They were running along a winding gravel road heading inland, and Jacobsson lost sight of the woman as she disappeared around a bend. When she reached that same curve she found herself looking at a straight stretch of road, but the woman was gone. She must have veered off into the woods. The question was: which way did she go?

Jacobsson stopped to catch her breath as she looked around and listened for any sound, but she heard only the faint rustling of the wind in the trees and the carefree chirping of birds. She took a minute to weigh up what would be the best course of action, given the situation. If the woman was armed, it might be wise to wait for back-up.

Suddenly, she heard the snap of a twig to the right of the road and caught a glimpse of a shadow among the trees.

Jacobsson instantly crossed the road and set off. Branches and twigs slapped against her as she weaved her way forward. Now and then she could make out a figure up ahead, but it was a dense forest, which made it hard for her to move quickly. She was scared of stumbling on a tree root or stones and then losing sight of the woman. She ran as fast as she could, all the while trying to take care where she put her feet.

She wondered for a moment whether she ought to fire a warning shot but decided against it.

By now Jacobsson had a painful stitch in her side. They should never have eaten hamburgers before going to the funeral.

In her mind she pictured the woman's face. She had classical features and looked to be about the age the witness had estimated, between thirty and thirty-five. In spite of the risk, the woman and the man called Degen had both come to the funeral, which indicated recklessness and a lack of judgement. Hadn't they realized what a gamble it was?

*

The woods began to thin out. Up ahead Jacobsson caught a glimpse of a solitary farm and a road. She tried to pick up speed, but her body refused to cooperate. Now, every step was torture. She was soaked with sweat, and her clothes were sticking to her skin. When she reached the asphalt road, she stopped and leaned forward with her hands on her knees as she tried to calm her ragged breathing. She glanced in both directions. Nothing. Not a soul, not a car in sight. The road stretched out before her, quiet and deserted.

Jacobsson wiped the sweat from her forehead. She discovered that she'd left her mobile in the camera case, which was back in the church.

She straightened up and headed for the farm to ask for help.

1994

When the ferryboat docked at the terminal in Visby, it was 8 p.m. and dark. They had bought tickets using false names and were scheduled to go back on the ferry that left in the morning at seven. They had exactly eleven hours. Degen had borrowed the delivery van they were driving from a friend who owed him a favour because Degen had helped him rob a kiosk a few weeks earlier. The van had stolen licence plates and, if everything went to plan, it would be impossible to trace. Jocke was driving, since he knew the roads best.

Terese's stomach churned as they drove down the ramp and entered the harbour area. It felt strange to be back on Gotland. When she'd left several months ago, she had been angry, sad and hurt. So she was surprised to find herself feeling almost happy at the sight of the familiar buildings close to the harbour and the three black towers of the cathedral. Beyond the bend in the road was the Catch 22 restaurant. It was open all year round, so presumably customers were sitting at the rustic tables right now, eating dinner in the soft glow of candlelight. She felt a pang of regret. Everything could have turned out so differently.

In the distance she could see the steep cliffs of Högklint in the cold light of the pale moon shining in the autumn sky. None of them said a word as they drove. Everything had been carefully planned, and they knew exactly what they were going to do.

When they took the turn-off towards Högklint, there were no other cars on the road. The flat landscape lay dark and desolate all around them. The bright shop signs in Kneippbyn looked ghost-like in the autumn dark as they drove past. The theme park was closed for the winter.

The road twisted more and more as it climbed the steep slope. The few houses they passed looked vacant; many were used only in the summertime and stood empty all winter. It was also a school holiday for all the children, and the people who owned these houses were well-to-do and could probably afford to spend the holiday abroad. That was another reason they'd chosen this week. The family always went away to visit friends who rented a house on Gran Canaria for the autumn half-term. Just to make sure, Degen had phoned the restaurant and asked to speak with Palle. He was told that Mr Stenfors was abroad and wouldn't be back until the weekend. Jocke had pretended to be the twins' uncle when he rang their school, and was told the same thing. If Terese were still living with the Stenfors family, she would have gone with them. She would have been soaking up the sun with all of them right now, instead of finding herself here. What an absurd thought.

The closer they got, the more nervous they all felt. They parked the van in a grove of trees a good distance from the house, just to be on the safe side. There was no hurry. It would be better if they waited until later to strike so they could then drive straight back to the ferry and get away as fast as possible. The less time they spent on the island afterwards, the better.

It was now 8.45 p.m. They wore trainers, sweat-pants, dark running jackets and baseball caps to give themselves the appearance of three young people out jogging, just in case they were unlucky enough to run into anyone. Though that was highly unlikely. The house stood all alone on a cliff, and the closest neighbour was a kilometre away.

Even so, they closed the van doors quietly, locked up and then walked quickly towards the house. The only sound was the crunch of the gravel under their feet and the rustling of the wind in the pines. Now and then they caught a glimpse of the moon through the trees. It was almost full. They didn't speak as they walked. When the house came into view, they had the final confirmation that the family was away. The house was dark except for the outside light and a lamp in the front hall. Terese knew that particular lamp was always left on whenever the family was not at home. Only the smaller car stood in the driveway. They always left the big car in the airport's guarded long-term parking lot when-ever they travelled abroad. Since it was an expensive vehicle with special tyres that were particularly desir-able, Palle thought the car would be safer there than left at home. Terese heaved a sigh of relief. The three split up, and Terese walked around the house to make sure the family hadn't changed the alarm system since the summer. In the meantime, Jocke and Degen scouted the property to see that everything was quiet.

Then they returned to the van to have a smoke. It was now nine thirty. They decided to wait until midnight before striking. Then there would be almost zero chance that anyone would come walking past. Until that time, there might be people out with their dogs or dedicated joggers who ran late at night, even though it was dark and chilly. The thermometer in the van showed seven degrees Celsius; the temperature would drop further as the night progressed. Terese shivered and took one last drag on her cigarette before climbing into the front passenger seat. Two and a half hours left. It was going to be a long wait. Degen got out a Thermos he'd filled with coffee on board the ferry and offered some to his friends. He was always so considerate.

Terese leaned back and closed her eyes. She wished the time would pass quickly so they could get this over with. It had been her idea, and they had to pull it off or they would be lost. Robbing the house that belonged to her former foster family would solve all their money problems without hurting anyone. The family was away, so they wouldn't notice a thing until they came back home. Of course, it would be unpleasant for them to discover that someone had broken in, but they could install a new alarm and take other security precautions. And besides, everything that was stolen would no doubt be replaced by the insurance company.

The burglary was their secret. They hadn't mentioned their plans to anyone, nor would they ever do so in the future. Terese was fully aware that she would come under suspicion since, until recently, she had been living with the family. But if they were clever and left no traces, the police wouldn't be able to do a thing. And they had gone over every detail with the greatest care, again and again. Nothing could go wrong.

Terese shivered once more. She couldn't help feeling guilty. No matter how angry and sad she had been when she left the family in such negative circumstances back in August, she did understand why things had ended as they had.

She couldn't really blame Susanne. The woman had done her best and was only looking out for everyone's well-being. In her heart, Terese knew that she herself was responsible. She'd been given every advantage by a nice family. She had her own room with everything she could possibly need and a summer job in a cosy restaurant. And she was supposed to have enrolled in secondary school in Visby, where she would have been able to make new friends. But instead of seizing the opportunity, she had ruined everything, even though she knew full well she could have done things differently. She wasn't stupid.

Yet it was partly their fault, too. If only they had been more tolerant and given her a second chance instead of just throwing her out. As soon as they experienced the slightest unpleasantness in their perfect lives, they refused to go on. They lived as far from reality as they could possibly get. Her reality, at any rate. When she thought about that, she felt her anger soar. They could only blame themselves.

In any case, that was how things had turned out, and right now she and her two best friends were in desperate need of money. The situation was dire. Degen had put off making the advance rent payment for the flat in Vällingby again and again, but he couldn't do it any longer. Next week the payment was due. And then there was the money Jocke owed to his drug dealers. If he didn't pay up, it might cost him his life. They were in real trouble, and this was the best idea she had been able to come up with. Palle and Susanne had expensive paintings on the walls and several small sculptures worth hundreds of thousands of kronor. That's what Kristoffer had told her. She also knew that in Palle's home office there was a safe, and one day she had discovered the combination when she was looking for cash in the room. That was shortly before the big confrontation, so she'd never had a chance to try it. But if Palle hadn't changed the combination, it would be child's play to get into the safe. And from what she understood, it was where he put large sums of money that he brought home from the restaurant.

She lit another cigarette and closed her eyes. Degen and Jocke were both dozing in their seats. There was nothing to do but wait until midnight. They would follow their plan to the letter.

A while later Terese was awakened by a sound. She gave a start and sat up. Her heart was pounding, and the next instant her mouth went dry. There was no mistaking what she had heard.

A car drove up the road and turned towards the house.

When Knutas came to, he found a rough tongue insistently licking his cheek. Blinking at the light, he looked up and saw the black cat, who had crept over to him and apparently decided to give his face a good wash. The cat's soft fur tickled his nose, making him sneeze, but the cat was unconcerned and merely kept on with what it was doing. He had no idea how long he'd been lying there on the hard floor of the stable. Slowly, he hauled himself into a sitting position as searing pain shot through his skull. The back of his head hurt terribly. He couldn't bring himself to open his eyes all the way but made do with squinting.

The cat leapt out of his way but retreated only a few metres. Then it sat down and resumed its grooming, this time licking its own fur.

Cautiously, he raised his hand to touch the back of his head. It was sticky with blood, and the size of the wound frightened him. Shit. The man had really clobbered him. Then he noticed a shovel that had been tossed on the ground some distance away. It was red with blood.

Light was shining in through the dusty windows of the stable. He heard the horses moving about in their stalls. They were no longer eating. Dinnertime was over. I've certainly made a mess of things, Knutas thought, feeling resigned. Degen had eluded them. He hoped that Karin had had better luck.

His head was bursting, and he felt sick to his stomach. He sat still for a few more minutes, waiting for the worst of the pain to subside. Two kittens crept cautiously towards him. They seemed to decide that he wasn't dangerous, because they lay down on his legs and began sleepily blinking their eyes.

Knutas noticed that his service weapon was gone. Degen must have taken it. He fumbled for his mobile, but that, too, was missing. Hadn't he called for back-up? Where the hell were they?

At any rate, he still had his watch. Three fifteen. He didn't remember exactly when he'd rung headquarters, but the church service had started at two o'clock, and it had been going for only about fifteen minutes when he and Jacobsson had noticed the two individuals at the back of the church. So it couldn't be more than forty-five minutes since he'd made the call.

The kittens scampered off as he began crawling over to the wall so he could hold on to it as he got to his feet. Very carefully, he stood up, but the dizziness was even worse.

At that moment someone came walking towards him.

Pia Lilja couldn't believe her eyes when the church door opened and a man wearing a hat and sunglasses came rushing out, followed closely by a woman similarly disguised. They raced across the church yard, both of them losing their hats in the process. The woman turned out to have dark hair gathered in a long plait. Pia instinctively lifted the camera up to her shoulder and filmed the fleeing couple as they disappeared down the road.

The next instant the door opened again, and she saw Anders Knutas and Karin Jacobsson come storming out of the church with weapons drawn. Pia thanked her lucky stars she'd been ready with the camera. Without a clue as to what was happening right in front of the lens, she filmed both officers as they, too, disappeared down the road. Then the church door opened a third time, and Johan came out.

'What the hell is going on?' he shouted.

'I was going to ask you the same thing,' replied Pia, putting down the camera now that everyone had vanished from sight.

Johan told Pia about the mysterious woman sitting next to him and the man in the row behind who had simultaneously leapt up and rushed out of the church.

'Do you think they're the ones?' exclaimed Pia excitedly. 'Degen and the girl?'

'Good Lord,' said Johan, slapping his forehead. 'You could be right. What the hell do we do now? We need to notify the police.'

He rang the duty officer in Visby and explained the situation. At first the officer sounded sceptical, but he changed his tone when Johan told him that Jacobsson and Knutas were chasing the two suspects. Reinforcements were promised as soon as possible. At that moment melancholy organ music could be heard playing inside the church. The situation seemed totally surreal.

'We can't just stay here,' said Pia. 'The funeral won't be over for a good half-hour. Let's go over to the road and check things out.'

They walked across the gravel-covered space. A short distance away they found a woman's black hat and, a bit further along, a man's hat.

'We really shouldn't touch them, but we can't just leave them here,' said Johan. 'They might get blown away, or someone might take them.'

'Wait a minute. Don't pick them up yet,' said Pia. 'This would be a great place for you to do a piece to camera, here in the church yard with the hats on the ground. "Here's what the victim's two friends left behind", or something like that. It'll only take a minute. Let's do it.'

Johan shook his head, but he was inclined to agree. Television was at its best when the reporter was on site as the action played out and able to follow what was going on in real time. He squatted down and quickly said a few lines while Pia filmed him. Then he gingerly picked up each hat by the very brim and ran over to the car to place them carefully on the back seat.

After that, Pia and Johan raced over to the road, but they saw no sign of the police officers or the couple they'd been chasing. So they stayed where they were, waiting to see if anyone would come back.

After a while they heard sirens off in the distance. Reinforcements were on the way.

The hotel was in the harbour area, right across from the terminal for the mainland ferries. Several hours had passed, seeming to drag by very slowly. He had begun to think that he'd chosen the wrong hotel, or that the individuals he was waiting for had been caught by the police. But then they had turned up. The couple got out of a taxi and took a good look around, as if they were worried about being followed. The man had a hunted expression. As soon as he was out of the cab, he lit a cigarette, turned his back and began smoking furiously. The woman cast a wary glance around her and then went over to stand next to him. They both smoked without saying a word.

He studied them intently as he hid behind the newspaper he was pretending to read. When they had finished smoking, they quickly went over to the hotel's revolving doors and slipped inside. He put on his sunglasses and followed.

The lobby was crowded because a new group of tourists had just arrived. Thirty or so people had pushed their way over to the counter and were eagerly waiting to check in.

He sat down on a bench outside the front entrance, lit a cigarette and settled in for another long wait. He'd brought along the evening papers, which he leafed through so as not to draw undue attention to himself.

Less than an hour later Diego González came out of the hotel, walking past without giving him even a glance. Degen strode across the car park and headed down the hill to the harbour. He had changed his clothes, but he was still wearing his sunglasses.

Quickly, the man got up and followed.

González went across the street and tried the doors to the ferry terminal, but he soon realized it was futile. The place had closed for the night. The next boat to the mainland wouldn't leave until seven in the morning. Then he strode past the big containers stacked on the wharf and the few remaining moored pleasure boats bobbing in the water. Near the tourist office he crossed the street and walked past the restaurant, which was now closed for the season.

He kept a decent distance so Degen wouldn't know that he was tailing him. Very few people were on the street at this time of night on a Monday. González stopped at the tobacconist's and yanked on the door handle. It, too, was closed, which prompted an annoyed look from Degen.

He ducked behind a pillar, hoping he hadn't been seen. A man with a dog came walking along the pavement. When he peered around the pillar, he saw González saying something to the dog owner, who then pointed, as if giving directions. After that, Degen crossed Donner Square and disappeared inside the Wisby Hotel.

The man wasn't sure what to do next, so he decided simply to wait. Why had González gone into the hotel?

Why would he risk going out in public at all when he knew that the police were looking for him? It didn't make sense. After several minutes González reappeared, holding a pack of cigarettes. He took a look around before heading back the same way.

And the man followed.

Johan and Pia came away with footage they could never have anticipated getting when they had left the office a few hours earlier. On their way back, Johan had talked non-stop on his mobile with various editors at the main office in Stockholm. Everybody wanted to broadcast a story about the funeral of the murdered Jocke Eriksson, the commotion that subsequently arose and the police hunt for his suspected companions. Regional News had obtained exclusive film of everything. Both Johan and Pia were fully aware that, as soon as the first report was shown on TV, they would be swamped by requests from news-paper editors from all over Sweden to buy their photos. The security-van robbery in the sleepy town of Klintehamn that had led to the death of a six-year-old girl and then the brutal murder of one of the robbers had exploded into a sensational story. There was tremendous interest now that something had finally happened, after there having been no new developments over the past week.

Pia's eyes were sparkling with satisfaction. She was the person in possession of the hottest pictures in Sweden at the moment, and she was elated.

When they got back to the office, Pia uploaded the images on to her computer while Johan began writing his first report. They had an hour before the material had to be sent to Stockholm. They sat next to each other, editing the pictures together so that Johan could sync his report with what would be displayed on screen.

The footage of the two suspects rushing out of the church was a bit shaky, but it did show a man and a woman racing across the church yard towards the road. By chance, Degen had turned to look back, and his face was clearly visible. The camera stayed with the fleeing couple until they disappeared from view. Johan and Pia decided to include the entire sequence without cuts. The drama of the scene far outweighed the less than desirable quality of the footage, though they did blur the faces of the suspects to hide their identity.

Then in the footage the two police officers emerged from the church with their weapons drawn. They paused for only a second, but Pia had reacted quickly and managed to capture on film the moment when Knutas and Jacobsson looked around in confusion before they took off after the couple.

'Good,' said Johan appreciatively. 'Great job.'

'Not bad, huh?' Pia agreed. 'Pretty amazing, even if I do say so myself.'

The next person to appear in the video was Johan, moving towards the camera. At that instant another figure also appeared, right behind him.

'Look!'

'Who's that?' asked Johan.

'No idea. I didn't see him come out of the church.'

Pia paused the film and slowly reversed it, frame by frame. The person's face was hidden behind Johan, though there was no doubt it was a man. They could see he was wearing a dark suit, but that was about all.

Johan threw up his hands.

'Where did he come from? And where did he go?'

'I have no idea. I didn't notice him at all. I was too busy filming you and everything else that was happening.'

'I don't get it. I was sitting in the second-to-last pew, and it took me only a moment to get up and leave. And we're talking about just a minute or so after the police stood up in the organ loft. This guy must have been awfully fast.'

Again Pia rolled back the film and then replayed it several times. No matter how hard they looked, all they could see was the man's shoulder.

'It's impossible to tell who he is,' said Johan, sighing. 'Everyone had on dark suits, for god's sake. Except for the bikers and the bums. And Jocke's brother, of course. The hippie.'

'What should we do?' asked Pia. 'Should we include the image and a comment?'

'There's nothing to say about it. All we can say is that the church service was interrupted. This guy could be anyone. Maybe he was just curious and wanted to find out what was going on outside. Maybe he saw no reason to stay in his seat.'

'You're right,' said Pia. 'Let's just drop it.'

Johan was still staring at the man's shoulder. He had an uneasy feeling that refused to go away. Who was this man standing so close to him? Could it be Jocke Eriksson's killer? The man who was cold-blooded enough to have slashed his victim's throat?

1994

'What the hell?' hissed Degen at the sight of the dark vehicle that had pulled into and parked in the driveway.

'That's their car,' whispered Terese. Her heart practically leapt out of her chest when she saw Palle and Susanne get out, followed by the twins. She and Degen had crept over to the edge of the property and were peering at the house from behind a tree. Jocke had stayed in the van.

With growing frustration, they watched as the family unloaded suitcases and bags and then went inside. Lights immediately went on in all the windows. Terese and Degen hastily drew back when the outdoor spotlight was switched on. It was so bright that half the surrounding garden was illuminated.

'Shit, shit, shit! There goes our whole fucking plan!' Degen spat out the words.

Terese was speechless. Thoughts whirled through her head. What did this mean? They weren't supposed to come home until Saturday, and today was only Thursday. She didn't understand. They'd been told the same thing when they rang the school and the restaurant.

Her courage sank. Now they wouldn't be able to carry out the burglary. All their plans were ruined, and she didn't even want to think about how they were going to manage to pay for the flat and Jocke's debts. She glanced at her watch. Eleven fifteen. She needed a smoke. And time to think. She didn't dare light up here, in case somebody opened a terrace door or one of the windows to air the house. She tapped Degen on the shoulder.

'Let's go back.'

He nodded. Only when they had walked down the gravel road and were a good distance from the house did he speak.

'What the hell are we going to do? Why are they already home?'

'Something must have happened.'

When they got back to the van, they found Jocke smoking a joint.

'What are you doing?' snapped Degen. 'This is not a good time for you to be getting high.'

'But you guys were gone so long,' complained Jocke. 'And that car drove past. I got nervous.'

'Just relax, for god's sake.'

'What's going on?'

'The whole family's come home,' said Degen. He sank on to the passenger seat with a resigned sigh.

'Does that mean you want to give up?' exclaimed Jocke, his eyes wide.

'I don't know. Let me think about it,' said Degen, annoyed. He leaned back and closed his eyes, slowly rubbing his temples.

Terese didn't say a word. Her mind was a total blank.

For a while none of them spoke. Terese lit a cigarette. Her mouth was dry, and she got out a bottle of water from the cooler that Degen had packed.

'Damn it. The whole plan is wrecked,' she said with a sigh.

'But why?' said Degen. 'Why can't we do it while they're all asleep? After such a long trip, they must be exhausted. Nothing will wake them up. Where are the bedrooms?'

'Upstairs,' replied Terese. 'At the other end of the house.'

'And where is the safe? We can focus all our attention on the safe. That's the most important thing.'

'In the home office,' said Terese distractedly.

'And where's that?'

'On the ground floor, at the opposite end of the house from the bedrooms.'

'And the house is made of limestone, right? That means the walls are super-thick.'

'I could play music full blast in my room, and you could hardly hear it in the living room and the kitchen. Sometimes it felt like I was home all alone, even though everyone else was there.'

'OK. That's good,' said Jocke eagerly. 'Nothing more to discuss, right? We'll wait until we're sure they're all asleep, and then we'll go in.'

Degen and Terese exchanged glances.

'On one condition,' Terese finally and reluctantly said. 'The only thing we'll take is what's in the safe.'

'That's fine with me,' said Degen.

'Me, too,' Jocke agreed.

Degen fixed his eyes on his friends.

'Now all we have to do is wait.'

At seven o'clock the investigative team gathered in the conference room. Jacobsson was in charge of the meeting because Knutas was at home in bed, suffering from concussion after having been hit over the head with a shovel. There was every indication that the blow had been delivered by the man they'd been seeking for the past two weeks. They still knew only his nickname: Degen. He had escaped, as had his female companion, whose identity continued to be a mystery. Jacobsson started off by summarizing what had happened at Jocke Eriksson's funeral. She then told the team how Knutas had been struck down by one of the robbers.

'The first patrol officers who arrived on the scene in Tofta quickly located Anders. He was taken to hospital, where the doctors diagnosed that he has mild concussion. He'll probably be back at work tomorrow. Roadblocks were set up, and police dogs were brought in to search the area – unfortunately, without result. We have no idea where the suspects went. The premises of the Road Warriors motorcycle club have been searched, in case the suspects have connections there that no one wanted to tell us about. We'll keep the place under surveillance tonight.'

'How did Jocke's family react?' asked Wittberg.

'None of them appears to know who the man and woman are, but they'll let us know if the pair should unexpectedly turn up. Even though the robbers got away this time, there are a few positive developments. Both dropped their hats outside the church. We sent the hats to the forensics lab, along with the shovel that the man used to strike Anders. So we may find a DNA match in police records. Now we also have a much better description of who we're looking for.'

'And we've even got pictures of them,' Wittberg added. 'They were part of the lead story on the local news. Pia Lilja was apparently outside the church, and she got everything on film.'

'I know. We need to get hold of those pictures,' said Jacobsson. 'Can you take care of that, Wittberg?'

'Sure. That'll give me a chance to have a good chat with the luscious Pia. It'll be a pleasure.'

Jacobsson assigned various tasks to the officers. In spite of the late hour, everyone was eager to get to work. As she was leaving the conference room, Wittberg stopped her.

'How come you've started calling the boss by his first name?' he asked.

'What? Did I?'

Much to her embarrassment, Jacobsson felt herself blushing.

'Yup. You said "Anders" several times.'

'So what?'

She turned away and hurried down the corridor.

As soon as the meeting was over, Jacobsson went to her office and called Knutas. The phone rang for a long time

291

before he finally answered. He sounded groggy, almost as if he were drugged.

'Hi. How are you feeling?' asked Jacobsson with concern.

'Oh. Hi. I'm OK. Just a little tired.'

'Did you get some sleep?'

'Uh-huh.'

He didn't seem to be in any shape to talk on the phone.

'Are the children at home? Could I speak to one of them?'

'No,' he said.

'What do you mean by "no"?'

'They're not here. They went to visit Lina in Copenhagen.'

'What are you saying? Isn't anyone there with you?'

No reply.

'Hello? Anders? Are you there?'

'Uh-huh.'

'Is anyone there with you?'

'Anyone? No.'

'I'm coming right over. I'll be at your place in fifteen minutes, max. If you can manage it, go and unlock the front door.'

'It's not locked.'

'OK, then. I'll be there soon. Bye.'

She slammed down the receiver and grabbed her jacket. She stuck her head in the door of the office where Kihlgård was working, poring over a stack of documents while he ate a hamburger.

'Hey, I have to go over to see Anders. He doesn't sound good, and none of his family are home. You're in charge while I'm gone.'

292

'All right. That's fine. We'll keep working. Say hi to Knutie.'

The house on Bokströmsgatan was almost completely dark when Jacobsson arrived. Only one lamp was on in the front hall, and through the living-room window she could see a bluish flickering from the TV. She opened the front door and closed it behind her.

'Hello! I'm here!' she called, but there was no answer.

She glanced in the kitchen, which was empty, and switched on a light. Several dirty glasses and plates were on the worktop, and the cat's food dish and water bowl were both empty. What sort of family is this? she thought. They don't even come home when he's been hurt? Then it occurred to her that Knutas might not have told them about the events of the day and having concussion. That would be so typical of him.

She found him stretched out on the living-room sofa. He had propped a few pillows under his head and he lay there with his eyes closed and the remote in his hand. Some sort of music programme was on TV. A woman wearing a blue sequinned gown was singing hysterically. Jacobsson took the remote away from Knutas and turned off the TV. She switched on the floor lamp, but tilted the shade so the light wouldn't be so glaring.

'Anders?' she said softly. 'Are you awake? I'm here now.'

He stirred a bit, made a few smacking sounds with his lips and then opened his eyes. His face lit up when he saw who it was. He smiled wanly.

'Karin. What are you doing here?'

'But we just talked about it on the phone. Don't you remember?'

He turned on to his side and buried his face in a pillow as he stretched out his hand towards her.

Karin wondered whether she ought to take him back to the hospital. He seemed totally out of it. She felt his forehead, then checked his pupils and pulse.

'Have you taken any medicine?' she asked. 'Any painkillers?'

Before he could answer, she noticed a packet of pills underneath a newspaper on the coffee table. A glass half filled with water stood next to it. The medicine contained morphine, and four of the tablets were missing. She phoned a nurse she knew who worked at Visby hospital. It was past ten at night, but she didn't care. The woman answered at once and told her that the pills were quite strong and that extreme fatigue was a natural reaction, especially if a person took four tablets. The maximum recommended dosage for an adult was two in twenty-four hours, but it wasn't dangerous to take four, particularly if the patient was a large adult man in his prime, the nurse reassured her. She should just put him to bed, but since he'd suffered concussion, he shouldn't be left alone overnight.

Good Lord, am I going to have to sleep here, too? wondered Karin.

She needed to ring Lina. She found Knutas's mobile and scrolled through his contacts to the appropriate number.

'Hi!' said Lina happily.

Karin could hear the sounds of a restaurant, with conversations and laughter in the background.

'Hi, this is Karin, Anders's colleague from work.'

'Oh? Hi.'

Lina's voice changed a bit, taking on a worried tone.

'I'm calling because Anders has got concussion. But maybe you already know that?'

'No. I had no idea. What happened?'

'It's just slight concussion, and he's been to hospital to have it looked at, so it's not serious. I thought you knew, and that somebody would be at home with him. But when I rang him from work tonight, I found out he was here alone. The children are with you in Copenhagen, is that right?'

'Yes. They've taken a few days off from school to come over and visit my mother, who has just turned seventy. There was a big birthday party for her this weekend,' she explained apologetically.

'Well, Anders didn't sound very good, so I phoned the hospital, and they said he shouldn't be left alone overnight. So I'm wondering if there's someone I could call. Otherwise, I'm fine with staying here and sleeping on the sofa.'

'Can I talk to him?' said Lina.

'I'm afraid not. He's totally out of it.'

'My god. When did he get concussed? How did it happen?'

Karin explained the whole series of events, and Lina gasped in dismay just as the noise in the background got even louder.

'Oh, poor Anders. I can't understand why he didn't phone us. If you could stay overnight, I'd be very grateful. There are sheets in the big white linen closet on the upstairs landing.'

'OK,' said Karin. 'Now I'd better see to your husband. Bye.'

She ended the conversation and couldn't help feeling a certain glee because Lina was obviously feeling guilty. She managed to wake Knutas up enough so that he could make his way upstairs, use the toilet and then crawl into bed. In the meantime, she cleaned up in the kitchen and filled the cat's food dish and water bowl. The minute she did that, the cat appeared. Then Karin turned off the lights downstairs and went up to look in on Knutas. She had no intention of spending the night on the sofa.

He was already in bed and sleeping soundly. She used the toilet, then took off her clothes, except for her knickers and vest. After that, she got in next to Knutas, lying down on Lina's side of the double bed. She gently stroked his forehead and cheeks as she listened to his steady breathing. She felt so safe.

And then she fell asleep.

The September evening was unusually warm, and Degen slowed his pace as he left the town behind and strolled along the deserted harbour. He lit a cigarette. He wasn't exactly thrilled about returning to the hotel room. All Terese did was cry. He had tried his best to comfort her, but he was sad, too. It was a relief to get away for a while; out here he could almost relax. The ferry terminal was closed, and not a soul was visible on the inside of the enormous glass windows.

They had missed the last boat, which left at four forty-five. Now they would have to wait until seven in the morning, if they dared take the ferry at all. They had already discussed what might be the best alternative. There was a risk the police might be watching the first departure of the morning. They could always bide their time and stay at the hotel for a few days until things had settled down a bit. The police had limited resources, so they couldn't very well spend several days checking out every ferry passenger. Yet it would also be risky to stay here. They knew no one on Gotland who might help them with as simple a matter as getting food. The hotel restaurant was open only for lunch. There wasn't even a bar or anywhere to buy cigarettes. That was why Degen had decided to go out, even though they were both aware of the danger. But there was nothing else to do. Neither of them could make it through the night without cigarettes.

Finally, they had agreed it would be better to leave in the morning, taking a chance that the ferry would not be under surveillance. That was their decision. They would have to check in at least half an hour before departure. It was going to be a sleepless night but, luckily, they'd brought along some whisky.

Degen thought about the disaster at the church. That had been a very close call. They had known that the police were hot on their trail and might turn up at the funeral. An officer had already been to the Thai boxing club, but Degen's trainer, Amanda, who was also one of his girlfriends, had phoned to say that she'd erased all his information from the club records.

But none of that had really mattered. They had to go to the funeral, even though they both knew it was a reckless thing to do. They couldn't let Jocke down and not turn up when he went to his final resting place. They had simply had no choice.

Degen lit up again when he came to the last pier. A few boats bobbed about at their moorings. The place was deserted and quiet. Then his mobile rang. It was Terese.

'Where are you? Why is it taking so long?' she asked, sounding worried.

'It's OK. I got the cigarettes. I had to make a detour to another hotel to buy them. Everything's closed in this bloody place.'

'What are you doing now?'

'I was taking a walk along the harbour, but I'm heading back now. I'll be there in ten minutes.'

'Promise? You shouldn't be walking around town. What if the cops see you?'

'I know, I'll hurry. Just take it easy.'

When he reached the most remote section of the harbour area, where the big containers were lined up, he noticed that someone was following him.

Twenty metres behind him he saw a solitary man whose face was hidden by a dark baseball cap. He was tall and brawny and seemed to be quite young, maybe around thirty. It was hard to determine his age because by now it was pitch dark, with only an occasional street lamp casting patches of light in the harbour. The man was not a cop; that much was clear. But what was he doing here? Degen looked about for a dog, thinking the man might be a dog owner who was out for a late-night walk.

He started going faster but noticed the man did the same. Now he was getting nervous. What the hell was going on?

He ducked behind a container to see if the man would keep walking. Maybe this was all just a coincidence. But when Degen slipped out of view, the stranger paused to look around, as if he'd lost sight of his quarry. Degen's heart was pounding hard. What the fuck should he do? Try to overpower the guy with some Thai boxing kicks? He thought about what had happened to Jocke and began to shake.

Tentatively, he peeked out from behind the container and saw the back of the man, who had stopped very close by but had then decided to walk around the container. As the man turned, light fell on his face and Degen got a good look at him in profile. There was something familiar about the man. Then the stranger disappeared, and Degen realized that he needed to move or he would be discovered. Slowly, he crept around the container and ended up behind the man who had been following him. For several seconds he considered pouncing on him and hoping for the best, but he decided against it.

Degen then took a chance and ran over to the next container. He pressed his body against the side, caught his breath and tried to collect his thoughts. He was one step closer to the hotel; that was where he needed to go. Back to Terese. This was crazy. How was he going to get away from this guy? And where had he seen him before? He searched his memory. Then he peered around the corner and saw the stranger coming straight towards him. He turned around and ran for the next container. Maybe someone else would turn up. He was almost hoping to see a police car.

For an insane moment he contemplated stepping forward into full view and asking the man what he wanted. Instead, he cautiously crept over to the corner of the container, listening for any sound. Was the man back where he'd left him, or had he moved over here, too? Degen squinted into the dark. Nothing. He waited. No movement. Not a sound. Then he set off running but suddenly found the stranger right in front of him. He turned in panic and raced out on to the pier where the boats were moored.

Too late, Diego González discovered that there was no way back.

1994

The minutes crawled by. The temperature quickly dropped, and it was cold inside the van. Terese regretted not having brought along a proper jacket. They smoked and drank Coke to keep themselves awake. They'd finished the coffee long ago. Every so often they would take turns sneaking over to the house to find out if Palle and Susanne had gone to bed. Not until three in the morning was the last light switched off. They decided to wait at least an hour to be sure that everyone was asleep.

At four thirty, Degen started up the van and slowly drove towards the house. They wanted to park as close as possible so they could get away fast, but they didn't want to wake the family. He parked the car down on the road, facing the right direction for their escape. The outdoor lights at the front of the house and lining the driveway had been turned off, so it was pitch dark when Degen stopped the van. Jocke was no longer sober enough to be entrusted with the driving. He'd managed to smoke several joints and was noticeably high, but there was nothing to be done about that now.

They'd planned their gear down to the smallest detail. They got out the torches and pulled on the black ski masks before leaving the van, the key ready in the ignition.

With all their senses on full alert, they moved through the dark. Terese tapped in the code to disarm the security system. She prayed silently it would be the same code they'd had when she lived here, but nothing happened. She tried again, but the alarm didn't switch off. What the hell? She was seized with panic. The house was equipped with an alarm which immediately summoned the police, and it wouldn't take long for the cops to make it out to Högklint, which was only about five kilometres from Visby.

'What the hell is happening?' hissed Jocke impatiently. 'Don't you know the code?'

'No. They must have changed it. I need to think for a minute.'

Degen and Jocke looked annoyed as they surveyed the property. Not a sound came from the dark. In the distance, they could hear the waves striking the shore. Terese was thinking frantically. So many times she'd searched every nook and cranny of this house when no one was at home and she was trying to find some cash. That was how she'd come across the place where Palle had hidden the combination to the safe. But she also recalled a note on the inside of a kitchen cabinet. The note listed the names of each family member, which had something to do with the alarm code. The family was very strict about turning on the alarm whenever they left the house. Palle brought large sums of money from the restaurant and kept the cash in his home office – not that anyone had actually told her about this, but she had often seen him arrive home carrying a special cash

302

bag, which he would then take into his office. Then he would close the door and stay there for a while.

When Terese lived with the family, she was told to memorize the code then in use. It was 520502. She once asked Kristoffer what the names on the note inside the kitchen cabinet meant. Three were written in red and one in green. Then he told her in great secrecy that the green name was the current code, and they changed the colour of the name every time they changed the code. She had to promise, cross her heart and hope to die that she would never tell anyone that he'd explained the system to her. She promised. To make the code easier to remember, it was always the birthdate of one of the family members. 520502 was Susanne's birthdate. But now it had obviously been changed. So she just needed to remember the birthdates of the other family members. Palle had celebrated his birthday while she lived with them. It was in July. But what day and what year? She remembered that he was a little older than Susanne. Maybe by three years.

She tried various combinations without success. Degen kept looking at his watch. He was clearly itching with impatience. What about the kids? She remembered their birthdate because they were born the day before Christmas Eve. Kristoffer had told her that. How old were they now? They must be twelve. She did a quick calculation to work out the year of their birth. Even though it was so cold that her breath came out in a big cloud, she could feel drops of sweat on her forehead. Finally, she decided that they must have been born in 1981. With trembling fingers, she tapped in the code. The alarm switched off.

She took a deep breath and pressed the door handle down.

Malin and Sofia had been taking power walks together ever since they first met on the day they happened to drop off their kids at the nursery at the same time. By now, their children were teenagers, but they had still kept up the routine. Three times a week they would meet, always early in the morning, an hour before breakfast and before their families awoke. All year round, no matter what the weather, they would walk briskly as they discussed all sorts of topics: job situations, parenting problems, general gossip and their marital relationships. The latter was a favourite subject, and they kept returning to it again and again, especially lately. Maybe this had something to do with their age. The children were growing up fast, so they now had more space and time to think about their own needs.

They crossed Almedalen and walked down towards the harbour. It was only a little past six o'clock on a beautiful, quiet morning.

'If you've been together as long as we have, everything gets to be so predictable,' complained Sofia as they strode along the dock. 'You know exactly what's going to happen at all times. You know your husband better than a pair of old shoes. Our marriage fell asleep years ago and has gone stagnant. So what do we do to inject some life into it? Buy more expensive wine for dinner or take a trip to a more exotic destination and convince ourselves that we're happy? But don't you think we're just fooling ourselves? Life goes on, the days come and go, but nothing happens. It's really getting to me. I think I'm going to go mad with boredom.'

Malin was listening with only half an ear. She'd heard this same complaint many times before. Suddenly, she stopped.

'Look. What's that?'

On the ground in front of them were several dark patches.

'Is that blood?' exclaimed Sofia. She stepped down on to the boat pier, keeping her eyes fixed on the ground. The patches continued on past the moored pleasure boats.

'It must be from a fishing boat,' said Malin, who was still standing on the dock. 'Just forget about it.'

'But there aren't any fishermen around here. We need to find out where the blood came from.'

A mixture of fear and excitement was audible in Sofia's voice. Malin stayed where she was while Sofia went on alone. The bloodstains led to a big motorboat at the very end of the pier. Without hesitation, Sofia climbed on board.

'What are you doing?' shouted Malin.

'The blood came from the boat! I just need to find out if anyone needs—'

She fell silent abruptly.

On the deck she saw a man whose head had been practically severed from his body.

Sofia was no longer bored.

It was very dark in the bedroom. The pain in his head was almost gone, his mouth was dry and his tongue felt thick. Knutas reached over to the nightstand for his glass of water, which was half full. The water was lukewarm, but it tasted fine. Then he noticed that something was different. He could hear someone breathing. For a microsecond he thought that Lina had come home, and his first reaction was relief.

He turned over and discovered a small figure curled up on the edge of the bed. On Lina's side. The hair sticking up from the covers was dark, the cheek suntanned. On the shoulder he saw a butterfly tattoo. That was something he'd never seen or even known about. Cautiously, he reached out, wanting to stroke that shoulder. But he stopped in mid-air and drew back his hand. What was Karin doing in his bed?

He sank back against the soft, downy pillow and stared up at the ceiling. He tried to recall what had happened last night. He'd been chasing Degen, who had hit him over the head. Then he'd been taken to hospital. The diagnosis was concussion. After that he'd been sent home in a taxi. The children were visiting Lina in Copenhagen. He could vaguely remember that Karin had come over sometime later in the evening. But after that he drew a blank.

He turned on to his side to check the time. Five thirty. He didn't know how long he'd been asleep. His head felt heavy but no longer throbbed.

He crept out of bed and went into the bathroom. He took a long shower and washed his hair. Then he dabbed on some aftershave before returning to the bedroom. Karin still seemed to be sleeping. He put on clean underwear and crawled back into bed. He didn't want to give up the unreal feeling of lying in the same bed as Karin.

When he lifted the covers he saw that she had on only knickers and a vest. She was turned away from him. Her body was so small, her limbs so slender. The complete opposite of Lina. He wondered why she had decided to sleep in his bed. What did she mean by doing that?

He turned on to his side, keeping his distance as he looked at her shoulder and her hair. He wanted to reach out and touch her but didn't dare. At that moment she stretched, yawned and turned over. In the dim light her face was now right in front of his.

He wanted to see how she looked, so he switched on the bedside lamp. She grunted and quickly disappeared under the covers.

'Good morning,' he whispered.

She peeked out. Only her brown eyes were visible.

'Good morning.'

'May I ask what you're doing in my bed?'

'I'm taking care of you. You're ill.'

'I don't feel ill.'

'That's great. I must have cured you.'

Her eyes sparkled. Knutas now reached out his hand to pull back the covers, which hid half her face.

'Hello,' he said gently. 'Mind if I have a look at you?'

She smiled, revealing the familiar gap in her teeth. He'd never seen it so close before. He moved nearer, until his face was only centimetres away from hers. He wanted to kiss those soft lips and put his arms around her. The strong attraction he now felt made him dizzy. He noticed that he was shaking. She lay there motionless, without saying a word. As if she were waiting.

Just as Knutas was about to reach for her, the shrill ringing of a phone pierced the room.

The sun shone high above Visby harbour; the boats bobbed on the glittering water. The warmth of summer still lingered. It would have been an idyllic sight were it not for the crime-scene tape, the police vehicles and the forensics officers wearing gloves as they combed the wharf area, looking for evidence. A cluster of passers-by had stopped to gawp at what was going on, and reporters had already gathered outside the blue-and-white police cordon.

Knutas and Jacobsson, who had been so rudely interrupted when they were about to have a romantic interlude, arrived together from Bokströmsgatan. They were escorted over to the boat at the centre of all the action. There they were harshly brought back to reality and immediately had to step into their professional roles. For the moment, the magic was gone.

When they caught sight of the body, they were instantly reminded of images from the day when Jocke Eriksson was found murdered in the outhouse. There was no doubt this was the same killer. The victim's throat had been slashed in the same way, and the blood had gushed out to soak his whole chest. Countless bloodstains were also spattered over the entire deck. Jacobsson had to press a tissue to her mouth.

'Did you find any ID on him?' Knutas asked scene of crime officer Erik Sohlman, who was busily taking skin scrapings from under the victim's fingernails.

'Look at this.' Sohlman turned over the victim's wrist. 'You were right. He has the exact same tattoo as Jocke Eriksson.'

'Anything else?'

'His wallet and mobile are gone, but we did find something in his jacket pocket. Just wait a minute while I finish this.'

Knutas waited patiently as he tried to focus on what the deceased man looked like, while at the same time blocking out the horror of the scene. This was undoubtedly the man in the hat who had been in the church and then rushed out. As he fled, he had dropped his hat and revealed a shiny, black mane of shoulder-length hair. His hair looked just as beautiful and vibrant now, though everything else about him had changed.

Knutas looked around. Jacobsson had already left the boat and was standing on the dock talking to a police officer. She had probably seen enough.

Sohlman had now finished collecting material from under the victim's fingernails. From a box he took out a plastic bag containing a small pill packet.

'Have a look,' he said triumphantly. 'This was the one thing the killer missed.'

He handed the bag to Knutas.

It was a small blister pack of cortisone tablets. And affixed to the packet was a label. Knutas smoothed out the plastic bag to read what it said: '750519 González, Diego.' With a pleased expression, he looked up at his colleague.

'Bingo!'

Pia Lilja dropped Johan off at the police cordon and then drove around the harbour and parked the TV van on the other side. She climbed over a wall, carrying her camera and gear, and made her way to the other pier, beyond the spot where the body had been found. On this side there were no police barriers. If she could manage to get up on one of the packing cases lined up along the edge, she would have a perfect view of the boat and the dead man. She realized they wouldn't be able to use any of those images for their TV report, but she still wanted to gather all the material she possibly could. The more footage, the better. This new murder was such a big story that at any moment a regular invasion of photographers and reporters would descend upon Visby. Pia wanted to be the first to get footage, and she also wanted it to be the best.

Right now, the body was still clearly visible, but the police would soon put up some sort of covering to block it from view. She thought they'd probably leave the body on the boat until the ME arrived. The next instant, she heard a police helicopter approaching from the sea. Apparently, the ME was on his way.

She was sweating in the heat. She studied the packing cases stacked on top of each other, trying to work out how she could climb up on them. She was looking for the best footholds. She was glad she had such long legs.

She pushed a few wisps of hair out of her eyes, hoisted the camera on to her shoulder and began climbing. It wasn't easy, and several times she almost lost her balance. She knew this was risky. If she dropped the camera, it would be all over. Plus the camera was worth at least a hundred thousand kronor. But it's probably insured, she thought as she climbed higher.

Johan stood beyond the police tape, feeling his frustration grow. A man had been found dead. That was all he knew. But it was easy to conclude the death was a homicide, considering the number of police detectives who were on the scene, not to mention all the forensics officers who were collecting evidence. The reporters kept vying to wring a few comments from the officers, but they were largely unsuccessful. For the moment Johan could do little more than watch and wait.

The crowd of spectators grew by the minute. The crime, whatever it entailed, had been committed in the middle of the harbour area. He was starting to wonder if it was somehow connected to the Jocke Eriksson murder. Suddenly, his mobile rang. When he took the call, he heard Pia's excited voice.

'This is so big. You have no idea.'

'What do you mean?'

'I managed to climb up on a bunch of packing crates on the other side of the pier, and I have a clear view of the whole boat. You know what?'

'No. What?'

'There's a dead man on the deck and a ton of blood all over the place. Luckily, I brought along a telephoto lens, and I can see the poor guy has had his throat slashed.'

'My god! Just like Jocke Eriksson.'

'And guess what else. The murdered man is the guy we think is Degen. The one who ran out of the church along with that woman.'

Johan swallowed hard.

'Are you sure it's him?'

'Yeah. I am. I'm absolutely positive.'

Everyone's eyes were fixed on Knutas as the investigative team gathered for a meeting later that morning. Only Wittberg, who was in the middle of a phone conversation, was missing. When Knutas passed his office, Wittberg had signalled that he would come as soon as he could. Since the phone call seemed to be about something important, Knutas had decided not to interrupt.

'As you all know, we now have another murder on our hands,' Knutas began. He grimaced when he realized what a poor choice of words that was. Then he cleared his throat and went on. 'The dead man's throat was slashed in exactly the same manner as Jocke Eriksson's. The victim's wallet and mobile were gone, but in his jacket pocket we found a packet of cortisone tablets labelled with his name and date of birth: Diego González, 19 May 1975.'

'Just as we thought,' said Sohlman.

'González had been convicted of a number of different crimes,' Knutas continued. 'The Stockholm police know him well. He was in and out of prison his whole life. He was registered at an address in Vällingby, which is a suburb north-west of Stockholm. The victim had the same tattoo on his wrist as Eriksson. I think we can assume that the initials "J" and "D" stand for their names. The third initial must be for the name of the as yet unidentified woman who was in the church and fled with González when Karin and I caught sight of them.'

He cast a glance at his colleague and for a nano-second felt himself get lost in her big, doe-like eyes. He pushed aside the image of her wearing only underwear and turned to look at Sohlman.

'OK, Erik, tell us about the crime scene.'

Sohlman got up and pulled down the screen at the front of the room. Then he went over to his computer to project the photos. Jacobsson, who sat closest to the switch, turned off the lights. The first image was horrify-ing. In the middle of Visby harbour, among the bobbing pleasure boats, a blood-soaked man was slumped on the deck inside the cockpit of a luxury motorboat. The contrast was so extreme because of all the blood sprayed over the gleaming white surfaces of the boat. The victim was leaning forward with a gaping wound in his throat.

'This is Diego González, also called Degen,' said Sohlman. 'Like Jocke Eriksson, he was killed by a deep gash to his throat. He was also stabbed multiple times in the stomach. All indications are that the murder occurred after a fight. González has defensive wounds on his arms and shoulders. There are also skin scrapings under his fingernails, which we're sending to the lab for DNA analysis.'

'How long had he been dead when he was found?' asked Kihlgård.

'I'd say eight or nine hours. That means the murder was committed sometime around ten or eleven last night. The gash in his throat was done by a left-handed individual, which is further confirmation that we're dealing with the same perpetrator. The ME flew here by helicopter this morning, and he's at the harbour now, examining the victim at the scene.'

No one spoke but they continued to study further photos.

'So now our perp has killed Jocke Eriksson and Degen González,' said Jacobsson pensively. 'That means there's probably one more potential victim. The unidentified woman. The third bank robber.'

'Whose name probably starts with the letter "T",' said Knutas. 'But who is she? Which names for women start with "T"?'

'Tullikki,' teased Jacobsson.

'What sort of name is that?' asked Knutas, frowning. 'And how the hell do you spell it?'

'Just like it sounds,' replied Jacobsson with a grin.

Knutas couldn't help smiling. He felt a surge of warmth inside, and his knees went weak as he blushed like a schoolboy. He hoped no one noticed. It wasn't good to be sitting here joking in the midst of this highly serious situation.

His thoughts were interrupted when Wittberg came into the room.

'Did you find out anything?' asked Knutas, even though it was clear from Wittberg's expression that he was bursting to tell them something.

'It turns out that Degen González has a connection to Gotland. He was sent to the Hassela young offenders institution in Klintehamn and stayed there for almost a year, from November 1993 until September 1994.'

'In Klintehamn?' said Jacobsson. 'How old was he back then? Eighteen? Nineteen? And Jocke Eriksson lived in Tofta, which isn't far from there. And they were born in the same year.'

'Patrik Rosén too!' exclaimed Kihlgård. 'He's the same age, and he's from Klintehamn.'

'Good. Now we're getting somewhere,' said Knutas. 'We need to find out if Rosén recognizes the name Diego González. And someone needs to go out to Hassela in Klintehamn. The rest of us will keep on mapping out the last hours of González's life. Since the harbour murder has already attracted a lot of attention from the public and in the media, we'll have to hold a press conference this afternoon. Can you make the arrangements?' he asked Norrby.

The police spokesman nodded, with a rather grudging expression.

Kihlgård got up from the table.

'When in god's name are we going to get any food in this place?'

1994

The minute they stepped inside, Terese was seized with a feeling of unreality. The smell of the house was so familiar, and yet she was here under different circumstances, with an entirely different purpose in mind. They paused in the front hall to listen for any sounds. No one seemed to have heard them come in. The pale glow of the moon streamed through the window, lighting up the walls and the cold stone floor. The crowns of the pine trees outside swayed faintly in the breeze, sending shadows dancing across the sparsely furnished space. Terese immediately headed for the home office at the other end of the house. The door to her old room stood ajar. She felt a pang in her chest at the sight of that luxurious bed.

She stopped when she noticed on the wall a framed photograph that hadn't been there before. It was a black-and-white picture. She saw herself, suntanned, happy and relaxed, together with the twins. How healthy she looked. Her eyes sparkled and her teeth gleamed. In the background was the huge sandy beach at Tofta. The camera had caught all three of them laughing. She remembered that day so well. Susanne had taken the snapshot this summer when they'd gone to Tofta to swim. Tears welled up in her eyes, and she brushed them away with annoyance. This was no time to go soft and weepy. I'm just tired, she thought. It was close to five in the morning. Quickly, she turned away and continued down the corridor.

She heard Degen and Jocke whispering excitedly in the kitchen, followed by a faint rattling sound. They must be gathering up some things. She chose not to think about that. She needed to focus on what was most important. The door to Palle's home office was closed. Panic surged inside her. She just hoped it wasn't locked. That was a distinct possibility, she now realized, since the family had been away. Palle might have taken extra security precautions. She reached out to turn the door handle, and to her great relief the door opened, with a slight squeak. The desk stood in its usual place, and the room looked exactly as it had when she lived with the family up to a few months earlier.

She hurried over to the window, desperately hoping that he hadn't changed the place where he'd hidden the combination to the safe. She checked underneath the windowsill. There it was. The slip of paper was still taped there. Simple. The combination, which consisted of eight digits, was not one she recognized. He must have changed it later in the summer. She'd discovered this hiding place when she'd come into the room looking for money, but she was drunk and ended up on the floor after stumbling. When she'd glanced up, she noticed the slip of paper and thought it looked strange. As if it had been taped there for a specific reason. And it had been.

But that was right before her stay with the family ended, and she'd never had a chance to try out the combination back then. Now she wrote the numbers on a piece of paper that she'd brought along. Then she took down the books on the shelf that hid the safe. Carefully, she pressed in the numbers and pulled the door open with ease.

Terese gasped when she saw what was inside, and for a moment she lost all sense of time and space. There were stacks of thousand-kronor bills. There had to be more than a hundred thousand kronor. She also saw several boxes piled on top of each other. She couldn't resist opening one. It was lined with dark-blue silk and held a silver necklace as well as a pair of earrings with glittering gemstones. She swallowed hard and turned to look at the door. Not a sound was audible. She didn't dare call out to the others, for fear of waking the family, who were all in bed upstairs.

Instead, she got out the cloth bag she'd brought along and began stuffing everything from the safe inside it. The sight of all that cash was thrilling. This was going to solve all their problems. It was more than enough, and there was plenty of room in the bag for everything. Then she closed the safe, stuck the paper with the combination in her pocket and checked to make sure she hadn't disturbed anything before she switched off the light and left the room. Only when she was back out in the corridor did she see what the other two were doing. They were in the living room, in the process of taking down a big painting from the wall above the sofa.

'What are you doing?' hissed Terese. 'We said we'd only take what was in the safe.'

'But this is a fucking Andy Warhol. He signed it himself. Check it out.' Degen shone his torch at the signature. 'Even I know this thing's worth a fortune.'

'OK, but hurry up. I've emptied the safe, and there's more than enough cash. We need to get out of here.'

The painting was so cumbersome it would never fit in any bag. Degen simply stuck it under his arm. Jocke grabbed his own bag, which looked heavy. Terese realized that, contrary to what they had all agreed, her two friends had been helping themselves to plenty of things while she emptied the safe.

It was high time for them to leave. Dawn wasn't far off, and they didn't want to be seen driving the van in the area.

'Just one more thing,' whispered Jocke, reaching for a bronze statuette that stood in a niche. He managed to pick it up but then lost his balance and fell full length on to the floor with a crash. The statuette slipped out of his grasp.

Terese froze. The next second she heard the creak of the stairs and someone shouting.

After that everything happened so fast. Even though they had agreed that no weapons were necessary, Jocke pulled a gun out of his jacket pocket. Swiftly, he turned, and in the same instant that Terese caught sight of tousled hair, frightened eyes and a suntanned face, a shot rang out, and Susanne fell to the floor in the living room. Blood ran from her chest.

Then a terrified man's voice shouted: 'What the hell is going on here?'

Palle made it down only one step before another shot was fired. He fell forward, and his body lay on the stairs. A slight movement in one arm caused Jocke to fire more shots in quick succession until the man lay still.

Then the worst thing of all happened.

First a panic-stricken voice.

'Mamma! Pappa!'

The gangly boy on the stairs, the terrified look in his eyes when he caught sight of his parents, motionless and covered in blood. And his expression when the bullet struck his stomach, when his body was pierced by a terrible force, and he fell, too. Jocke then fired several more shots.

Terese reacted instinctively. She ran up the stairs, tore off her gloves and felt for a pulse, sobbing.

'What the fuck!' shouted Degen. He grabbed hold of Jocke and tore the gun out of his hand. He picked up the bags filled with loot and shoved Jocke in front of him. 'Come on! We have to get out of here!'

Terese came to her senses and obeyed mechanically. All three of them rushed out of the house and over to the parked van. Terese noticed that tears were pouring down her face.

The image of how Kristoffer had died, right in front of her eyes, would haunt her for the rest of her life.

He was alone in the house. Outwardly, everything looked the same as it always did. The red-and-white checked curtains at the window gave the place a cosy look, as did the rows of geraniums on the sill. The clock on the kitchen wall ticked quietly. The smell of coffee still lingered from breakfast. He wiped a few crumbs from the table. Calmly and methodically he filled the dishwasher, then turned on the radio. The same news was repeated over and over: This morning a man was found dead in Visby harbour. The police suspect murder. Blah, blah, blah.

He heard what they said, but it had nothing to do with him. He no longer cared about anything. He felt as if he were standing outside of it all. Things hadn't gone as he'd expected, but that didn't really matter. Degen González had turned out to be as strong as an ox, and for a moment he'd been afraid of being overpowered there on the wharf. He'd been chased up on to the boat, but then he'd managed to deliver a blow to his opponent's stomach, and that had decided how it would all end. The sight of blood gushing out of his victim was the stimulus he had needed to keep going. He was totally focused and experienced a feeling close to pure joy as he slashed Degen's throat. Maybe he was going mad. Yet he felt an inner satisfaction, a sense of calm that he hadn't experienced in years. Justice had been done, order had been restored. There was no other path to take.

He poured himself the last of the coffee and went outside to sit on the terrace at the back of the house. Sheep were peacefully grazing in the pasture, the church gleamed white against the blue sky in the distance. Kristoffer was at school, and Marianne was at work. He'd taken the whole week off from his job at the estate agent's, saying that he needed to spend time redecorating the bathroom.

In fact, he was quite proud of himself. It was amazing that he'd managed to pull everything off so far, without arousing the slightest suspicion either at home or at work. The washing machine was going, and in a few minutes he would set about cleaning the inside of the car.

He finished his coffee. The most important part still remained. He had been saving her until last. First, she had to go through the same thing that he'd experienced: losing the people who meant the most to her.

He took the photo out of his pocket and saw her smiling up at him. The sun shone on her hair.

He hoped she realized what was in store for her.

Johan and Pia were back at the editorial office, having a quick sushi lunch in front of their computers, when the receptionist rang to say they had a visitor. They looked at each other in surprise. They weren't expecting anyone, and it was rare for someone to turn up there without phoning in advance.

'Who is it?' asked Johan.

'He says his name is Sonny Jonsson,' whispered the receptionist on the phone. 'He looks like he's from some motorcycle club. He's wearing leathers and one of those waistcoats that says "Road Warriors" on the back. Lots of piercings and tattoos. Looks really tough.'

'Don't worry. He's OK,' Johan told her. 'I'll be right down to get him.'

It was the day after the murder of Diego González, and Johan and Pia were up to their eyes in work. The main office in Stockholm had decided to send over an additional reporter and camera person to help out. They were expected to arrive on Gotland later that afternoon. It was a good thing, because the two of them couldn't possibly handle everything on their own.

Sonny Jonsson had a strained look on his face. He declined the offer of coffee, and then they all took seats in the small conference room.

'So what's going on?' asked Pia.

Sonny ran his hand over his shaven head.

'I'm only telling you this because Degen was murdered, but it has to be off the record. OK? You can't breathe a word about this information coming from me.'

'Sure. We always protect our sources,' said Johan. 'But we can't promise not to use whatever you tell us in our reports if we think it's important. We won't divulge where we got the information.'

'Not even to the police?'

'No. Not even to them. I guarantee it.'

Sonny leaned forward and lowered his voice, as if afraid that someone else might hear what he said, even though the room was on the top floor of the building.

'What I'm going to tell you is based on my own suspicions. That's all. I haven't told this to anyone else, not even Maddis. OK?'

'Sure,' said Johan and Pia in unison, giving him their full attention.

'Well, it was a fucking awful thing that happened here on Gotland sixteen years ago. In 1994. A whole family was shot in their house up in Högklint. You heard about it, right?'

'Of course we remember what happened,' said Pia. 'Don't we?' She poked Johan in the side. 'Everybody in Sweden was talking about it. The police never caught anyone, and the case was never solved. It's been discussed lots of times on various TV shows, most recently as a feature on *Wanted*.'

'Exactly,' said Johan. 'As I remember, the killings occurred in connection with a burglary.'

'That's right,' said Sonny. 'The family was in bed asleep when the burglars struck. The mother, father and one of the twin boys died, but the other brother survived. He was shot, too, but he managed to pull through.'

'And?' said Johan. 'What's your point?'

'The fatal shootings in Högklint occurred in the autumn of 1994. During that time Jocke was often in Stockholm, and we didn't have much contact with each other. But I know that he was spending a lot of time with Degen and that bird. And, by the way, I remember now what her name was. Terese.'

'My god!' exclaimed Johan. 'Are you sure?'

'I know at least her name started with a "T". I'm positive about that. Like in Jocke's tattoo. "J", "D" and "T". And I'm pretty sure it was Terese.'

'Do you recall her surname?' Johan asked.

'No. But I remember that the attempted rape happened the summer before the family was killed, and that Jocke stayed away from the club – and I think from Gotland – for several months afterwards.'

Sonny stood up.

'That's all I have to say. I'm telling you this for Jocke's sake. So now it's up to you to do more investigating, if you like.'

He headed for the door but then turned around.

'He was a decent guy. It was all the fault of those fucking drugs.'

As soon as Sonny left, Johan and Pia sat down at their computers. Johan got the first hit.

'Her name is Terese Larsson, and she was a foster child who had been placed with the family in Högklint.'

Pia leaned back in her chair.

'Good lord!'

'She came to stay with the family in May 1994, but she left only four months later. In August.'

'And you think that—'

'I'm starting to think that the murders of Jocke and Degen have something to do with what happened in Högklint.'

Pia stared at him.

'But then that means—'

'That Terese Larsson is next in line.'

Terese was huddled on the window seat, staring at the deserted harbour area spreading out from the hotel. She had to phone the receptionist to ask if she could keep the room for a few more days. No problem. It was low season. She was badly in need of a smoke, but she had no more cigarettes, and she had to avoid going out at all costs. Although, sooner or later, she would be forced to do so, since there was no room service in this shitty hotel. They hadn't thought of that when they booked the room. They had planned to stay only one or two nights. But now Degen was dead, and here she sat. Stunned, paralysed, panic-stricken. The only thing she could bring herself to do was follow the news coverage on the radio and the TV.

The darkness of the past twenty-four hours had brought an endless pain; it was the worst night she'd ever been through. She had waited and waited. Called Degen's phone number over and over without getting an answer. She was filled with worry and dread but still hoped he would finally turn up. And give her a perfectly natural explanation for why he'd been gone so long.

Towards dawn she was seized with the icy realization that he was not coming back. Then she became convinced the police had caught him and it was only a matter of time before they knocked on the door of the room. Degen had taken a key card with him, so it would be easy for the police to find the right hotel. But no one came. When she listened to the morning news on the radio, she found out why Degen had never returned.

She had wailed her grief into a pillow, curled up in a foetal position, and whimpered for hours. Thoughts raced through her head. She had no idea what to do next. On and off, she felt an inexplicable calm come over her, and her mind felt totally empty. She lay on the bed, filled with apathy and staring vacantly into space.

By afternoon her stomach was screaming with hunger, and her body burned with a craving for cigarettes. She was going to have to go out. There was no other option. Yet she didn't really care any more. Let the cops come and get me, she thought. Or that fucking murderer. Just go ahead and kill me. I have nothing left to live for.

The only people who meant anything to her were gone.

She took a shower and got dressed. Then she put on her big sunglasses. Made sure to put her wallet, mobile and key card in her handbag. She didn't want to speak to anyone at the front desk.

Then she opened the door and stepped out into the silent hotel corridor.

This new interview with Patrik Rosén had produced results. He must have got the wind up him, thought Knutas, as he sat in his office and filled his pipe while he read the notes Jacobsson had taken during the interview.

Rosén had suddenly decided to come clean and admit that he had been selling marijuana to Jocke Eriksson for years. He grew his own plants at home, which he claimed to harvest only for his personal use, with one exception. Jocke was an old friend; they'd known each other since they were kids. Rosén hadn't mentioned the fact that they knew each other because he was scared that his drug dealings with Jocke would come to light. After he was assaulted in the restaurant, he'd apparently decided it would be better to accept whatever legal punishment he might have to endure. Or maybe he'd received even worse threats.

It would be worth talking to the members of the motorcycle club again, thought Knutas. Jocke and Sonny Jonsson had had a close friendship, and the latter had expressed concern over his friend's use of drugs. So the assault could have been a form of revenge, since Patrik had supplied some of the drugs that had been Jocke's undoing.

*

Wittberg knocked on the door of Knutas's office. He looked pale under his suntan as he held up the papers he was carrying and waved them in the air to show his boss.

'I think I've worked out how everything is connected. And I know who the woman is. The third robber.'

'What? Are you kidding? Sit down and tell me.'

Wittberg sank down on to a visitors' chair in front of Knutas's desk.

'It's an awful story,' he began, shaking his head. 'Do you remember what happened in Högklint in the autumn of 1994? The family that was shot by burglars?'

'Yes,' said Knutas, looking confused. 'I didn't handle the case. Another detective was in charge, but I definitely remember it. And the perpetrators got away. But didn't one of the sons survive?'

'Exactly,' said Wittberg grimly. 'Listen to this. I started checking on that car rental. The killer rented the Toyota Corolla under the name of Alvar Björkman. Remember that we found only a few people in Sweden with that name, and here on Gotland there was only one: an old man living on Fårö. But then I checked for women with the maiden name of Björkman who live on Gotland. That was how I traced Anna Björkman, whose married name is Magnusson. She lives in Vibbe. What interested me about her was that she has a sister whose married name was Stenfors and who lived in Högklint. The sister turned out to be the mother of the family who died on that November night in 1994. Susanne Stenfors.'

Knutas tapped his chin.

'And?'

'Do you remember what the father's name was? The one who was also killed?'

'No,' said Knutas, perplexed. 'I recall that he owned a restaurant, but—'

Wittberg gave Knutas a long look and leaned forward. 'That's right. The Catch 22 down on the harbour.'

'So what was the father's name?'

'He was called Palle. Remember? Palle Stenfors. But his real name was Per-Alvar.'

Knutas stared at Wittberg. He was dumbfounded.

'The car was rented under the name of Alvar Björkman. The perpetrator was actually giving us a hint, but we didn't get it. Susanne and Palle Stenfors had twins: two boys, Daniel and Kristoffer. They were twelve when it happened. One of them died, but the other survived. Daniel Stenfors was wounded, but he managed to pull through. And you know what?'

Knutas shook his head.

'The family had a foster child living with them that summer. Before the shooting. A girl from Stockholm who'd had a rocky childhood, since her parents were junkies and alcoholics. She was questioned after the murders, but she had a cast-iron alibi. Nothing was discovered linking her to the crime. She had moved away several months earlier, since things weren't working out between her and the Stenfors family. Do you know what the girl's name was? Terese Larsson.'

'"T" as in Terese,' said Knutas, and he reached for the phone.

He poured the last of the coffee from the Thermos and sat down at the kitchen table. Through the window he could see that a few leaves were starting to turn red. A portent of autumn. It reminded him of back then, early November 1994. He remembered looking out of the window at the blazing red leaves on the trees when he woke up in hospital and found out that his whole life had been shattered. After that everything was black. As if a shutter had been pulled down over his life and destroyed everything. Everything he'd once had. He was only twelve years old. At that moment something inside him was crushed. Something that could never be repaired.

It was through his work as an estate agent that he was one day suddenly confronted with his past and forced back to that fateful night. He had repressed most of what happened. In spite of intense psychological counselling immediately afterwards, followed by years of therapy, he couldn't recall anything that might have helped the police. All he knew was that there were three intruders. And they all wore masks.

On that night in early November he and his family had gone to bed late. They had arrived home sooner than expected from Gran Canaria, where they always used to spend the autumn holiday. The restaurant had suffered a serious leak, and his father needed to come home. His parents had decided the whole family might as well return at the same time. He remembered that he and Kristoffer didn't really mind. Coming home earlier meant they would have a chance to spend time with their friends during the remaining days of the school holidays. They had already made plans to go to the swimming pool with Rasmus the next day. Rasmus's father had promised to take them.

That night a deafening bang had awakened him. He later realized it was a gunshot he'd heard. He jumped out of bed and, when he opened his bedroom door upstairs, he heard screams and more shots. He dropped to the floor and then squirmed his way forward to look down and see what was happening. Three masked strangers were frantically shouting at each other. One of them was holding a big black sack.

His mother lay lifeless and covered in blood on the living-room floor. She was wearing a pink nightgown. He saw his father collapse on the stairs as Kristoffer was on his way down. One of the masked intruders had a gun, which he was firing wildly. Someone screamed. He watched as his brother was shot in the stomach and fell. One of the burglars ran up the stairs and bent over him, muttering something inaudible. The last thing he saw was the burglar in the front hall raise his gun once again.

A burning pain in his head, like fire. And then nothing.

He awoke to find Rasmus's father patting him on the cheek. Then the ambulance. The hospital. The next time he came to, his Aunt Anna was sitting on the edge of his bed. Her face was pale and contorted with pain. It took time before he fully understood what had happened. That his mother, father and Kristoffer were dead. That they no longer existed. That they had all been murdered.

Then came the funeral. The emptiness. He moved in with Aunt Anna and Uncle Björn, who lived in Vibbe, only a few kilometres away. That was where he grew up. And he never returned to the house in Högklint. He never went anywhere near it.

After graduating from university and spending several restless years on the mainland, he came back to Gotland and started working for one of the large estate agents. He met Marianne, who was sixteen years older than him, and they bought a house in the country. She gave him a son, and they named him Kristoffer.

One day he was in charge of an open house viewing at a summer cottage in Åminne. Only a few people turned up, and one of them was a man who was clearly dodgy – probably involved in criminal activities and possibly a drug addict. He brought along a friend who had thick, curly blond hair. The friend was a cheerful and talkative fellow, but he seemed slightly out of it. Daniel noticed that he had a tattoo on his wrist. There was something about that tattoo. Just initials, but he wasn't able to see what they were. He forgot all about it, as he was busy showing the cottage. A few people signed the list to indicate they were interested, including the suspicious guy with the tattooed friend. And that was that.

When Daniel got home in the evening, he couldn't stop thinking about the tattoo. And suddenly he knew where he'd seen it before. He began searching through some old photos. He'd saved everything, not wanting to throw anything out after his family died. And he found the picture he was looking for. Gradually, he realized what must have happened after recalling something that had occurred while Terese was living with them.

She was standing in the kitchen, looking defiant, her long, dark hair hanging loose down her back. She held up her bare arm, fist clenched, to show off her new tattoo. Three letters inscribed on her wrist. The initials of her own name and the names of her two best friends. And now he remembered their names. Jocke and Degen.

In the next instant a fragmentary image flitted through his mind, a memory that took his breath away. He was inside the house at night. Awakened by a scream, a gunshot. First his mother, then his father and Kristoffer. And when his brother fell, a heart-rending shriek. He heard that shriek again. He could hear it echoing inside his head right now.

She had been disguised from head to toe. It had been impossible to tell that the burglar was a girl. She rushed up the stairs to where Kristoffer lay and tore off her gloves. That was when he saw it. The tattoo on her wrist. The next instant he was also shot and everything went black. He had never been able to remember exactly what happened. Not until now, after the open house, when he saw that tattoo.

He finally understood how everything was connected. And he was filled with rage.

Terese walked briskly up the hill to the Statoil petrol station, which sold both groceries and takeaway food. There she loaded up on everything she thought she might need for the next few days. Plus a whole carton of cigarettes, just to be on the safe side. She was longing for something strong to drink, but it was too far and too risky to go over to the state off-licence. The popular Östercentrum shopping centre would be crawling with police. Luckily, Degen had brought a bottle of whisky in his suitcase, and they hadn't yet opened it.

Weighed down by her purchases, she went back to the hotel. She was on high alert, but hadn't noticed anyone following her.

She ate some food, opened the window and then got into bed with the whisky after piling the pillows behind her back. She lit a cigarette and slowly exhaled a cloud of smoke. She was thinking about Jocke and Degen. Both had been murdered in the most brutal and cold-blooded way, but she refused to allow herself to cry right now. What the hell was she going to do? Who was this killer? And what did he want?

She held up her wrist and looked at the tattoo. Gently, she ran her finger over the three letters. Their initials intertwined, symbolizing the fact that they would always stay together. They were the only people who meant anything to her.

She remembered the day they got the tattoos. They went to a tattoo parlour in Visby and then celebrated afterwards with a few beers at a place on the harbour. They kept looking at each other's wrists to compare the tattoos. They were all thrilled. When she got home she had shown her wrist to Kristoffer and Daniel, and they were suitably impressed. Tears welled up in her eyes as she thought about them and that whole tragedy. And the terrible events of the past few weeks.

The next moment she froze. She sat there, staring into space. Slowly, her thoughts coalesced into a pattern, and the connections began to make sense. Suddenly, she understood why her friends had been killed. It was crystal clear. And she knew who had done it. Somehow he must have found out who they were. After all these years the truth had finally caught up with them.

'But why now?' she whispered into the silence of the room. 'Why did you wait so long?'

She knew it also meant that she was next, and she realized she didn't stand a chance. Either the police would get her, or the killer would. The only question was who would be first.

She raised the whisky bottle to her lips and took a swig. The alcohol deadened the worst of her fear.

Basically, she no longer cared what happened. She had nothing left to live for. Absolutely nothing.

A face appeared in her mind. Kristoffer. His warm brown eyes and thick dark hair, the dimples in his cheeks. He had been so fond of her, looking at her with sheer adoration. For some inexplicable reason, he had liked her just the way she was. And she had killed him, even though she hadn't fired the shot. Snuffed out the life of that young boy who had his whole future ahead of him. All for the sake of a stupid burglary. She didn't deserve to live.

She had killed yet another child. The girl outside the bank who had swerved into the road on her bicycle after the robbery. Because of Terese, two children had lost their chance to grow up. And Susanne and Palle would be alive today if she hadn't thought up that whole burglary idea.

Again she pictured Kristoffer lying on the stairs. She saw him fall and then die right before her eyes. That was the worst thing of all. She couldn't even go to his funeral to show her respect. She had never visited his grave or brought him a single flower.

She took several more swigs of the whisky and then got out of bed.

She now knew what she had to do.

The police immediately sent out an all-ports warning for the two suspects. Lars Norrby issued a press release asking for any leads from the public or any other information pertaining to the two individuals. Reporters started phoning, and Norrby had to handle all the calls himself. The investigative team was totally focused on trying to locate Terese Larsson and Daniel Stenfors as quickly as possible. A patrol car was sent out to the farm in Stenkumla where Stenfors lived, but he was not at home, and his wife thought he was at work. At the estate agent's, the police learned that Stenfors had taken the entire week off. No one knew the whereabouts of the man who had murdered two people in cold blood.

A number of officers were working hard to find Terese Larsson. They assumed she was still on Gotland, so they set about contacting every hotel, youth hostel and cottage-rental service, initially concentrating their efforts on Visby. It didn't take long before they found the hotel near the harbour where a couple calling themselves Mr and Mrs Nilsson had arrived two days earlier.

The receptionist said that she'd paid particular attention to the man and the woman because they had seemed very stressed when they checked in, and then they never left their room. They paid for two nights in advance, and in cash, which was highly unusual. The man had not been seen in the past twenty-four hours. In the morning the woman had rung the front desk from their room to ask if she could stay a few more days, but she couldn't say exactly how long. She had refused to let the cleaner into the room, saying that she didn't want anything done while she was there.

The mysterious guest had left the hotel only once, returning with several carrier bags of food from the Statoil petrol station. According to the receptionist, the woman was in her room now.

Knutas and Jacobsson decided to go over to the hotel in person. They brought along two colleagues in case Terese put up any resistance or tried to flee.

They parked both police vehicles outside and hurried into the lobby. The woman at reception identified herself as the clerk Knutas had spoken to on the phone.

'She left in a cab,' the clerk said apologetically, as if it were her fault the woman had got away.

'Bloody hell!' exclaimed Knutas. 'Do you know where she was going?'

'No. I'm sorry. I haven't got a clue.'

'Could you please ring the taxi company for me?' said Knutas with annoyance, as he turned to his colleagues. 'Karin and I will follow the route of the cab. In the meantime, I'd like you to search the room. But get Sohlman over here, just in case. You never know what we might find in there.'

'I have Gotland Taxis on the line,' said the receptionist, handing the phone to Knutas.

'Thanks,' he said with a nod. 'This is Detective Superintendent Anders Knutas. We're looking for a woman who ordered a cab to pick her up at this hotel about an hour ago. Can you find out where it went?'

'What's the name?'

'Try Nilsson.'

A few minutes later they had their answer.

'The cab dropped her off at Norra Cemetery at 11.57.'

'What's the time?'

The cemetery was a kilometre outside Visby. It was beautifully situated on a hillside that extended along the coast. The trees were gradually beginning to change colour. Autumn was on its way.

Terese got out of the taxi and looked around. She had never been here before and had no idea where the family was buried. But she had all the time in the world, and there wasn't another person in sight. The neatly raked gravel paths stretched out before her. Slowly, she made her way forward, reading some of the inscriptions on the headstones, looking at the flower arrangements. All the graves seemed to be well cared for. Everything was lovely and well tended, which showed a real respect for the deceased.

It didn't take her long to find what she was looking for. The headstone was dark grey with a gold inscription: Palle Stenfors, Susanne Stenfors and Kristoffer Stenfors. All dead on the same day. 4 November 1994.

She knelt down.

They had been willing to take her in. She could have had a family. But how had she responded? How had she thanked them? She was overwhelmed by so much pain she could hardly breathe.

When she calmed down, she decided what her next step would be. It was unavoidable.

She got out her mobile from her purse and rang for a taxi. She had to go back.

To the place where it all began.

The cab drove through the city and then continued south. Terese remembered when Viveka had picked her up at the airport on that first day on Gotland. It had felt so liberating to get away from Bagarmossen and her parents. Back then, everything was new. Back then, she didn't know what awaited her.

Her heart beat faster as the cab passed Kneippbyn. She hadn't been back here in all these years, but the road was so familiar. They drove past the turn-off to the viewpoint at Högklint and continued uphill. Finally, the cab turned on to a small gravel road leading up to the remote location of the solitary house. She asked the driver to stop before reaching the driveway, paid the fare and got out. She wanted to walk the rest of the way.

Gravel crunched under her feet. A few houses had been built nearby since she'd lived here, but they seemed to be summer cottages. She didn't see a single person or car.

An icy shiver ran down her back when she caught sight of the fence next to the narrow drive. It looked exactly the same. She paused to light a cigarette, then continued on, but at a slower pace. When the house came into view between the pine trees, she felt a throbbing inside her head. The property was unchanged. The land stretched out before her, rock-strewn but otherwise bare and flat. The white plastered limestone house stood on a rise, untouched by rain and wind. The distinctive wooden shutters had been removed, and a guest cottage had been built nearby. Otherwise, everything looked the same.

There was no car in the driveway, and the whole place seemed deserted. She checked the name on the letterbox. It had been changed. It now said 'Martland', which was not a name she recognized. She opened the gate and slowly approached the house. She saw the big windows of the living room that reached from floor to ceiling. She saw the patio furniture on the wooden terrace. Further on she saw the window of her own bedroom. She recalled lying in that wonderfully soft bed, listening to the silence and looking out of the window. How she had savoured the sense of calm that enveloped her there.

She went over to the living-room windows and peered inside. New furniture. Not the same minimalist style she remembered.

Suddenly, images began flashing through her mind. Jocke holding the gun, Susanne screaming as she fell. Palle, who was shot before he even understood what was happening. And then Kristoffer. Screams. Chaos. Dead bodies. They had fled in panic.

Degen had said they still had time to catch the ferry. Then came the unbearable waiting at the terminal, all three of them convinced the police would arrive and arrest them at any second. She was in shock, apathetic. Then they were waved on board with all the other passengers. They had reserved a cabin, and they locked themselves inside. The crossing to the mainland was a nightmare. Hours of terror, expecting the cabin door to be torn open as the police rushed in. But nothing happened.

When they drove off the ferry in Nynäshamn, she remembered how Degen's legs were shaking as he smoked non-stop. But they saw no police on the dock. They drove straight back to the run-down block of flats in Hagsätra where they had been staying temporarily. Somehow they'd managed to bring with them all the cash and most of the other loot they'd gathered.

For weeks they simply lay low. The police contacted Terese, and she was certain they'd be arrested. But they merely interviewed her several times. Her best friend Jessica had vouched for her, giving her a watertight alibi. Several cops had searched the flat but found nothing.

For a long time there was speculation in the press that the murders had something to do with Palle's restaurant. It turned out he'd been cooking the books. He'd also been conducting an illegal gambling club at the weekends. The police seemed to put all their efforts into following that theory, which of course led nowhere. The weeks turned into months, and the case remained unsolved.

Degen, Jocke and Terese stayed away from each other for almost a year before daring to re-establish contact. Even then they continued to keep their close friendship secret from the rest of the world, just to be on the safe side.

Suddenly, Terese's thoughts were interrupted by a creaking sound coming from further along the terrace. Abruptly, she turned around.

Someone was coming straight towards her.

Before Knutas could put down the phone, the woman in the dispatch office of the cab company said, 'Wait a sec. A taxi picked up a customer at Norra cemetery fifteen minutes ago.'

'Where was the cab headed? And who was the passenger?'

'Just a minute and I'll contact the driver. I think he still has the customer in his cab.'

Knutas waited tensely, hardly daring to breathe. Then the woman was back.

'He dropped off the customer at Rövar Liljas Väg up in Högklint a couple of minutes ago.'

'And who was his passenger?'

'A woman. She was alone.'

Knutas and Jacobsson ran for their car. Jacobsson hit the accelerator and headed for Högklint.

'She's gone back to the house. Why in the world would she want to go there?' said Knutas grimly.

'That's the big question,' said Jacobsson. 'Although it's not unusual for criminals to return to the scene of their crime. But I'm surprised she would dare. Should we call for back-up?'

349

'Definitely. I'm sure the killer is after her. He might be on her trail this very minute.'

Knutas phoned headquarters and asked for several patrol cars to be sent to the address in Högklint where three members of a family had been murdered sixteen years earlier.

When they turned on to Röver Liljas Väg, Jacobsson slowed down. The area seemed deserted. Only a few houses were visible through the pines, but most of them appeared to be summer cottages that had already been closed up for the winter. The duty officer had given them the address, and they soon found their way to the house, which stood all alone on a hill. There were no cars in the driveway near the garage, so that was where they parked. They took out their service weapons and quickly went up to the front door, looking around them, but there was no one in sight.

Knutas tried the door. As expected, it was locked.

Jacobsson climbed up on to the upstairs balcony to survey the grounds. Suddenly, she gave a shout.

'There's a car parked at the edge of the woods.'

They hurried over there and found a black SUV at the side of the road. Knutas rang a colleague and asked him to check the licence-plate number. He said he would wait.

'The vehicle belongs to a Daniel Stenfors,' said the officer after a moment. 'It's registered to an address in Stenkumla.'

'Damn,' said Knutas.

Just then two patrol cars drove up.

Back-up couldn't have come at a better moment.

Terese didn't recognize him at first. He was tall and brawny. His face was pale, his hair brown and combed smooth. But his eyes were the same dark brown colour. Just like Palle's. And Kristoffer's. She caught only a glimpse of them before she turned on her heel and ran across the grounds, out through the gate and over to the path that wound its way down to the sea. He was close behind. On the cliff she turned left and continued through a sparsely wooded area that extended along the precipice. She could hear him breathing hard. She picked up speed and ran for her life.

After a hundred metres she turned to look over her shoulder and saw that he was still following. She was panic-stricken and yet she also felt an almost elated sense of indifference. Whatever happens, happens, she thought. I don't care if I fall off the cliff and plunge into the sea, or if you cut my throat. Everything is fucked up anyway. But just let me run for a while. Let me run like hell.

Her legs were pumping mechanically, as if of their own accord, carrying her over tree roots and rocks, traversing the rough terrain. Thirty metres below, waves were striking the stone-covered shore. A dark line of birds screeched as they flew past overhead. She thought about Jocke and Degen as she ran. I'll be joining you soon, she thought. Soon I'll be with you. Soon we'll see each other again, my heroes.

And she kept on running.

The police split up. Some headed off in their vehicles, taking the bumpy and barely passable road along the edge of the cliff.

Jacobsson and Knutas continued on foot, taking the sea path. They chose a route at random, not sure which way the two suspects had gone.

At the furthest point the cliff dropped precipitously to the stony shore far below. A low railing provided a flimsy barrier. The wind had picked up, and the waves were pounding the rocks. The sea spread out before them, grey and menacing beneath the gathering black clouds. The sun had disappeared, and a storm was on its way.

Jacobsson shouted, 'There's something down there! On the ledge below!'

They stopped to catch their breath. The distance was too great for them to see anything clearly, but they could make out two figures moving along the jutting cliff ledge up ahead.

'That must be them,' gasped Jacobsson. 'Shit.'

They started running again, and when they got closer they saw a big man and a slender woman circling each other on the ledge.

If only we can reach them in time, thought Knutas.

After Sonny Jonsson's visit, Johan had agreed with Max Grenfors, his editor back in Stockholm, that the best thing for him and Pia to do was to go out to the property in Högklint where the tragic drama had taken place sixteen years earlier. They needed to get some footage of the site. In the meantime, the Stockholm reporters would work on digging up all the facts about the case.

It took Johan and Pia a while to locate the house. When they did, they found a police vehicle parked nearby.

'What the hell?' exclaimed Johan. 'What are the police doing here?'

'This is the confirmation we needed,' said Pia triumphantly, parking right behind the police car.

She jumped out and raised her camera to her eyes. There wasn't a second to lose.

Johan and Pia ran towards the house but quickly discovered that there wasn't a single officer or anyone else in sight.

'We have no clue what's going on here,' said Pia. 'Maybe more police are on the way. If so, they might cordon off the property. You'd better do a piece to camera here right now.'

'You're right,' said Johan. 'Just give me a minute to put together what I'm going to say.'

While she waited, Pia filmed the house and the surrounding area, including the parked police car. Then Johan was ready. He took up position near the front entrance, holding a microphone in his hand. Pia started filming.

'It was here, inside the house you see behind me, in Högklint, outside of Visby, that a whole family was shot in the early-morning hours of 4 November 1994. The tragedy occurred during a burglary. A family friend found the victims inside the house later that morning. One of the twin boys survived the shooting. According to information obtained by Regional News, the police suspect that both murders committed on Gotland during the past weeks are connected to the tragedy in Högklint.'

Just as Johan finished his report they heard two loud bangs in quick succession off in the distance, down by the sea.

The gunshots made a flock of birds rise up from the cliffs. They screeched ominously as they flew off into the darkening sky.

The moment Terese climbed down to the ledge in panic, she realized she had come to a dead end. There was no way back. All around she saw only a sheer drop to the sea.

He was right behind her and, as he slid down the last stretch, she merely stood there, watching. He was tall and muscular. Nothing like the boy he'd been when she last saw him. This was a man standing in front of her. But his eyes were the same. Terese felt tears well up, and she was close to collapsing as she met his gaze.

'Forgive me, Daniel,' she pleaded. 'Forgive me. I never meant to—'

'Shut up!' he snarled. His dark eyes blazed with fury. 'You murdered my whole family. You ruined my life. And now yours is over. You're going to die the same way your blood brothers died.'

He took several steps closer. Terese saw the gleam of the knife in his hand. For a few seconds she weighed up her options. Then she was filled with resignation. She realized she didn't have a chance, and that she really didn't care. She had nothing left to live for. But she wanted him to know what had happened back then. That they hadn't intended for anyone to get hurt. That it was Jocke who had brought along a gun, without telling her or Degen. And that she would rather die by throwing herself off the cliff than have her throat cut.

'Daniel,' she began as they circled each other on the ledge. 'We were just going to break into the house and steal a few things. We were desperate. We didn't have any money. We thought you would be away the whole holiday, that the house would be empty. We rang the restaurant and the school to make sure. We had planned everything so carefully and borrowed a delivery van. We were just sitting out there waiting for midnight before we broke in. But then you and your family turned up.'

'Yes, we did. But that didn't stop you, did it?' Daniel shouted into the wind. Tears were running down his cheeks.

'No, unfortunately. I'm so terribly sorry, Daniel. I wanted to call it off, but—'

'Don't you dare shift the blame to somebody else, goddamnit!'

'No, I'm not. I take full blame. It was my idea, after all. But I just wanted you to know that we hadn't planned on hurting anyone. Degen and I had no clue that Jocke was armed. We weren't supposed to bring any weapons. He had stayed in the van, smoking dope, and when he pulled out that gun we couldn't stop him.'

Daniel's face was contorted in anger.

'You killed my brother and my parents!' he screamed. 'My whole family. We took you in, and you wiped us out. Destroyed us.'

He took a few steps closer. Terese backed towards the edge. His eyes didn't leave hers. The next second they heard a voice.

'Police! Put your hands up! And don't move!'

357

Abruptly, they both turned. Knutas and Jacobsson stood at the top of the cliff, pointing their guns at the man and the woman on the ledge below.

Terese stared up at them. Then she made up her mind and took a step towards the edge. Daniel Stenfors threw himself after her.

Two shots rang out almost simultaneously.

And it was over.

Knutas came home from work on Friday afternoon and took a shower. He was cooking dinner when Lina rang from the taxi to tell him she was on her way. This was the first time since she'd taken the job at the University Hospital in Copenhagen that she'd come home for the weekend, and he was feeling ridiculously nervous.

He and the children had cleaned the entire house. He had also bought flowers, which he'd put in a vase on the kitchen table. On the way home he had stopped to buy food: fresh bread, fruit, several different cheeses and Lina's favourite cold cuts. She liked the kitchen cupboards well stocked and a full refrigerator.

She won't have anything to complain about in that regard, thought Knutas with satisfaction. He sipped from a glass of red wine and hummed along with Simon and Garfunkel's 'Cecilia', a big hit in the seventies.

In his mind he went over the dramatic events of the past few days. First, the arrest of both Terese Larsson and Daniel Stenfors on the cliff ledge in Högklint. He and Karin had fired their guns when they saw what was about to happen. Terese was heading for the edge and no doubt would have jumped if Karin hadn't shot her in the leg. At the same moment Knutas had fired at Daniel, hitting him in the shoulder, which was enough to stop him from attacking Terese. Luckily, another patrol car had just pulled up, and they were able to grab both suspects.

They were taken to hospital. Neither of them had suffered life-threatening wounds.

The next day Knutas and Jacobsson questioned them. It was a sad story, in which one unfortunate occurrence after another had led to the fateful drama out in Högklint. But was it really just unfortunate circumstances that had caused the tragedy? Of course not. Jocke, Degen and Terese were all responsible for the terrible unfolding of events.

Terese made no attempt to evade blame. She had confessed to everything, and at long last the police had learned exactly what had happened.

Daniel Stenfors, on the other hand, showed no remorse. He seemed to think that his actions were justified, and he never wavered from that point of view. He was going to be evaluated by a forensic psychologist.

Just as the case was resolved, Kurt Fogestam had phoned from Stockholm. Vera Petrov and her husband, Stefan Norrström, who were being sought by the international authorities, had indeed been tracked down to Las Palmas in Gran Canaria. The information was now judged to be reliable. Knutas was due to fly there with Fogestam on Sunday to assist the Spanish police when they made the arrest.

But first Lina was going to arrive, and the whole family would have dinner together for the first time in a long while. He was tossing the salad when he heard the front door open. He felt a wonderful warmth spread through his body at the sound of her familiar, cheerful voice.

'Hello? I'm home.'

He went out to the front hall to greet his wife.

Acknowledgements

First, I want to thank my husband, Cenneth Niklasson, and my children Rebecka (Bella) and Sebastian (Sebbe) Jungstedt for their support, encouragement and love. Thank you for all that you give me every day.

Thanks also to:

Ulf Åsgård, psychiatrist and police profiling expert

Lena Allerstam, journalist

Magnus Frank, detective superintendent with Visby police

Martin Csatlos, of the Forensic Medicine Laboratory in Solna

Johan Gardelius, scene of crime officer with Visby police

Conny Lantz, East Coast Riders motorcycle club, Visby, and all the other club members

Ulf Byman, Thai boxing club Slagskeppet, Stockholm

Maria Ernestam, author

Gustav Åsgård, Loomis transport company

Ruth González Nuñez, manager of Hotel Riu Karamboa, Boa Vista

A big thanks to:

All the professionals at the Albert Bonniers Publishing Company, especially my publishers Lotta Aquilonius and Jonas Axelsson, and my editor, Ulrika Åkerlund

The cover designer of the Swedish edition, Sofia Scheutz

My press agent, Lina Wijk, and my PR person, Charlotta Wågert

My agents at the Stilton Literary Agency, Emma Tibblin, Nina Bennet and Poa Broström

And last but not least I want to thank all my fellow authors. Thank you for your support, inspiration and all the fun we have together.

Mari Jungstedt
Stockholm, March 2011

THE DOUBLE SILENCE

A group of close friends holiday on a remote Swedish island every summer. But this year, their trip won't go as expected.

A terrible series of tragedies unfolds, seemingly random, somehow all connected. To find the truth, Detective Superintendent Anders Knutas will have to look into the friends' tangled pasts.

What malevolent force has followed them to the island?

Or was it amongst them all along?

DARK ANGEL

Family ties can be dangerously tight.

Viktor Algard was in love. Reckless in the grip of passion, he left his wife and grown-up children to be with his new lover. His last act was a celebratory drink at a glamorous party . . .

Inspector Anders Knutas must find out who on the island of Gotland hated Algard enough to poison him. At first Algard's spurned wife seems like the obvious suspect. But a second attack confirms his suspicion that there's a more complex motive behind the murder.

If Knutas is to catch the killer, he must discover the truth that lies hidden at the heart of a broken family – and face some secrets within his own.